P9-DEX-725

THE
SHELL HOUSE

Also available by Linda Newbery:

The Nowhere Girl
Flightsend
From E to You
The Damage Done
No Way Back
Run With the Hare
Some Other War
The Kind Ghosts
The Wearing of the Green
Riddle Me This
The Shouting Wind
The Cliff Path
A Fear of Heights

THE
SHELL HOUSE

Linda Newbery

David Fickling Books

OXFORD · NEW YORK

OAK BROOK PUBLIC LIBRARY
600 OAK BROOK ROAD
OAK BROOK, IL 60523

A DAVID FICKLING BOOK

Published by David Fickling Books
an imprint of Random House Children's Books
a division of Random House, Inc.
1540 Broadway
New York, New York 10036

Copyright © 2002 by Linda Newbery

All rights reserved under International and Pan-American Copyright Conventions.
No part of this book may be reproduced or transmitted in any form or by any means,
electronic or mechanical, including photocopying, recording, or by any information
storage and retrieval system, without the written permission of the Publisher,
except where permitted by law.

Published simultaneously in Canada by Random House of Canada Limited,
Toronto, and in Great Britain by David Fickling Books,
an imprint of Random House Children's Books

"Water" from Collected Poems by Philip Larkin. Copyright © 1988, 1989 by the Estate of
Philip Larkin. Reprinted by permission of Farrar, Straus and Giroux, LLC.

www.randomhouse.com/teens

Library of Congress Cataloging-in-Publication Data
Newbery, Linda.
The shell house / Linda Newbery.
p. ; cm.
Summary: Seventeen-year-old Greg's interest in photography draws him
to a ruined mansion whose history becomes more personally relevant
as he slowly discovers the tragic events that led to the destruction
of the house during World War I.
ISBN 0-385-75011-0
[1. Self-perception—Fiction. 2. Interpersonal relations—Fiction.
3. Homosexuality—Fiction. 4. World War, 1914–1918—Fiction.
5. England—Fiction.] I. Title.

PZ7.N4715 Sh   2002
[Fic]—dc21
2002020663
Printed in the United States of America
August 2002
10 9 8 7 6 5 4 3 2 1
First American Edition

To the other A.C., with love, thanks and admiration; also to the real shell house and its Friends, especially my mother, Iris Newbery, whose caryatid photograph provided the starting point.

Water

If I were called upon
To construct a religion
I should make use of water.

Going to church
Would entail a fording
To dry, different clothes.

My liturgy would entail
Images of sousing,
A furious devout drench,

And I should raise in the East
A glass of water
Where any-angled light
Would congregate endlessly.

Philip Larkin
from The Whitsun Weddings

He couldn't face going back indoors.

If he walked in, their faces would look up at him, polite, expectant; they would be ready to make allowances. The meal would be finished: his plate and his scattered cutlery would have been removed from the table, his toppled chair replaced. His mother would have said something to smooth over his rudeness, and the others would make sympathetic noises, some of them genuine.

No-one understood. They would be having coffee now, passing the cream, passing the sugar, in the large room with the windows closed against the spring evening, as if nothing had changed.

*Every*thing had changed.

At the top of the steps to the garden, he filled his lungs with cool air. It was dusk. Light from the windows fell on the terrace, and a fountain played below. Its soft, regular trickle ought to have been soothing, but nothing could soothe him; he had to get away, down the steps, out of sight of the house. Mown lawn welcomed his feet, yielding silently to his tread. The cool toughness of cypress leaves brushed his face as he pushed through a row of conifers; the air smelled of grass and damp earth. He closed his eyes as memory surged through him like the delayed after-shock of pain. He felt detached from his body: from his walking feet, his breathing lungs, his mind registering smells and sounds.

In the lower garden, he paused for a moment to listen, looking in the direction of London, thinking of Kent beyond, and the coast. People said that you could sometimes hear the guns, even at this distance. Nothing. He felt oddly disappointed, hearing only the whirr of moth wings, seeing the flicker of a bat; an owl hooted down in the woods. Nothing else disturbed the silence.

He lowered his head and walked on, down a flight of steps towards the glimmer of water, along a mossy path to the grotto.

Chain gang

Greg's photograph: a huge eighteenth-century mansion standing alone. It is built in classical style: weighty, monumental, symmetrical. The frontage is of Portland stone; twin flights of steps rise to the pillared main entrance. The central section is surmounted by a decorative triangular panel sculpted with reclining figures and a Latin inscription. At a glance, you'd think you were looking at a stately home — a National Trust property, perhaps. Only when you look properly do you see that the door and windows are blank, that there is no roof, and that the house is an empty shell.

'You can't do it,' said Faith. 'You can't make a bargain with God.'

Greg would always remember her saying that, in the grotto, where cold sunlight on the lake rippled patterns of light on the curve of the wall. She sat shrugged into her fleece jacket, her hands tucked up inside the sleeves; her eyes were dark and intense. She

3

was a girl in a shell, cupped and held like a pearl in an oyster. He saw her as part of an accidentally beautiful composition: dark hair and eyes, scarlet fleece, tile fragments in a swirling pattern behind her. *Frame, click!* went his mental camera. These were the photographs that stayed in his mind: the ones he hadn't taken.

The first time they met, at the end of summer, he saw her as bossy, imperious. She manipulated him.

He was trespassing. The burnt-out mansion was visible from the main road: sometimes a silhouette on its ridge, sometimes golden in sunlight. Out on his bike with hours of Sunday freedom ahead, he had let curiosity reel him in. He cycled past the sign that said GRAVENEY HALL – PRIVATE on the lodge gates, and on down the long driveway to the ruined mansion, with its commanding position over acres of wheatfields and woods. If it hadn't been for the cars parked along the front drive, he would have poked about, inside and out, taking photographs, ignoring the DANGER signs. He hadn't expected anyone to be here, and was annoyed.

The day was still and humid; sweat trickled between his shoulder-blades and down his back. He leaned his bike against the fence and stood gazing up at the vast shell. Must have been some fire, he thought, to destroy a place this size. It was roofless, open to the sky. All the doors and windows were huge, as if the house had been inhabited by giants.

Most of the outer walls were intact, but through a door beneath the steps he glimpsed piles of collapsed brick, and nettles and even slender trees growing out of the debris. Although the house must be past repair, he saw people working inside, a team of them: shovelling, hacking at the layer of sediment that coated the ground, carting stones in wheelbarrows. A woman with a tray of mugs was picking her way across the rough floor. He hung back, expecting to be challenged, but they were all absorbed in their tasks.

Retreating, he found a way through the makeshift fence that ran along the farthest side of the house, making the place look like a building site. The house was almost as deep as it was wide; there were remains of brick walls here, perhaps from extensions or a conservatory. Making his way round to the back, he emerged into an expanse of derelict garden. He saw a pair of stone summerhouses, and a balustrade dividing the garden into two levels. From the driveway, you wouldn't know this was here at all. He took two photographs, imagining how the garden must have looked a hundred and fifty, two hundred years ago. There must have been statues, fountains, the lot, and a whole team of gardeners. The outlines were still visible: the bases of statues, and a raised walk of rough grass down the whole length, with sunken areas either side. And this was only the formal part. He guessed that there would have been more: a kitchen garden for the house, orchards, wooded areas down in the valley.

No-one stopped him as he crossed to the far side of

the garden. There was a large area of grass beyond, roughly cut between trees, some sort of crumbling stone tower on the far side, brick outbuildings to his right. Beyond the tower, the ground took an abrupt plunge down a bracken-covered hillside, at the base of which he saw the gleam of water and the domed roof of another small building. A temple or summerhouse? Drawn by his photographic instinct, liking the idea of a small classical building almost overwhelmed by wilderness, he began to push his way down the slope. The tough, dried fronds of bracken resisted his progress, backed up by brambles and nettles. Thorns tore at his shorts, nettles prickled his legs, and he would have turned back if the watery gleam hadn't spread itself, to his surprise, into a large stretch of lake. Well, a place the size of Graveney Hall *would* have a lake, a piece of landscaping on a grand scale. He imagined a picturesque island, a boathouse, women in long dresses (Edwardian? Victorian? Longer ago than that?) decorously taking the air, and swans and ornamental ducks coming to be fed.

It was so quiet here. The voices of the workers couldn't carry this far. Even the birds were silent in the heat of midday; he heard the *crukk* of a coot, the faint rustle of leaves, and that was all, apart from his own feet brushing through vegetation. He pushed on down to the water's edge, seeing the surface all hazed over with pollen and the quick silvery flip of a fish breaking the surface. He paused to rub at a nettle-sting on his calf, noticing a trodden path along the shore where it would be easier to walk. Heading for the summerhouse, he threaded his way down the slope.

The shore path was of dried mud. He slid down the last bit of the bank and looked out over the water. Dense slopes of trees rose on all sides, holding the lake beneath a bowl of sky. The nearest end bristled with reeds or sedges; in the faint breeze the stalks moved against each other with a small sighing sound. A moorhen bobbed out of view among them. Greg walked on towards the summerhouse, his feet slapping on hard ground. They obviously went in for summerhouses, whoever had lived here; had to keep their delicate aristocratic skins out of the sun, he supposed.

Closer to, he could see that it wasn't so much summerhouse as grotto; open-fronted, it was built in a curved shape, like a cupped hand or an oyster-shell. He heard the plash of water inside, and glanced in, seeing that the inner curve was a mosaic of tile fragments, blue and white. And a girl was sitting on a stone bench, startled, staring back at him.

Damn! He wanted the place to himself.

He backed off two paces. 'Oh, sorry. Didn't know there was anyone here.'

The girl held a hand to her throat. 'I heard your feet coming, but you still made me jump.'

'Sorry,' he said. In this setting he could have seen her as water-nymph or wood-sprite, except that she was obviously a modern girl: splayed bare legs with feet in grey trainers; short denim skirt and a skimpy red T-shirt. Her hair was long, dark and sleek.

Recovering from her surprise, she regained that air of self-possession girls seemed to convey so easily. She made Greg feel like an intruder. Which he was.

'What are you doing here?'

Greg shrugged. 'Trespassing, I s'pose.'

'You are – there's no public footpath.'

'I can read. Saw enough PRIVATE signs. You?'

'I'm with the volunteers. I come here a lot.'

He noticed, by her feet, a raffia basket, sagging, displaying its contents: a bottle of Perrier, a mobile phone, a paperback book and a rolled-up sweater. She held a spiral-bound notebook, now slammed shut, her place kept by a pen. The bench she sat on was marble, a curve, in two halves, round the interior of the grotto. A grotesque stone head, set between the bench's two sections, spouted water from its grimace of a mouth into a pool, which decanted into a thin channel running out and down to the lake. The base of the pool was set with pebbles, not tiles like the rest. Greg smelled the water and damp moss – a cool respite from the heat outside.

The girl was still looking at him, requiring him to account for his presence.

'Who are they, the volunteers?' he asked.

'Friends of Graveney Hall. They're restoring the place.'

'Oh.' Moving forward, he waggled the toe of one trainer in the ribbon of water. He thought of the place tarted up into a National Trust kind of stately home, with visitors' car parks and gift shops and guide books. 'Why not leave it as it is?'

'If it wasn't for the Friends,' the girl retorted, 'the whole place would be demolished by now, turned into a country club or a conference centre. You'd prefer that?'

'No,' he conceded. 'But a group of volunteers, restoring that enormous house? I'd have thought it was past help.'

'The house, yes. They'll never do more than tidy that up a bit. The grounds aren't past help. That's what they're concentrating on.'

'You're not one of them?'

She looked at him. 'My parents are. My father's a landscape gardener. He's leading the project. I help out sometimes, when I want.'

Stepping inside the grotto, he traced with one hand the pattern of tiles on the wall nearest him. Most of the fragments were blue and white, like the Willow Pattern design, with occasional deep red; each piece was firmly embedded in plaster, the whole design coated with glaze. *My father's a landscape gardener.* Yes, he would be. She had that sort of voice. She probably called her parents Mummy and Daddy.

'Do you trespass here often?' she asked him, with an irritating little giggle.

'Never been here before. Saw it from the road and thought I'd have a look round, take some photos.'

'Is that your job? You're a photographer?' the girl said, looking at the camera slung round his neck.

'I wish. I'm still at school.'

'Oh. I thought perhaps you were from the local paper or something. They sometimes give us a bit of coverage.'

'Then I wouldn't be trespassing, would I?' Greg countered.

'What are the photos for, then?'

'I like ruins.'

'You don't have to fight through brambles to get to them.' She was looking at his legs. He glanced down and saw two long scratches, across one knee and the other shin, beaded with drops of blood. He should have worn jeans; the irritation of nettle-stings prickled his legs all over.

'You came down the slope?' She indicated with a turn of her head.

'Yeah.'

'There's a better way. I'll show you.'

She was gathering her things together, stuffing the notebook into the basket. As she leaned forward, a silver cross on a chain round her neck swung forward, catching the light.

'Wait.' Greg wanted to look at the grotto. 'This place – it's amazing.' The tiles made swirling patterns – loops, waves, curls like tentacles. He thought of someone standing here with a heap of tiles, smashing them into bits with a hammer, choosing each fragment, then placing it in the mosaic of cool colours. 'I wonder who made it?'

'Oh – the gardens were laid out about eighteen hundred. It's probably a bit later than that, wouldn't you say? More romantic than classical.'

Her assurance irritated him. He had been wondering about the individual, not trying to pin it down to an architectural period. She was, he thought, about his own age, possibly younger; it was hard to tell with girls. She was skinny enough for twelve, poised enough for eighteen.

'What about the main house? When did that get burnt down?'

'Nineteen seventeen.'

'In the First World War,' he said, sure of something.

'Mm. Nothing to do with the war, though. It started with a kitchen fire, they think.'

'They?'

She made an impatient gesture. 'People who know about the history of the house.'

'Could have been a bomb, I suppose – we're not that far from London.'

'*First* World War, not Second,' she said, with a trace of scorn. 'Years before the Blitz.'

'London was bombed in the First World War. Near the end.'

'I didn't know that.'

Greg, with GCSE History still recent, did know. He shrugged, wanting to convey *You don't know everything*. He turned away and stood looking at the lake, wondering how deep it was. The sand or mud of the shallows near his feet was gradually obscured by thick tangles of vegetation – too weedy for swimming. A pity. Hot and sweaty as he was, the thought of plunging into coolness was as desirable as an iced drink. He thought of Jordan at the pool, his taut body piercing the surface in a racing dive. Perhaps there had been a diving board here, once, before it got so weedy and neglected.

'Coming? I'll show you that path.' The girl slung her bag over one shoulder.

'If you want.'

She turned towards the farthest end of the lake, keeping to the trodden path. He followed her, taking in the fall of hair over brown shoulders, the narrow waist and the vulnerable backs of her knees. He could make something of this, if he wanted to, for Gizzard: he heard himself saying, 'I met this girl . . .' 'Yeah?' Gizzard would say, his face alert with interest. Girls meant sex to Gizzard, and that was about all.

She turned, shaking back her hair. 'What's your name?'

'Greg. Yours?'

'Faith.'

Oh yeah, he thought. Posh.

'Don't tell me,' he said to the back of her head. 'You've got two sisters, Hope and Charity?'

'Ha ha.' She didn't turn round.

Abruptly, she veered away from the lake into what looked like a dense slab of shrubbery, mounting two steps half-hidden in grass. There was a narrow path, marked by log steps, cutting diagonally up the slope between hollies and sapling beech trees. Definitely easier than the way he'd come down. She went up quickly, with long agile strides. Following, he glimpsed smooth inner thighs and a flash of white knickers.

'Didn't you mind being down there on your own?' he called.

'Mind? Why?'

'Well . . . anyone might be prowling about.'

Reaching the top of the slope, she turned to face him. 'No, not here. That's why I like it. There's no-one around.'

'But there could be. I was.' Greg resented being dismissed as *no-one*.

She looked at him levelly. 'Well, I've got my mobile, in case I thought I was being attacked.'

'What were you writing, anyway?'

'Nothing much.' Her mouth curved in a secretive smile. 'Ideas. I like being on my own.'

'So I interrupted.'

'Yes, you did.' She looked at him for a moment with that same half-smile. 'But now you're here, I'll show you round, if you like.'

'OK.'

They walked across the rough grass of the orchard. Passing closer to the brick outbuildings, Greg saw that they formed a stableyard, built round three sides of a cobbled square. The stables were all shut up, but another large building, adjoining, had its double doors thrown open. Inside, someone was sawing; he heard a shout and another voice in answer.

'They're lovely old stables,' Faith said, 'and that's the Coach House. Used to be, anyway. We use it now to store stuff, and to have lunch when it's raining. And that's where we have the exhibition.'

She was sounding proprietorial now, as if she ran the whole show.

'Exhibition?'

'When we have open days. Next one's the second

13

Sunday in October. You ought to come, if you're interested. There'll be photos and stuff, and guided walks. They raise a lot of money for the Trust.'

Greg didn't answer; it didn't sound like his sort of thing, being led round like a tourist. He preferred trespassing.

'Are they here every day, those workers?' he asked.

'No, just weekends. I told you, they're volunteers. They don't get paid or anything.'

Greg heard a toilet flushing. A bearded man came out of the Coach House, glanced their way, then strode across the grass towards them, looking quizzically at Greg.

'My father,' Faith said.

The man wore shorts, walking boots and a grubby polo shirt stretched over a large belly; his legs were muscular and very hairy. He looked considerably older than Greg's dad and, as far as Greg could see, nothing at all like Faith.

'Hello!' He held out a hand. 'Michael Tarrant. You didn't say you had a friend coming,' he added to Faith.

'Forgot,' Faith said. 'This is Greg.'

Reluctantly, Greg held out his hand, which was wrung rather than shaken in a strong, painful grip.

'Pleased to meet you, Greg,' Michael Tarrant said. Smiling teeth appeared rather unexpectedly between gingery moustache and gingery beard, as if he had no lips. 'Good to see young people taking an interest. Actually, you've come along at just the right moment. Feel like lending a hand for half an hour?'

'Well, I—' Greg looked at Faith, but she offered no support. Her father, not waiting for an answer, turned to lead the way across to the main house.

'We could do with some extra muscle power. We're making a new track round the south side. It's got to be ready for Open Day. Laying the hardcore's a back-breaking job.' He clapped a hand on Greg's back. 'We've got a chain gang going, but an extra pair of hands at the business end would make all the difference.'

Oh well, he could hardly refuse . . . He allowed himself to be led towards the half-made track, where a small group of people laboured with wheelbarrows and shovels.

'This is Greg,' the man announced. 'Friend of Faith's. He's offered to pitch in.'

Offered! But there were welcoming smiles all round. The chain gang consisted of two men and three women, none of them young. A white-haired woman, straightening stiffly with a hand clamped to her side, handed him her shovel. 'Here you are then, Greg. I've done enough for now. I'll do my back in again if I'm not careful.'

'How lovely to have a strong young man to help,' said a woman with a yellow bandanna knotted over her hair.

Feeling rather foolish, Greg took the shovel. The track they were laying was extensive; he could see the rutted outline they were filling with broken brick and clinker, presumably brought out from the cellars of the house. Half an hour's work wasn't going to make much impression! He'd put in a token effort, then make some excuse. Michael Tarrant set to with a grunt, up-ending a barrow that stood nearby; another man trundled up with a fresh load. Greg started scraping the stuff about. The grating of shovel on coarse brick set his teeth on edge.

'You're at Faith's school, are you?' Michael asked him.

Greg hesitated, for some reason unwilling to end the pretence that he was a friend of Faith's.

'Oh, but I thought Faith went to St Ursula's?' called out the woman in the bandanna.

'They have boys in the sixth form,' Michael explained.

Right. Faith was a St Ursula's girl; he might have guessed. 'No, I'm at Radway.'

'Oh, the comprehensive?' Michael said, as if he'd vaguely heard of such things. 'Sixth form?'

'Yes, just started.'

St Ursula's was a private school, an old brick mansion behind high walls. Its girls (the All Saints, Gizzard called them) wore strict uniform and generally regarded themselves as several notches above the plebs from the comprehensive. Gizzard claimed to have lost his virginity to one, last summer in Epping Forest; starved of boys till Year Twelve, he claimed, they couldn't wait to get their hands on willing male flesh. Greg considered adapting his version of meeting Faith in the light of this new information.

But where *was* Faith? Shovelling, getting hotter and

hotter, he looked round for her. She was nowhere in sight; how had she managed to escape this penal servitude? She must have slipped away, back to the solitude of her lakeside grotto. She'd be laughing at him, having delivered him into the clutches of the Übergruppenführer.

But she hadn't corrected her father when he assumed they knew each other. He couldn't make her out; couldn't decide whether she'd been friendly, or had simply found an easy way of getting rid of him.

Gizzard

Greg's mental photograph, black-and-white: the edge of the lake. Shallow water, pierced by reeds and sedges. The surface is lightly ruffled by wind. Reflected sky is seen in the ripples, caught by fast shutter-speed; otherwise the water is in shadowy darkness.

'Thought you were at Gary's,' Greg's mother said when he got in. She refused to use the name Gizzard. She was frowning in concentration over her icing-nozzle, carefully marking white lines on a rectangular green cake. Looking more closely, Greg saw that it was a football pitch, meticulously proportioned, of course. Whatever his mother did, she did to perfection.

'How do you know I wasn't, then?'

'He phoned. Thought you might want to go round later.' She seemed to speak without breathing, balancing her icing-bag, squeezing it just enough to produce a steady, shining ooze. He didn't know how she got the lines so straight.

'Oh. I might. I'll ring him back in a minute.'

'So,' she said, squinting at him, 'where *have* you been?'

With his back to her, taking a Coke out of the fridge, he said, 'Just out and about on the bike. Nowhere in particular.'

His mother straightened, tilting her head at the cake. 'D'you want to get yourself some lunch? We've had ours. I'm not cooking till tonight.'

'Had some, thanks.'

'McDonald's, I suppose. I don't know why you spend your money on Big Macs when you can eat for nothing at home.'

Greg didn't put her right. 'That looks good,' he said, nodding at the iced football pitch.

'For first thing tomorrow. Then I've got a mermaid to do.' She nodded towards another pair of sponges cooling on a rack.

Greg had liked cake, once. Now that Julie's Party Cakes was taking off, he was used to seeing them dotted about the kitchen in various stages of completion – nude or iced, made to resemble country cottages, dinosaurs, cartoon characters or treasure chests. Sometimes there would be a traditional wedding cake, with tiers and supporting pillars. As long as he didn't have to eat one, that was OK. The smell of them cooking was enough – sugary, laced with vanilla, cloying the air of the kitchen. The basic sponge recipe was always the same, unless it was a rich fruit mix for a wedding cake, in which case the smell was spicy and faintly alcoholic. Either way, Greg had had enough of cake. Julie's Party Cakes had given him a taste for hot savoury food, meaty food, man food – anything but cake.

'Is Dad back from golf yet?'

'Yes, upstairs, on the Internet, I think.'

'Right, so he's out of circulation for the next three hours.' Greg had been thinking of doing a bit of web-surfing himself, but his dad's laptop was out of action and there was only one computer. Reluctantly he considered his homework, decided it could wait, and wondered whether he wanted to go round to Gizzard's.

'You're going to miss Gary,' his mum had been saying all through the summer holidays, and now that school had started, 'It must be odd without Gary.' Surprisingly, it wasn't. Gizzard – Gary Guisborough – had been Greg's best friend since Year Seven, but had now left Radway for the sixth-form college in Hunsdon, ten miles away. His course, Media Studies and Sociology, sounded more fun than school and AS levels – 'But then,' Greg's mum kept saying, 'Gary's not academic.' According to her, Greg *was* academic. He wasn't so sure, himself. His GCSE grades last month had been better than expected, provoking an outburst of champagne and congratulations and even a special cake with WELL DONE GREG! in a looped icing flourish. It was because his parents weren't academic that they so desperately wanted Greg to be. And if his sister Katy didn't get top results in her SATS tests this year it wouldn't be for lack of parental pushing.

His mother had finished marking in the lines. From

a cardboard box on the worktop, she took tiny plastic goalposts and footballers.

'Man United v Chelsea?' Greg suggested.

'Don't know – they just asked for red and blue. I don't think I'll go as far as painting names on the shirts.' She looked at her watch. 'Katy's friends are coming round with a video, so I hope you weren't planning to watch TV.'

'I wasn't,' Greg said. 'Friends – what, Lorrie, as in face-like-the-back-of-a, and the gormless ginger one?'

'Lorrie and Sarah, that's right.' She gave him a teasing look. 'The Greg Hobbs Fan Club. And don't be unkind about Lorrie. She can't help being a bit plain.'

That settled it: he was going to Gizzard's. He could have listened to his Walkman in the garden or up in his room, but the girls wouldn't leave him in peace for long. Last Sunday morning, after he'd been out running, he'd heard them giggling on the landing while he was in the shower. That Lorrie – he wouldn't have been surprised if she'd tried the door; she'd have peeked through the keyhole if there had been one. Sarah, who rarely spoke, flushed fuchsia-pink whenever he appeared and, according to Katy, had written his name all over her new pencil-case, adorned with hearts. Girls! Some of them were all right, but not when they invaded his home in tittering huddles.

That was a funny thing about Gizzard leaving, too. When Gizzard had been around, he was the one who attracted all the girls. He was easy, cheerful, popular; he did it without appearing to try. Although he had been overtaken in height by Greg, there always seemed, somehow, to be a lot more of him. And now that there was no Gizzard, there was more of Greg. Girls outnumbered boys in the sixth form, that was why. The term was only two weeks old but already Greg felt more conspicuous. It wasn't because of anything he did; he just was.

The Guisboroughs lived only two blocks away; hardly worth taking the bike, though Greg did. Gizzard was in the garden, sprawled on a lounger and plugged into his Walkman. He raised a can of lager at Greg, then pulled a spare one from under his seat and passed it over.

'Come and sit down, Tiger.'

'Tiger?'

Gizzard mimed teeing off. 'Woods. Thought your dad must have dragged you off to the golf course.'

'No chance. He'd have me signed up as a life member if I showed my face there again. Sad, isn't it? He's got this fantasy about going off together every Sunday morning. You know, man-to-man chats on the fairway. Male bonding in the bar. Showing off his son and heir to his golfing buddies.'

'Miss out the stuff with birdies and niblicks but show up at the bar. I would.'

Gizzard's mother, plump and impossibly young-looking with the same floppy hair as Gizzard, smiled vaguely from the patio and turned the page of her magazine; she wore white shorts and a halter top, showing an amount of tanned skin and cleavage that Greg would have been mortified to see displayed by his own mother. What he liked about coming to the

Guisboroughs' was that you never had to do anything other than be there. You never had to make polite conversation; you just joined in the sitting, or sunning, or watching the football, or whatever was going on. Even the dog, a fat golden Labrador, was an expert in relaxation; he raised his head from the grass and thumped his tail twice in welcome, then closed his eyes again. Greg's family owned two neurotic cats that were always screeching when they got under his feet or sending his heart into overdrive when they rocketed out from under his bed.

'So where were you, then?' Gizzard asked.

Sitting on the grass, Greg took a swig of lager. 'Out on my bike.'

For some reason he didn't feel like explaining about Graveney Hall, nor about Faith. Gizzard would think he was a plonker for letting himself be press-ganged into what had turned out to be a couple of hours' manual labour. Unexpectedly, though, Greg had enjoyed it – and not because of the welcoming flattery of the volunteer group. For all their references to his strong young muscles, he'd found it hard to match the older people for strength or determination. He'd been flagging long before they showed any signs of taking a break, and had to force himself to keep shovelling. But it had been rewarding, seeing the trail of hardcore extending towards the garden entrance, imagining it as a proper finished track.

Sprawled on the grass next to Gizzard, Greg flexed his arms. He was going to be stiff tomorrow. Definitely not as fit as he thought, not in the upper body, anyway. When the workers finally downed tools, they had invited him to share their lunch, a huge picnic over in the Coach House, set out on trestle tables. Everyone, it seemed, had contributed something – sausage rolls, pork pies, salads, fruit, fudge brownies. With a little encouragement, Greg had tucked in. People emerged from all over the gardens, some two dozen of them. 'Oh, you're Faith's young man?' one of the men said, with a quaintly old-fashioned turn of phrase. Why did everyone think he must have something to do with Faith? Presumably because they were the only two people under forty. But there had been no sign of her.

'How's the old slave-ship, then?' Gizzard asked.

Greg shrugged. 'OK. We've got a couple of new teachers – Art and Physics.'

'Young? Female?' Gizzard's eyebrows rose suggestively.

'No. Both male.'

Greg hadn't seen Faith again before he left. He hadn't felt like searching for her. With all that work to be done, how did she get away with not helping? He got the impression that her dad couldn't bear to see anyone without a pickaxe or shovel in their hand. As soon as lunch was eaten, people started to drift back to their jobs; Greg found Michael and said, untruthfully, that he had to go.

'Well, thanks for your help,' Michael said. 'See you next weekend, if you like? We're always here Saturdays and Sundays.' Not bloody likely, Greg thought, cycling down the rough drive; you're not getting more free labour out of me. Anyway, he had his Saturday job. But now he found that Graveney Hall was on his mind: the burnt-out shell on its shoulder of land, the austere lines, the contrast between ruined building and fertile fields all round like a tide lapping at a shipwreck. He'd taken only five or six photographs, having been so successfully hijacked. Next weekend, or maybe one evening, he'd go back for a proper exploration, keeping well clear of Faith's dad.

'Who d'you go around with now, then?' Gizzard asked.

'Jordan, mostly. You know? Jordan McAuliffe. We're in the same tutor group now.'

Gizzard frowned. 'Dark hair? Hardly ever speaks?'

'He's OK when you get to know him. He's a brilliant swimmer, did you know? Butterfly and freestyle.'

'How would I? He's never said more than two words to me.'

'No. Well.' Greg didn't find this surprising. Jordan McAuliffe had been in a different form throughout school, and was in any case a reserved, self-contained boy – the opposite of Gizzard. 'He trains at the pool. He was there a lot over the summer.'

Gizzard grinned. 'While you were doing your *Baywatch* bit? Cor, I'd have swapped my holiday job for yours like a shot!' Being pool guard, in Gizzard's view, gave endless opportunities for eyeing semi-naked girls. In fact, it was more a case of watching mesmerized while the fitness fanatics ploughed up and down, or warning kids not to dive-bomb each other in the paths of struggling infant doggy-paddlers.

'I wouldn't fancy being rescued by you,' Greg said. 'You nearly drowned me, that time in life-saving practice.'

'Don't s'pose I'd bother. You can look after your-self.' Gizzard yawned. 'We're getting the barbecue out later. Want to stay? Mum, it's OK if Greg troughs with us, yeah?'

'No problem,' his mum said, not looking up.

'I've got my homework still to do,' Greg said.

Gizzard grinned. 'Keep forgetting you're still a schoolboy. Don't worry about it – what are Monday mornings for?'

Next weekend, Greg thought with the doomed sense of a resolution that would never be kept, he was going to get it out of the way on Saturday before starting at the pool, not leave it till Monday morning. 'I'll have to ring Mum, or she'll cook dinner for me.'

'Fine.' Gizzard swung his legs round to one side and glanced at his mother to see if she was still listening. 'There's this girl in my Media Studies group, right?' he began, confidingly man-to-man. 'You ought to see her . . .'

Only half-listening, Greg lay back on the grass. There always was some girl. Sherry, this one was called, or maybe it was Cherie like Mrs Blair, but he'd given up bothering to remember their names. Supplying enough *mms* and *uhhs* to satisfy Gizzard, he narrowed his eyes against the brightness of sky.

Again, Graveney Hall came back to him, filling his mind. He thought of the way the trees opened up suddenly to reveal the glint of water, deep-shadowed on the far side; the stir of rushes as the air sighed through the stalky mass. It was in his mind, more real and vivid than the images stowed safely in his camera. Some of his mental snapshots would be translated into real ones for his art project, if he got the chance. Close-ups, he thought: the ripple of water, the spear-thrust of rush, black-and-white to bring out pattern and light. And the grotto – yes, colour for that, the swirl of blues and whites . . . He might tell Jordan; he was more likely to be interested than Gizzard, who would dismiss the place as a dismal old ruin.

'Sherry's got this friend, nearly as lush, not quite, but she'll do for you,' Gizzard was saying. 'How about it, then, next Saturday night?'

'Uh-uh. Thanks but no thanks.' Last time Gizzard had tried to fix him up, it had been a disaster.

'What's up with you, then? Met someone else at school?'

Greg shook his head, rolled over to reach for his lager can, put it to his lips and up-ended it, shaking out the last few drops.

'Apart from Jordan the Turbo-charged, I mean,' Gizzard said, with a sideways look.

Greg lowered the can and returned an *up yours* sneer.

'Just winding you up, dollop!' Gizzard gave him a friendly punch. 'Like getting blood out of a stone, it is, talking to you. Fancy watching the match?'

1916, midsummer

Last night I saw the ghost of France
Rise from her grave to mourn.
She gazed down at her bleeding corpse
With ~~many~~ wide-mouthed gashes torn.

Her flesh was ravaged and defiled
By those who came to save;
With mine and ~~shell~~ ~~spade~~ shell and trenching tool
We mauled her to her grave.

Friend or foe, what difference
When both brought only pain —
But, when our wounding feet are gone
~~Will~~ might she yet breathe again?

Last night, alone and wakeful
While men around me slept,
I felt the sighing of her bones
And cold tears as she slept.

Edmund Pearson

28

'I've heard that this next push should be decisive,' Edmund's father said, at tea. 'Maybe it won't be many months more.'

'Something must be done to relieve the pressure on the French. They can't hold out indefinitely, around Verdun.' The Reverend Tilley liked to give the impression of being party to the latest news. 'You'll be going back at just the right time, Edmund. I wish I were going with you.'

Why don't you, then? Edmund thought, irritably. Wasn't there anything else to talk about, apart from the war? *Someone's got to stay and keep up morale at home*, the vicar would say next, with a regretful sigh. This, apparently, meant sermonizing on the evils of German militarism and choosing hymns like *Fight the good fight with all thy might*. 'Can it be right to take up arms, to kill another human being?' Edmund had asked him, at the outbreak of hostilities nearly two years ago. 'When God wills it so,' had been the Reverend Tilley's prompt reply.

But how did you know what God willed and what He didn't will? How could you know it wasn't your own will, disguising itself? Edmund crumbled cake on his plate, thinking that if he hadn't been prepared to be a soldier, and therefore to kill Germans, he wouldn't have met Alex. He would have gone off to Cambridge according to plan, as his father had done at his age. He would go there still, after the inconvenient interruption of the war – if he survived, as everyone seemed oddly confident that he would. To his father and the vicar, it was as if the British army had merely been awaiting the return of Lieutenant Edmund Pearson before sweeping on to victory.

The maid, the pretty one, brought more hot water in a shining silver pot. She bobbed a curtsey as she placed the pot on the table, which already bore a ridiculous amount of bone china, linen and silverware just for three people to have scones and cream and a cup of tea. In France, in the front line, there would be a battered tin mug and strong tea tainted with petrol from the cans the water had been carried in. Edmund would have preferred that. Home, with all its comforts and routines, seemed abnormally normal, shockingly familiar.

Edmund, with his father and the vicar, was sitting out on the terrace, supposedly enjoying the fine midsummer weather which was gracing his last week of convalescent leave. Their chairs faced the balustrade, so that they could gaze over the gardens and out to the fields and forest. Since the gardeners had enlisted – all but Baillie and his remaining son, the dull-witted one, who kept order as best they could – the gardens were less manicured than usual. June growth flourished all the more for the comparative neglect, with buttercups and campions daring to show their blooms alongside the choicer plants. Beyond the ha-ha, acres of Essex countryside spread themselves in the patterns so familiar to Edmund from the framed estate map that hung in his father's study: fields of wheat and barley, copses, grazing land. Beyond, to the south and west, the farthest reaches of Epping Forest were hazed in fresh green.

It was for this he was fighting, Edmund told himself. If the German army had its way it would sweep on over the Channel and across the English coast. He imagined these fields – his own fields – sliced up into trenches, bristling with barbed wire and pitted with shell-holes, like the front lines in France and Belgium. England had entered the war to support the Belgians; but to Edmund, future landowner, it was the land itself that was the victim, hacked and mutilated. It was bad enough in winter, worse in summer. The front line and its debris made an ugly gash across the French landscape at a time when the meadows should have been lush with grass, the trees graceful in new leaf and full of the twitter of nesting birds.

The vicar took another scone from the tiered plate. 'Of course the French haven't got the leadership we have. Haig's been biding his time, but this will be a master plan.'

Master plans, new pushes – they cost lives, Edmund knew that. To the vicar and his father it was like bringing on a new spin-bowler in a cricket match; an interesting tactic, when viewed from the sidelines. Edmund knew that the front-line soldier saw the war not in terms of master plans, strategies or maps of Europe but as a few hundred yards of scarred earth, another day survived, another wiring party accomplished without shameful loss of nerve. On his way back from Arras, injured, he had seen a batch of new recruits arriving in Boulogne, many of them alarmingly young; some had looked like schoolboys.

But at least they had chosen to enlist. Now the Government was bringing in conscription.

'So, Edmund,' the vicar said, noticing his withdrawal from the conversation, 'five more days at home, then back to your unit?'

Edmund nodded. His father said, 'The Fitches are dining with us tomorrow.'

The two men exchanged glances. Edmund knew what that meant.

'Good,' said the vicar, sipping tea. 'And how is Philippa?'

'Very well,' said Edmund's father. 'Looking very well indeed last time I saw her.'

At this point Edmund was supposed to betray interest. Instead he looked away, towards the ha-ha. Slipping a hand into his pocket he felt the smooth rectangle of a letter; he touched it, caressed it. As soon as the tiresome vicar had gone he would read it again, though he already knew its contents by heart. He closed his eyes, taking pleasure in the deep, yearning ache that was his constant companion; more painful than the shell-fragment that had embedded itself in his leg, because he didn't think he could ever be cured. He didn't want to be cured.

Realizing that Reverend Tilley was addressing him, he called himself to attention. The vicar was still going on about the Fitches. 'I'm sure young Geoffrey wishes he were in your position. Another eighteen months and he'll be old enough to enlist.'

'Then,' Edmund said, 'we must all hope that the war goes on long enough.'

The vicar decided to take this as a joke. Edmund's father heard only the sharpness, and gave him a reproachful look. Edmund looked straight back at him. It was his father's fault, since he chose to arrange these ordeals. Tea with the vicar today, dinner with the Fitches tomorrow . . . it was unbearably tedious. And pointless, if they only knew.

The Fitches were old family friends, with a large house in Ongar. Their daughter, Philippa Fitch – her name was like a tongue-twister, or the start of a comic verse – was destined to be Edmund's wife, if his father had his way. This dinner party was carefully timed so that Philippa could see Edmund in his uniform, modestly playing his part of wounded hero about to return to the battlefield. The supposed romance between Philippa and Edmund was being carefully orchestrated by both sets of parents. A marriage would be a way of uniting the two families. After an appropriate interval, according to the plan, Philippa would obligingly produce a son, heir to the Graveney estate, and the future would be assured. Philippa was a pleasant young woman, well-mannered, accomplished and pretty by anyone's standards, with a pale complexion and a mane of rich chestnut hair, artfully arranged by her maid. She had large dark eyes which constantly darted and flickered in Edmund's direction; she listened attentively to everything he said, as if expecting nuggets of insight and wisdom to drop from his lips. She knew how to play her role.

There was one very large obstruction to this

marriage, something that would have shocked and horrified Edmund's parents if they had been able to begin to understand it, the Reverend Tilley even more. Everything was the wrong way round. *Thou shalt not kill*, the Commandments said, but that was all changed in wartime, when *Thou shalt kill*, like it or not, and with the approval of God's deputies if not of God Himself. And if killing could be good or bad, so could loving, it seemed. Love thy neighbour, but not too much. Love thy neighbour with everyone's blessing if her name is Philippa Fitch, but not if his name is Alex Culworth. That kind of love was reprehensible, damnable, contemptible. Edmund could imagine the vilification he would get from the vicar if he found out. But the idea of confiding in him was laughable. The vicar, a long-standing friend of Edmund's father, was like a tedious uncle – a frequent visitor to the house, fond of good dinners, vintage wines and circular conversations.

Edmund amused himself by imagining Alex here now. No respecter of convention, he would be sprawled on a chair with unconscious elegance, long legs stretched out. Alex and the vicar! Edmund found himself smiling at the thought. He could imagine how Alex would draw out the older man, questioning him with open-faced sincerity about the conduct of the war, innocently leading him into confusion, self-contradiction and bluster. Alex's cleverness and barbed wit did not threaten Edmund now, as they once had. Alex had a way of looking at him, no matter who was present – a swift, reassuring glance that was as good as a declaration.

'Excuse me.' Edmund pushed back his chair. He had tolerated the conversation for long enough.

Reverend Tilley also rose to his feet and proffered his hand. 'Well, good luck, my boy. I don't suppose I shall see you again before you leave. My thoughts go with you.'

Edmund sincerely hoped not. He suppressed a smile, composed his face into an expression of pensive gravity, and walked away down the steps, past the fountains and formal beds to the grass walk that led to the ha-ha. He stood there for a few moments, feeling the sun warm on his back, looking out over fields of ripening barley. He knew that they could see him from the terrace, and were fondly imagining, no doubt, that he was savouring the peace and harmony of the garden and the productiveness of the farmland, his inheritance; looking forward to the time when he would walk here with Philippa on his arm and an infant or two romping at his feet.

'Alex . . .' he said slowly, lingering over the separate sounds for only the green ears of corn to hear.

Wanting to be out of sight, he turned away through the orchard and walked towards the stableyard. It was deserted and unswept; all the horses, apart from the old pony that pulled the gardener's cart, had been requisitioned by the army. Edmund could see the gardener's son, the one he knew as the idiot boy, pushing a wheelbarrow, with his odd ungainly gait. He was concentrating hard, gripping the handles tightly, his mouth open; he did not notice Edmund.

Leaning on the Coach House wall, Edmund took off his uniform jacket and slung it on the mounting-block, first taking Alex's letter from one of the pockets. Unfolding the pages, he held them to his mouth. One more week.

Jordan

Greg's photograph: at the swimming pool, from the poolguard's chair. The water is cool and aquamarine, shimmering in artificial light. Most of its surface is undisturbed. The first swimmer has just dived in and is swooping low under the water. The long human shape flickers against pale-blue tiles.

On Tuesday evening Greg cycled over to Graveney Hall, taking his camera in his rucksack. The weather was still very warm for September; the ground was dry and dusty. He passed a couple of dog-walkers on the driveway, but there were no cars parked along the front of the house. He dismounted and stood looking at the façade. This time, there was nothing to stop him having a proper look round.

Abandoned, the mansion was eerie, standing sentinel over its fertile acres. It was a house out of time. The fire that had destroyed it had also preserved it; the nearby towns had expanded, motorways had been built, the M25 had circled London, cutting off

Graveney Hall from the forest, but the wreck of 1917 still stood. Rather like the *Mary Celeste*, Greg thought – an abandoned hulk, empty, mysterious. Its blank windows made him think of a skull's empty eye-sockets. He felt dwarfed by its height and scale, reduced to insignificance, standing and staring, as so many must have stood and stared before.

It was rather an ugly building – imposing and magnificent rather than beautiful. The square brick extensions at either side of the stone-faced central part could have been added at a later date. The ornamental panel which crowned the central section, shaped like a flattened triangle, was state-of-the-art décor of the period, he supposed, looking at the reclining figures, harps and flowing vegetation.

Signs on the frontage warned DANGER, KEEP OUT. STRICTLY PRIVATE. But what damage could he do? He wasn't stupid enough to risk climbing rickety walls or staircases, and it must be safe enough to enter the building; people had been working inside on Sunday.

Parts of the lower frontage on this side were boarded up with corrugated panels, but the door beneath the twin flights of steps – the one he'd glanced through last time – was a makeshift wooden panel, left as an entrance. Carefully, he pushed it open and stepped through.

It was like entering a cathedral, but one open to the sky. He was standing on a concrete floor littered with silted mud and fragments of brick. Looking up, he saw a huge fireplace on what would have been the first floor, suspended in mid-wall; he could see that the upper rooms must have been enormous. Above him had probably been a drawing room or dining room, giving, at that height, the best possible views over the countryside and forest. To his left, the floor gaped, revealing more rooms below – cellars or kitchens, he thought. Since humans had moved out, vegetation had moved in. Clumps of nettles clung between bricks; brambles, willowherb, and even the sapling trees he had noticed before had found rootholds. A swallow swooped low over his head as he stood there.

He began to make his way through to the rear. He was thinking of what Faith had said, about the place being a prime site for development as a country club, hotel or conference centre. He disliked the idea, but now wondered why. This house was a relic of an age when the rich were very rich and the poor were nothing. Dozens of poorly-paid labourers must have sweated and toiled to build the place; teams of servants would have slogged long hours so that the owners could live in luxury. Wouldn't it be better turned into a facility for everyone to enjoy? The land itself must be worth a packet, at a time when farmers could make a fortune by selling off odd corners of fields for house-building. But country clubs and hotels were only for the well-heeled; there would be no change there. His instinct was that the mansion should be left as it was. To pull it down would be to destroy the past with it, to state that the twenty-first century had no room left for this great, sprawling reminder of an older way of life . . .

The hairs rose on the back of his neck as he became aware of a strange keening sound. At first he thought it was some creature, a fox or a cat, trapped in the ruins. He stood and listened, trying to locate the direction. Then the voice took on a distinctly human tone, and was joined by another, rising in a banshee wail. Kids, mucking about! Greg's anxiety turned to annoyance. They were taunting him, creeping up close, hooting, staying out of sight. He heard a jeering laugh and another drawn-out, wavering cry. Then a Tarzan yell from somewhere above his head made him jump. He looked up and saw, balanced on the edge of a staircase, a skinny boy – wavering, losing balance, arms flailing. Greg caught his breath. The boy laughed and dodged back out of sight – only pretending. Kookaburra laughter rippled to his left. There must be three or four of them.

Irritated, Greg continued to pick his way through to the back of the house. The voices followed him, like sparrows mobbing a magpie. The glimpse he'd had was of a boy, thirteen or so, in jeans and a yellow T-shirt. Moronic, climbing around in an unstable building! But Greg was unlikely to catch them – they knew their way around. It must be their illicit playground.

Emerging at the foot of the steps leading down from the first floor to the garden, Greg looked to his left. Past the brick wing of the building were the remains of another low structure reaching along the edge of the garden; could have been a covered walkway or pergola. He stepped out into the garden and stood looking and listening. Silence. Then:

'Tosspot!'

'Prat!'

There were three of them halfway along the walk-way, running, leaping over blocks of stone, knowing he was too far off to catch them. He wasn't going to make a fool of himself by trying. They were making for the main driveway. A moment later he saw them riding away on bikes, which they must have hidden in a ditch or behind bushes, or he'd have noticed them. Well out of his reach, they rode slowly, swerving across the path, sliding into turns. One of them gave a mocking hoot and raised two fingers.

He walked slowly along the way they had left. The low structure, marked by remnants of pillars at varying heights, led to a large octagonal area of foundations. A conservatory, he supposed. At the farthest end, his eye was caught by something bright, where a section of wall still stood. DEAN WOZ ERE announced itself in spray-paint. Going closer, Greg smelled dry ash and saw the scattering of cans and litter in the burned circle of a fire.

Yobs. Morons.

He took out his camera: focused, clicked, without being sure why. Then he thought of his bike, vulnerable there in the driveway, and went to check it; he wouldn't have been surprised if they'd sprayed that as well or kicked the spokes in. He found it unharmed, but resolved to be more careful where he left it in future.

Mindless little oiks! He resented the way they'd tainted the place. They could have gone into the forest

41

to light fires and muck about, but the PRIVATE and KEEP OUT signs here were as good as an invitation. He could hardly blame them for trespassing when he was doing the same himself. But he was here as careful observer, not leaving markers like a tomcat spraying its territory, or clambering all over the building at the risk of bringing it down.

With any luck, they'd break their stupid necks.

Keith, the pool manager, had asked Greg if he could continue to do the early Wednesday slot as well as all day Saturdays. It meant hauling himself out of bed at first light, but was otherwise no hassle; the early morning was a training session, no-one likely to get into trouble, with the coach watching his group closely. The pool guard was a token presence.

Greg did his routine jobs – checking the water temperature, taking a sample to be measured for chlorine, putting out lane markers – then got up on his high seat as the first swimmers started to arrive. He saw Jordan, in brief black trunks, come out of the changing room and walk to the deep end, dangling goggles from his fingers. Poised to dive, Jordan saw him and raised a hand, then took a neat header into the pool – the first to ruffle the turquoise-blue surface. Greg watched the deep, sure underwater curve, a long shape flickering against pale-blue tiles. It made him think of a line from a poem they'd looked at in English yesterday – something about 'swimmers into cleanness leaping'. Flipping over, Jordan put on his goggles and adjusted them, then did two lengths of leisurely crawl. The coach, a small wiry man in jog-pants and flip-flops, sent his group into their warm-up routine, gradually building up speed and effort. Greg watched Jordan. A strong swimmer himself but with neither elegance nor impressive speed, he envied Jordan's ability to make swimming so good to watch. When Jordan swam butterfly – a stroke which Greg could manage only as a laborious flounder – it was like watching a fast, graceful animal in its natural element. Poor or clumsy swimmers seemed to fight the water; Jordan rode it, like a human surfboard.

At school Jordan rarely mentioned the swimming, even though he turned up every day smelling faintly of chlorine and with hair still damp, and ate his breakfast in the sixth-form common room, usually before anyone else arrived. It was odd that someone so eye-catching and powerful in the swimming pool could be so unobtrusive at school. Jordan kept himself to himself, rarely speaking up in class. In some subjects he could get away with remaining silent and letting others answer the questions, but when he was forced to speak up – in English, particularly, where Mr O'Donnell insisted on everyone taking part – he usually said something perceptive. He certainly wasn't dim but, Greg realized, had an almost neurotic dislike of drawing attention to himself.

At the beginning of term he and Greg, finding themselves the only two boys in their English class, had sat together with the defensive instinct of boys outnumbered by girls, and discovered that they had other subjects in common as well as being in the same tutor group. It had become habitual for Greg to look out for Jordan in the mornings, in the common room. If Jordan arrived first, as he usually did, he would sit by himself in the corner reading the sixth-form copy of the *Guardian*, which he collected from Reception on his way in; if for some reason Greg were there first, Jordan would give his diffident smile and come over to join him. The predominantly-girl tutor group took little notice of Jordan, so successful was his fading-into-the-background technique. Which was strange, Greg thought, because Jordan was a handsome boy – more so than Gizzard, for instance, whose mouth was too wide and nose too podgy for conventional good looks. Jordan was tall, slightly olive-skinned, with springy dark hair and eyes that Greg had noticed were an unusual clear green. Clever, athletic, good-looking – he had all the qualities that could easily, in someone else, have added up to arrogance. Yet there was always something cautious and guarded about him.

That day in English, they were continuing the reading for their first coursework piece, on First World War poetry. Mr O'Donnell had given them various handwritten drafts of *Anthem for Doomed Youth* by Wilfred Owen. In one version, alterations had been made in another hand; these, Mr O'Donnell explained, were the suggestions made by another poet, Siegfried Sassoon.

'That Wilfred had really neat handwriting, didn't he?' said Bonnie Johnson.

'Yes, Bonnie – unlike yours,' Mr O'Donnell said

crisply. 'Now listen. When they met, at Craiglockhart Hospital in Edinburgh, Owen was definitely in awe of Sassoon. Sassoon was a few years older and already a published poet. Not only that, he had a reputation for bravery and dash in the trenches. He'd already been awarded an MC – a Military Cross – for conspicuous gallantry, after he captured a whole German trench single-handed. Poet-soldier – it must have seemed a potent combination to Owen, the younger of the two. It's not surprising he hero-worshipped Sassoon. *Anthem for Doomed Youth* is one of the poems Owen wrote at Craiglockhart. We're going to spend a bit of time looking at the drafts I've given you, comparing them.'

'What's the point,' Bonnie grumbled, 'if these are just the rough drafts? Can't we stick to the one in the book?'

Mr O'Donnell had a way of looking over the top of his glasses that could be completely shrivelling. Bonnie shut up and looked at the duplicated poems.

'If Wilfred Owen was so much, you know, in awe of Sassoon, like you said,' Madeleine Court pointed out, 'he might have agreed to the changes whether they were good ideas or not, mightn't he?'

'That's exactly what I want you to think about,' Mr O'Donnell said, 'by looking at each of the changes suggested by Sassoon, and at the finished poem. I want you to work in pairs, consider each one carefully, and think about what difference it makes. I'll give you fifteen minutes, then we'll hear what you've got to say.'

'Shouldn't it be *Anthem for Doomed Youth* by

Wilfred Owen and Siegfried Sassoon?' Bonnie said, recovering from the non-verbal snub.

Mr O'Donnell considered. 'If I help you with your coursework essay, will you write on it: *by Bonnie Johnson and Mr O'Donnell*?'

'That's different. You're paid to help me. You're a teacher.'

'And perhaps Sassoon taught Owen something. There are lots of ways of teaching that have nothing to do with school,' Mr O'Donnell said. 'Or not so much teaching, more a matter of Sassoon helping Owen to express what he wanted to say more effectively. Which, come to think of it, is exactly what I try to do with your coursework, Bonnie. Many people consider Owen to be the more promising poet of the two – in fact I think Sassoon himself thought so. Who knows what Owen would have gone on to write if he hadn't been killed?'

The class settled down to study the poem. Immediately Jordan pointed to the title: *Anthem for Dead Youth* in Owen's hand, with *Dead* crossed out and the word *Doomed* substituted in Sassoon's.

'You can see why that's better. *Dead* – well, they're dead already, corpses, finished. *Doomed* means they're fated, there's a death sentence hanging over them, they can't escape it. It makes you sorrier for them.'

Greg nodded. 'Yeah, that's good. And there's the sound as well – *doomed youth*. *Oo oo*. A sort of rhyme. What do you call it?'

'Assonance,' said Mr O'Donnell, looming over their

shoulders. 'Yes, Greg. And what difference does that make?'

He moved on to Bonnie, who had taken her mobile phone out of her rucksack and was reading a text message.

'Well, what difference does it make?' Greg asked Jordan.

Jordan's pen traced *oo ou* on the printed page. 'A longer sound. *Oo* instead of a short *e*. *Dead* is sort of cut off, finished – the sound as well as the meaning. *Dead youth, doomed youth* – I don't know – sadder again?'

Greg wrote *sadder* on his copy. 'How do you spell assonance?'

Jordan spelled it out, then pointed to the word *Anthem*.

'Churchy, like a hymn,' Greg said. 'The National Anthem – well, that's a sort of hymn, I suppose.'

'Does it have to be religious?' Jordan reached into his rucksack for a pocket dictionary. '*Anthem*,' he said, finding the place. '*A piece of sacred music sung in church. Any dignified song of praise.* And it's got *National Anthem: song used by any country as symbol of its national identity*'

'So you're right. It doesn't have to be religious. Ours is, though, 'cos it starts *God save our gracious Queen*.'

'Anthem is good. Ironic.' Jordan underlined it in the green pen he was using for notes. 'Because you read the title, *Anthem*, but in the poem there are none of the things you'd expect. Instead there's a list of no this, no that. *No passing-bells . . . no prayers nor bells . . .* I think he's saying none of that has any relevance any more – church, hymns, prayers.'

'Maybe he's even saying God's given up on them?'

'I don't know. Is it about God, or only about the rituals humans use to make sense of things?'

'Rituals, I suppose.'

'War makes all the old ones pointless and invents new ones of its own,' Jordan said, writing in the margin.

That was good, Greg thought. He wrote it down too, then looked more closely at Wilfred Owen's handwriting in the draft, noticing the firm downstrokes in black fountain pen, the precise shaping of the letters, the characterful *k*s and *p*s: it was neat but artistic. He imagined Wilfred Owen leaning over the page in just this way, considering his choice of words, crossing out, rewriting. Sassoon's writing, in pencil, was scrawly, less careful. What would Owen think now if he knew that teenagers in a classroom were studying his every word, every change of mind? He'd have been amazed, surely, to find himself revered as the voice of the Great War; maybe he'd have found it amusing. Greg knew that Owen had been only twenty-four when he wrote this, twenty-five when he was killed a year later. From the convalescent hospital he had returned to the front line, knowing what he'd be facing. Would he have thought it worth dying, to be established for ever as a war poet, never to have the chance to move on to other subjects? It occurred to Greg that an Owen tragically killed at twenty-five was more interesting than an Owen who survived to become crusty, grey and hard of hearing . . .

He was on the point of saying something about this to Jordan when the door crashed open and a Year Nine messenger came in. Chewing sullenly, the boy handed Mr O'Donnell a folded piece of paper. Mr O'Donnell, who had been explaining something to Jenny Sullivan at the front of the class, straightened and glared at him.

'You know perfectly well that's not the way to enter a classroom. Would you like to go out and try again? And get rid of your chewing-gum while you're out there.'

The boy, obviously not one to be intimidated by the curious eyes of sixth-formers, rolled his eyes. He slouched to the door, knocked, and came in again with mocking courtesy, proffering the note.

'Yes?' Mr O'Donnell prompted. 'Try using *words* if it's not too much effort.'

'Got this note.'

'What's your name?'

'Dean.' The boy's tone implied that everyone ought to know.

'Dean what?'

'Dean Brampton.' Again, the *What's it to you?* inflexion. The boy's gaze fell on Greg. Still chewing, he raised his chin and managed by a small adjustment of his features to give a look of contempt.

Dean. Dean woz ere.

There were lots of boys called Dean . . .

'Well, Dean Brampton, you can come back here at

break-time and we'll have a little discussion about manners and why they're rather important. And you can explain why you're still chewing gum when I just told you to get rid of it. Off you go.' Only now did Mr O'Donnell look down at the note he'd been given. He passed it, still folded, across the desk. 'Jordan, for you.'

Jordan read it. He didn't let Greg see, but Greg saw the expression on his face. Immediately Jordan got his things together, zipped his pencil case, folded his papers and stuffed them into his rucksack. Everyone looked at him. 'Got to go,' he said, pushing his chair back. He didn't ask politely, but this time Mr O'Donnell didn't pursue his crusade for good manners. He just looked at the open door with an anxious expression as Jordan's footsteps retreated down the corridor.

'What's that about?' Bonnie asked, aggrieved. 'Can we all go?'

At Jazz's

Greg's mental photograph: a packed room. The camera is held at head height, rather shakily. The shot is out-of-focus, as if seen through an alcoholic haze. There are figures, male and female: spiked hair, bare shoulders, one head aggressively bald. A girl's head is caught in mid-turn, long hair flying as if in a wind machine. Someone is raising two fingers at the camera, and someone else holding up a joint and grinning inanely. The air is blue with smoke.

With the new digital camera his parents had bought him for his birthday, Greg could download his pictures straight to the computer, bypassing the bother and expense of developing, then tinker with them using Photoshop. Last night he had downloaded his shots of Graveney Hall, and had cropped and enlarged and experimented. Finally he had printed out three, intending to show them to Jordan: the house from the dip in the driveway, then a view through the open doorway on the garden side, and the DEAN WOZ ERE rubbish and graffiti. In the common room at break he took out the three prints and looked at them, beginning to see how he could develop a sequence. From certain angles and in certain lights, you could easily think the house was still intact and inhabited; only at closer range did you see ruin and decay. If his photographs gradually closed in on the vandals' territorial marking, it would give a sense of – what was that word Mr O'Donnell had used the other day? – bathos, that was it. Grand and imposing from some views, derelict and litter-strewn from others.

Greg took out a slip of paper from his pencil case and re-read it. *In photography everything is so ordinary; it takes a lot of looking before you learn to see the ordinary. David Bailey*, it said, in Jordan's small, firm hand-writing. Jordan had read it in a magazine and copied it for Greg, knowing of his ambition to be a photo-grapher. They both liked the idea of *learning to see*. It was, Greg thought, more important than learning about apertures and exposures.

Where was Jordan now? Greg looked up at the doorway. He would have had Geography before break if he'd got back from wherever he'd been summoned. Madeleine, coming in, caught his eye and came over, with Bonnie trailing.

'Why did Jordan have to rush off like that?'

Quickly, Greg put his photographs away in their folder. 'Don't know – he didn't say.'

'Is he in trouble?' Bonnie asked eagerly.

Greg gave her a withering look. 'Yeah, caught

dealing crack behind the bike sheds, I bet.'

'I expect it's to do with his sister.' Maddy's friend Safia, who had been in Jordan's form last year, was getting coffee from the machine. 'She's always in and out of hospital. There's something wrong with her kidneys. He cleared off like that once before.'

'How old is she?' Maddy asked Greg.

Greg shrugged. 'Didn't even know he had a sister.'

'Honestly – blokes!' Maddy huffed, looking round at Safia. 'They go round together all the time and don't even know about each other's sisters!'

'We don't talk about that sort of thing,' Greg said, defensive.

'She's Year Ten, I think, only not here,' Safia said. 'She goes to St Ursula's.'

'Must be serious then,' said Maddy, 'if Jordan's gone haring off?'

Safia shrugged. 'I s'pose so. Don't know any more about it than that, only what Suzanne told me.'

'It must be so *boring*,' Bonnie said, 'going round with Jordan, after Gizzard. I wish Gizzard hadn't left – he was always good for a laugh.'

'Maddy doesn't think Jordan's boring, do you, Mads?' said Safia, with a teasing glance. 'She likes the silent type.' Maddy coloured up. Greg looked at her in surprise; she saw him noticing, blushed even more furiously and turned away. 'Oo-*oo*-ooh!' Bonnie crowed. Jordan would hate this, Greg thought: being the subject of who-fancies-who gossip. But Madeleine . . . maybe she was the sort of girl Jordan might like – bright, unflashy, with a mind of her own.

53

Jordan didn't reappear that day. Greg wasn't sure what to do, not knowing how drastic the situation was. It must have been more than a routine alarm: Jordan's face, when he read the note, had registered first mild curiosity, then shock and dismay. In the evening, he got the McAuliffes' number from Directory Enquiries, unsure whether to phone or not – he didn't know Jordan well enough to probe into a family crisis. But, in the end, he did phone; there was no answer, so he left a message on the answering machine and Jordan rang back just as he was thinking of having an early night.

'Greg? Got your message – sorry it's late.'

'Thought I'd better phone. I thought someone must have died or something.' *Stupid* thing to say!

There was a small pause, then: 'We've all been at the hospital.' Jordan sounded quite calm.

'Safia said it must be something to do with your sister.'

'Yes. Michelle. She's OK now, but she was taken ill at school – she was having trouble breathing, so they took her into hospital as an emergency. They're keeping her in for a couple of days. We've just been back to take the things she needed, and my mum's spending the night there.'

'What's wrong with her?' Greg asked, uneasy with illness and disease.

'It's a long-term thing. Her kidneys don't work,' Jordan said. 'She needs a transplant. But till that happens, she has to go into hospital three days a week for dialysis. That means being plugged into a machine

54

that filters all her blood. It takes five hours each time, and leaves her feeling washed out.'

'It's serious, then?' Greg managed.

'Oh yes, it's serious. She nearly died two years ago when she had acute kidney failure. And if she doesn't get the transplant she'll be stuck with this for ever. She's on a list, waiting. But she's not actually in danger now, if that's what you mean.'

'I didn't even know you had a sister.'

'Haven't I said? Yes, Michelle's great – imagine putting up with all that! But she does. I've got a little brother as well, Mark – he's only eight. If I'm a bit late tomorrow it's because I've got to get him ready for school and take him there – I'll have to miss training. Look, thanks for phoning. See you tomorrow, OK?'

Greg hung up and wandered into the kitchen, where Katy was arguing with their parents about getting her navel pierced.

'Oh, you're so *uncool*! Lorrie's mum let her do it! It's my body, isn't it? I'm not asking for you to *pay* for me to get it done! Why do I have to be the only one with parents who treat me like I'm six years old?'

'You are *not* going to mutilate yourself,' said their father. 'You're too young, and besides it looks tarty.'

'No, it doesn't! What do you know?'

'Give it a rest,' Greg said. He went to the fridge for a Coke.

She turned on him. 'Who asked you, gimp-features?'

'Katy, for goodness' sake!' Their mother was boxing up a cake, tying it with shiny ribbon and running the blade of her scissors down the ribbon-ends to make them spring into curls. 'If you can't speak nicely to *any*one, go to bed! And try to wake up in a better mood tomorrow. I think we've exhausted the subject. We've said no and that's it.'

Katy started banging about in the cupboard. She reached for a packet of biscuits, took one out and ate it, scattering crumbs. 'Why aren't there any chocolate digestives left? I bet Greg the Gannet's scoffed the lot. Anyway, you've got pierced ears, Mum, so how can *you* talk?'

'Tell you what, Katy, why don't you get your lips stapled together?' Greg suggested pleasantly.

Katy flounced out. 'I'm going to phone Lorrie. I need to talk to someone in*tell*igent.'

Their mother put the cake-box to one side and took the wire tray to the sink. 'Oh, dear. Teenagers!' She looked at her husband. 'What did we do to produce such a monster of ingratitude?'

'It's just a phase,' said Greg's dad, flicking through the local free paper.

'Lucky you've got me,' Greg remarked. 'Always charming, witty and sociable.'

'You had your moments,' said his mum. 'Still do, sometimes. How about making us all some coffee, love?'

Greg filled the kettle, thinking about Jordan's sister. What if it had been Katy rushed to hospital? Right now, he'd most likely think *bloody good job* – she was such a pain. But she was still his sister, and he'd have to forgive her for being as obnoxious as she liked if she had something awful like kidney failure. The threat of serious illness hanging over his family was hard to imagine – they were never ill, any of them, apart from ordinary coughs and colds. Really, when you thought of all the things that could go wrong, it was amazing that most people's bodies were in perfect working order. He saw Jordan's sister as a pale, sickly creature in St Ursula's uniform (unsettling, as he thought of St Ursula's as a posh school for daughters of the wealthy); then he pictured Jordan powering through the water, his shoulders gleaming. Michelle had drawn the short straw in that family, then.

'Doing anything this weekend?' he asked Jordan on Friday.

'Inter-club swimming Saturday night, at Chelmsford. Apart from that it's all family stuff. My grandparents are coming over to see Michelle – she should be coming home on Sunday. You?'

'Working Saturday. Nothing much else.'

It was Bonnie's birthday on Saturday, and she and friends were going to the Forest Tavern. Greg had been about to ask Jordan if he wanted to go – partly through curiosity about how things might shape up with Madeleine – but now thought better of it. Jordan gave the impression of having a full and well-organized life; even the hospital crisis had been swiftly assimilated, without fuss. On his return to school, he had answered Greg's questions without appearing keen to discuss the subject at length.

Greg ended up going to a party with Gizzard. He hadn't meant to, but the doorbell rang just as he was getting ready to go to the Tavern. Gizzard, gelled and grinning, was on the front doorstep.

'Hi, fleapit. Come to whisk you away from this humdrum life to a night of wine, women and song.'

'I can't sing.'

'OK, wine and women, then. Two out of three'll have to do. Your charabanc awaits.'

'My what?'

Gizzard waved an expansive hand, gesturing towards the road outside; Greg saw a Mini parked under the street-lamp.

'Shel's just passed her driving test. We're going out to celebrate, round a mate's house. Thought we'd take you along. You allowed out? We'll bring you back before you turn into a pumpkin.'

Greg didn't realize till he reached the car that there were two girls inside – he'd forgotten about Gizzard's attempt to set him up. Sherry/Cherie, in the driving-seat, was small and elfin, with a pert face and hair in short black spikes; the one in the back was all legs and breasts and sparkly hair. The Mini was a two-door, and he struggled past the forward-tilted front seat to squeeze in next to her.

'You don't know Tanya, do you?' Gizzard said, getting into the passenger seat.

'Not yet,' said the sparkly girl; she made a pretence of moving away, but they were both tall and the back seat was cramped, and Greg was very conscious of her thigh against his. She leaned forward between the two front seats as Sherry/Cherie drove away, continuing a muttered conversation that ended in peals of laughter from both girls; her long hair brushed Greg's arm, and he smelled musky perfume. She obviously thought she was sultry.

No, she *was* sultry. At the party – it was at the house of someone called Jazz, but Greg never did work out who Jazz was, nor even whether Jazz was male or female – she attached herself to him as if he were her project for the evening. Not knowing anyone, he didn't mind that at all; being with such a striking girl meant he didn't need to feel self-conscious, the way he sometimes did at parties. She'd seen him at the pool, she told him. She stood so close that he could see right down between her breasts; her musky scent filled his head. She wore a skimpy black top that ended well above her navel, which was pierced with a silver ring and stud. 'Did that hurt?' he asked, looking in fascination at the punctured flesh, thinking of Katy. 'Yeah, like hell,' Tanya said. 'Worth it though, wasn't it?' 'My dad thinks it looks tarty,' he told her. Her eyes stared at him, round and astonished. 'Your dad thinks I'm a tart? Do I know him?' Greg explained about Katy; she laughed. 'I like this sparkly stuff,' he said, touching; she'd put it round her eyes as well as on her hair. It made her dark hair looked spangled with raindrops.

They shared a bag of tortilla chips. He downed his beer, drank another, and another, and began to feel pleasantly vague. Tanya pressed herself against him and in a drunken sway he found that they were kissing. Her hands were twining round him, fingers pushing down inside the back of his jeans. There was something teasing in the way she looked at him: as if she were testing him, pushing to see how far he'd go. The room was smoky and hot and loud and he could hardly breathe. Her tongue was in his mouth; he could taste garlic. The thrum of the music sounded in his ears with a hypnotic beat.

'Let's go upstairs,' Tanya whispered, and nipped the lobe of his ear with sharp teeth. 'Jazz won't mind.'

She took his hand, pulling him through the crowded room. They'd reached the stairs before the thought reached his fuddled brain: Christ, was she intending to *do* it, right now, this minute? My first time, he thought, in a kind of delirium; at the house of someone called Jazz, on a bed piled with coats, with a girl called Tanya with spangles in her hair. It would be a triumph, an achievement, something to tell Gizzard about . . .

If he could do it. He felt as if his groin was on fire, but mixed up with it was sick panic – he had to get out, away from Tanya, away from this houseful of smoke and noise. He balked at the bottom of the stairs, resisting her grip on his hand. Tanya, already on the second stair, lurched back.

'What's up?' Her face loomed close to his; he saw spiky mascara and the gleaming white of her eye.

'Nothing.'

'Oh yeah?' Her hand was snaking down his body, flattening against the fly of his jeans, stopping there. 'I wouldn't call this nothing.'

'You can't be serious—'

'Who said anything about serious? I feel like it, that's all. And don't tell me you don't!'

Her hand continued to move against him, fingertips pressing, exploring – he closed his eyes, then opened them again and pushed her hand away. 'Leave off!' There were two people sitting at the top of the stairs, more voices on the upstairs landing.

'Oh, come on, Greg!' she said into the dip at the base of his throat. 'Don't wind me up. You fancy me, don't you?'

'Who wouldn't?' he answered evasively.

She nuzzled his neck. 'You scared or something? Don't tell me you've never done it? You'll be safe with me, I promise—'

He edged away. 'Course I have,' he lied.

'What, then?'

He gazed at a painting on the wall behind her, an elegant print of a tulip, black-framed. How could he explain? And who was she anyway? Someone he'd only just met. He didn't owe her anything.

He moved towards the door. 'Look, I've got to go, right?'

'You're joking!' Her face hardened. 'Stuff you! Go home to Mummy then. Loser!'

He nodded towards the jewel in her navel. 'In case you're interested, it *does* look tarty. Suits you.'

Her eyes narrowed and her mouth started to open; he saw her preparing a retort. Then the door to the main room opened and three people spilled out. In the confusion, Greg slipped out of the front door and slammed it shut behind him.

He stood on the doorstep, breathing deeply. He heard the bass thud from the stereo, laughter and a girl's voice shrieking from inside. The air was cool against his face. It was dark, but a smudge of moon showed edges of heaped cloud. He stood there biting his lip, ashamed and angry – angry with Tanya, angry with himself. Gizzard would hear all about this, with embellishments. They'd be talking about him, laughing, Gizzard and the two girls.

He could go back into the party and pretend to enjoy himself; maybe find some other girl, show that poser Tanya where she could get off. He needn't ring the doorbell and stand there like a nerd; he could go round to the open back door and just reappear, get himself another lager, find Gizzard and make the whole thing into a joke. He got as far as the side gate, saw the lighted kitchen window running with condensation, and an exhalation of fag-smoke from the extractor fan.

No. He'd had enough.

He walked away from the house. On the way, in the back of the Mini, he'd taken little notice of where they were going. He turned right, found himself in a cul-de-sac, and tried the other direction, at last reaching a road he recognized. The solitude, the silence broken only by occasional traffic, were like gifts he hadn't deserved. His head cleared and became his own again. If he'd had his bike, he'd have gone to the Tavern after all; he considered hitching a lift, decided he couldn't be bothered, and walked home.

His parents were watching a film; his mum looked

at the mantelpiece clock in surprise. 'You're not very late! Did you have a good time?'

'Great, thanks,' Greg said. He went straight up to his room and turned on his stereo.

Caryatid

Greg's photograph (colour): the female caryatid figure on one of the garden summerhouses at Graveney Hall. From ground level, a pillar of stone rises in an angular, widening coffin-shape, becoming the top half of a girl or woman. A draped cloth falls in folds around her waist; above she is naked, with graceful, muscular arms and small rounded breasts. In her arms she holds a garland of vines and fruit. The sunlight throws strong shadows on her face, exaggerating the classical repose of her features. On her forehead there is a medallion or brooch, from which the folds of stone fabric fall away like hair. Above her head, the stone becomes pillar again, rising to a decorative beaded edging, surmounted by balustrades. Moss or lichen gives a greenish shading. Ivy has found a roothold in the stone, and twines live and green around her head.

When he woke up, the sun was shining through his curtain and his mouth tasted of garlic. Remembering the party, he groaned and rolled over; then, giving up the attempt to fall back into sleep, he shoved off the duvet and went into the bathroom to shower, washing last night away. He gargled with his mother's mint stuff and cleaned his teeth, then stuck out his tongue to inspect it.

Dad would be up before long, getting ready for golf; his mother usually had a Sunday lie-in, and Katy rarely surfaced before eleven. Quietly Greg let himself out of the house, and got his bike from the garage.

The cool air revived him like a plunge into the swimming pool. He felt free, full of energy, cycling fast till he was clear of the town and heading towards the fringes of the forest. There had been a heavy dew, and the grass beside the road was shining, webbed with fine threads. It was very still, the *zizz* of his tyres almost the only sound.

On its ridge in hazy sunlight Graveney Hall was the ghost of itself, like the setting for a gothic film. Except that in the film it would be deserted, approached on horseback through swirling mists, whereas in fact there were a number of cars already parked along its frontage. They were keen, those volunteers. On the way here Greg had passed only a few dog-walkers, one jogger and a couple of kids delivering Sunday papers, but this lot had already clocked in. Parking his bike, he kept a wary lookout for anyone with shorts and a beard. He shouldered his rucksack and slung his camera case round his neck with the aim of appearing to be on a photographic assignment, in case anyone invited him to join in the back-breaking fun.

'Hello! Greg, isn't it?' Someone was calling from behind a Volvo hatchback. He looked round and saw the woman with the bandanna over her hair – a red one today. She came over, smiling broadly. She had gappy teeth and a sunburned face and a posh voice. 'You're becoming quite a regular! We'll be glad of your help, I can tell you.'

He indicated his camera. 'No, I'm taking photos.'

'Oh. Well, good – we need lots of those for our exhibition. Are you looking for Faith?'

'Not really.' He'd had enough of being pushed and pulled around by girls.

The woman took no notice. 'She's around somewhere – comes every Sunday, rain or shine. Off on her own most of the time. Well, I must get on. See you at coffee! Don't forget – in the Coach House, eleven sharp. Lovely to see you again.'

You'd think she was his auntie. He wouldn't mind coffee, though, having left home without breakfast. She strode back to her car, collected a big chill-bag and walked off, waving.

He wondered if he ought to tell someone about those yobby boys. First, he walked across to the corner of wall where they'd left their rubbish. This area didn't seem to be visited by the volunteers, whose efforts were concentrated on clearing the house floor and laying their track and working lower down the gardens, but Greg saw immediately that the boys had been back. There was an addition to the acid-green spray-paint: GREG H IS A TOSSPOT. His fists clenched. And they'd lit another fire: he saw fresh ashes in the burned circle, and the blackened remains of sticks and fag-ends.

That settled it – it *must* be that boy Dean from school, the one who'd brought the note for Jordan. What was it? Yes, Dean Brampton. Ignorant little yob! Why should he have it in for me? Greg wondered. Irritation prickled him: *every*one seemed to be getting at him. But if they came here regularly, he'd catch them sooner or later. Then he'd show that arrogant little oik and his friends what they could do with their spray-paint.

He crossed the garden, skirting bandanna woman and her group, who were only a couple of metres farther along their track than when he'd left them last week. Recognizing Faith's father among them, he accelerated his pace, swinging to their left. The woman's imperious voice carried across the grass: 'No, he's taking photographs today.' His role seemed to have become semi-official. Walking slowly through the wet grass of the orchard, he picked up a windfall apple and took a bite, then winced at its sourness and chucked it away. He was making his way to the lake, along to where Faith's log path made its secret descent through the shrubby thickets, when he saw her by the edge of the wood, her back to him. She was picking blackberries, dropping them into a blue plastic carrier bag; she wore jeans and a bright yellow T-shirt. While he wondered whether to speak to her or cut down to the lake on his own, she turned and saw him.

'Hello!' She didn't seem at all surprised. 'I hoped you'd come.'

'Oh, did you?' He walked slowly towards her. 'What, after last week? Handing me over to your dad, then clearing off?'

She laughed. She had white, even teeth and an infectious laugh; annoyed with her though he was, he couldn't help smiling.

'Dad kept going on about you all week – how good to have young people involved, how hard you'd worked, all that sort of thing.' She stooped to wipe juice-stained hands on the grass; the silver cross swung forward on its chain as she crouched.

'Why did you go along with him when he thought you knew me?'

Faith smiled. 'Easier than saying you were some trespasser who crept up on me down by the lake.'

'I didn't creep! And how come you don't get roped in to the slave labour? I don't see you sweating and straining.'

'I am helping, though!' Faith looked affronted. 'Mum makes blackberry pies and jam to sell at the open day. It all helps make money. Look! There's hundreds here – great big juicy ones. You can help if you like.'

'Well, OK.' He came closer to the mound of brambles, seeing the thorny stems heavy with clusters of blackberries, plump and glossy, and the drapery of spider-webs spangled with dew.

'We can get loads.' Faith pulled another plastic bag from her jeans pocket. 'Look out for maggots. I've seen one or two.'

'Does your mum work here as well, then?'

'Mm, every week – she's tidying up in the Coach House.'

The berries were asking to be picked, coming away easily from their stems; it was satisfying, dropping the warm fruit into his bag, feeling it gradually sag with their weight. He ate while he picked, feeling the sharp sweetness on his tongue and the fibrous pippiness.

'Breakfast,' he explained to Faith.

'Were you mad at me last week?' she asked.

'What do you think? Getting rid of me like that!'

'Oh no, it wasn't that. I was in the middle of something, that's all.'

'What?'

'At the grotto, where you found me – I go down there to be by myself. To meditate and pray.' She looked at him defiantly. 'No-one disturbs me down there.'

'Pray?' Greg echoed, not sure she was serious.

'Yes.'

'What, all day long?'

She shook her head. 'No, I think and read and walk about as well, and just look at the water and the trees. I suppose I think of it as my own special Sunday place. That's why I didn't like you being there at first.'

Greg looked at her sidelong. 'So you don't – you know – go to church; you go there instead?'

'Church on Sunday evenings. And to Bible Study class on Wednesdays.'

'Oh.' He was taken aback. The cross round her neck

wasn't a mere piece of jewellery, then. St Ursula's girl. Right. Religion probably came as part of the package. But it was more than a formality for her, if she spent time praying by herself.

'What do you pray about?' he ventured.

'Oh, things. There's always something. I mean big things, not just things for myself.'

'You've got the right name then. Faith.'

She laughed. 'That's no coincidence. My parents are both Christians, you see.'

'What if you hadn't wanted to be one?'

She looked at him. 'But I do. I am. If I didn't believe – well, what would it all be about?'

'What would what be about?'

'Life. Everything. What would it all mean?'

'OK, so what *does* it mean? You're telling me you've got it sussed?'

She was stretching deep into the bush, reaching for a cluster of berries, showing a strip of smooth flesh between jeans and T-shirt. A thorn caught at the yellow fabric; she stopped to free herself, then bent the stem down in an arc. 'It means living for God. For Jesus. Everything we do is for them. Without that, there'd be no point in anything. No meaning.'

'Shouldn't we work out our own meaning?'

'OK, so what's yours?' she asked, chin high.

'You do like to ask awkward questions, don't you? Only I'm not pretending to have the answers. What you said – is that what you've been taught? Or do you believe it for yourself?'

She turned to stare at him, holding the thorny spray

away from her face. 'Of course I believe it. If I didn't, it would just be . . .'

'Mm?'

'Like cleaning your teeth every morning and night. Like looking both ways before you cross the road. Just following rules, no more than that.'

'So you're a real born-again Christian? Or a born-into-it Christian?'

'Every true Christian is born again. Just going to church and reading the Bible doesn't make you a Christian. You have to know that Jesus died for you. No, more than that, you have to *feel* it. You have to know it inside yourself.'

Greg was beginning to feel preached at. 'So you know that Jesus died for you? He died for your sins that you wouldn't commit for another two thousand years?'

'He died to show me the way to God. And to show you.'

He huffed a laugh; she looked at him sharply but turned away to concentrate on her picking. He dropped a handful of berries into the bag, assimilating this new aspect of her. He felt, in a way, embarrassed; he wasn't used to having conversations like this. He knew other people who went to church, of course – there was a girl in his form who taught a Sunday school class. Some people rode bikes or played football, others went to church. But for Faith, it was obviously more than that. It was – well, real faith. He didn't know whether to feel amused, irritated or impressed.

'What about you?' Faith asked.

'What about me what?'

'What do you believe in?'

Greg puffed out his cheeks. 'I don't believe in God, no.'

'What, then? What do you think we're doing here?'

'I think we evolved from apes. I mean, God creating the world in seven days and all that – fine, nice story, when people believed the earth was the centre of the universe, but it doesn't make much sense now. Not since Stephen Hawking and Big Bang theories have proved it wasn't like that.'

'Proved? Aren't those just theories?'

'Better theories than yours, though.'

'I don't see that. The Big Bang doesn't rule out the existence of God.'

'The universe obeys its own laws – the laws of physics,' Greg said. 'There's no need for a God to have created it.'

'But God *made* the laws of physics. Otherwise, what? Scientists keep talking about the first few seconds of the universe, but what was before that? What made time and space?' Faith paused to suck a blackberry prickle from her finger. 'Anyway, go on.'

'Go on what?'

'About the Big Bang,' Faith said. 'How you understand it.'

Christ! (And he'd better not say *that* aloud.) He wasn't sure how much he *did* understand. It was a bit much to be called upon to account for his existence, the existence of the whole universe – all out of the blue on a Sunday morning when he'd come here to get away from last night. 'Well, it was about twelve billion years ago,' he began reluctantly. 'And our galaxy exploded from a singularity – the centre of a black hole. And maybe that's where it'll all finish up again, eventually – sucked back in. Don't they teach you about cosmology at St Ursula's?' It was easier to be flippant than to dredge up Physics lessons he wasn't sure he could pass on coherently.

Suddenly Faith was defensive. 'How do you know I'm at St Ursula's?'

'Your dad said.'

'Oh, he would!' Faith said, grimacing Katy-fashion. 'Why does he have to tell people that? It's like hanging a label round my neck: St Ursula's girl!'

'You don't mind hanging that cross round your neck. Isn't that a kind of label?'

Faith's hand went to her throat; she held out her silver crucifix as far as its chain would allow, as if using it as a charm to ward off evil. 'That's not the same thing at all. I choose to wear this – it's for me. Anyway, what about you? Sixth form or what?'

'Radway. The comp. Doesn't Daddy mind you hanging around with a pleb like me?'

'Don't be stupid; you're not a pleb. And I'm not posh just because I go to St Ursula's.' He had annoyed her; she was picking the fruit at accelerated speed, deciding her bag was full enough, pulling out another from her pocket.

'D'you know a girl called Michelle McAuliffe?' he asked in a gentler tone. 'Her brother's in my year.'

73

'Yes. She's the year below me, Year Ten. I don't know her well, but I know who she is.'

'OK, then. Why does God decide to give a fifteen-year-old girl kidney failure? Because he's so kind and concerned?'

Faith shook her head. 'We can't know why things like that happen.'

'So there is a reason?'

'God has a reason for everything. It's not for us to know. We just have to accept it as God's will.'

'So if it were you or me with duff kidneys, we'd have to say, *Oh dear! But I'm sure God must have a reason, so I'll have to put up with it.* Is that what you mean?'

'Yes, that's exactly what I mean.'

'And if you'd been on your way to Auschwitz and the gas chambers? Or buried in an earthquake? Or starving in a famine? All part of the great plan?'

She looked at him, puzzled. 'Why are you so angry?'

Only now did he realize how his voice had risen; he'd almost been shouting.

'I believe in God, you choose not to – why should that annoy you?' Faith asked.

'I don't know.' He pulled a stem towards him and plucked off the ripe berries, then released it so that it sprang back out of reach. He let go clumsily; a thorn pricked his thumb. He looked at the bead of blood before sucking his thumb clean, tasting the salt-sweetness. They carried on picking in silence, Greg trying to work out a proper answer for himself if not for her. A few times she glanced at him, seeming about to speak, but said nothing.

That was what was annoying him! She was waiting for him to come up with a reason, so that she could trot out her ready-made answer. It was like a barrier, a safety-belt. She wasn't having to think for herself. She was as well-rehearsed as a double-glazing sales-man. Before he could find wording for this that wouldn't be offensive, she stepped back from the bushes, tied the neck of her carrier bag and said, 'We've got quite a lot. Let's stop for a bit. I want to show you the most wonderful thing in the whole place.' Her voice was changed – soft, friendly. He knew she thought she'd won the argument.

'OK,' he said, glad to change the subject. He put down his bag next to hers – three bags in a row on the grass – and picked up his camera. 'What is it?'

She smiled over her shoulder. 'Wait and see.'

He expected her to go down to the lake, towards the grotto, but instead she walked back across the orchard to the formal part of the gardens. An electric mower trundled noisily along the main grass path; another pair of workers were cutting down brambles from a plinth that must once have supported a statue.

'There are photos of what this looked like in about nineteen hundred,' Faith said. 'It was fantastic – well, if you like that sort of garden, it was. All statues and fountains and curving steps, and clipped box hedges, and flower-beds perfectly weeded. You'll see the photos if you come to the open day. Here. Here's my favourite thing.' They had reached one of the pair of stone summerhouses that faced each other across the lower part of the terrace. 'You haven't seen her before, have you? Isn't she wonderful?'

They were looking at a female figure carved out of a supporting pillar. There were two of them, one on each side of the open front of the summerhouse, but Faith was looking at the left-hand one. The one on the right was damaged, most of its face crumbled away, but this one was perfect. Larger than life, she rose above them, holding a carved garland, one hand raised as if to pluck a too-tempting grape. Her face was very beautiful – straight Grecian nose, large eyes, an expression of calmness and strength. The green shading of moss or lichen made her appear more lifelike than if the stone had been scrubbed and pristine. The ivy twining around her head and shoulders gave the accidental finishing touch.

'That twiggy stuff – it makes her look like something from a legend,' Greg said. 'You know the woman with snakes for hair – one look at her and you turn into stone. Medusa, was it?'

'It's all right,' Faith said quite seriously. 'She won't turn you to stone. I've looked at her loads of times and it's never happened to me. She's not malicious, is she? You can see from her face. I wonder what she'd say if she could speak? I wonder what she's seen.'

'And there are two of them.' Greg looked at the other, almost faceless statue, spoiled by time and erosion. 'How come this one's so perfect when the other's all worn?'

'Something to do with the prevailing winds, Dad

says. This one's sheltered by the angle of the building. They're called caryatids.'

'Caryatids?'

She nodded. 'Supporting columns made into female statues. Male ones are called telamons. There are two of them over there.' She nodded at the opposite summerhouse; they walked across to look. The building was identical, but this time the statues were of muscular, bearded men, again holding wreaths of vines and fruit.

'They're lovely too, but not like my caryatid,' Faith said.

Greg opened his camera case. 'I'm going to take photos.'

He took several, from various angles, of both summerhouses, but concentrated on the caryatid, moving in close to get the shadows that threw her features into relief. Faith watched at first, then sat down on the steps; when the man with the mower had moved on, she walked along the main path to the far end and stood looking out across the fields. When he'd used up his disc, he went to join her. The garden simply ended in a bank of rough grass and thistles; two metres lower was a newly-ploughed field, curving down towards the valley. The smell of mown grass filled the air with summer.

'There used to be steps here and great wrought-iron gates,' Faith said. 'I've seen the pictures. But you can still see the ha-ha.'

'The what?'

'Ha-ha. This. Haven't you seen one before? What it

is – people who owned stately homes like this wanted to look out of their windows, or sit on their terrace, and see their land sweeping away into the distance. They didn't want it all chopped up by fences, but they needed to keep cows and sheep out of the garden. So instead of a fence they had a big drop like this, a sort of dry ditch. It keeps animals out but doesn't interrupt the view. I expect there's a wall underneath all this grass, to stop it from collapsing.'

'So why's it called a ha-ha?'

Faith giggled. 'Dad says it's because you're walking along and all of a sudden the ground drops away from your feet, and you go *A-ha!* I don't suppose that's the real reason, though.'

Greg turned his back on the ha-ha and looked towards the mansion. He imagined, on a day like this, ladies and gentlemen sitting in one of the twin summerhouses, and a butler crossing the terrace with a loaded tray. Polished silverware, there'd be, and linen napkins in stiff folds, and dainty things to eat.

He said to Faith, 'All this, just for one family! It must have been palatial! Who were they, the people who lived here?'

'The Pearsons were the last ones – till nineteen seventeen. Before that it was Sir Somebody Something and all his descendants. There's a leaflet – I'll get one for you later.'

A thought struck him. 'Your mum and dad – putting in all this work and effort on a place like this. Why don't they . . .'

Faith had stooped to pick a clover flower. She turned towards him, wary again. 'Yes?'

'I mean, they're Christians. Aren't there other things – more important things – they could be doing?'

'Like what?'

'Like making money for famine victims, or helping the homeless – this isn't really helping *people*, is it?'

Faith twirled the clover stem between her finger and thumb, then tossed it aside. 'Oh, there you go again – finding things to criticize! What about you? Why aren't *you* helping famine victims or the homeless if it's so important to you?'

'I didn't say it was! I was just saying, they're Christians. Shouldn't people be more important to them than statues and stuff?'

'What's it to you?'

'I'm just *asking*—'

'So when you're playing computer games or kicking a ball about or all the mindless things boys do, do you stop and feel guilty because you could be shaking a tin in the High Street or working for Oxfam? 'Course you don't. My parents aren't trying to make themselves into saints just because they're Christians – neither am I! It's up to us what we do in our spare time. Why should you criticize?'

'I didn't mean—' he began, but she was in no mood to hear his answer. She gave him a final glare and walked away quickly, taking long strides across the grass.

Bugger! He hadn't meant to upset her but she was

so easily offended, so touchy, on the subject of her faith especially. Why had she started on the subject at all if she didn't want to discuss it? She needn't have told him about the praying; at first she'd sounded proud of it, not in the least secretive.

Girls! He wasn't doing too well, one way or another. That was two of them he'd quarrelled with in different ways in less than twenty-four hours. He sat down heavily on the grass, wondering what was the matter with him. Reluctantly he remembered what an idiot he'd made of himself last night. He'd have to come up with a convincingly edited version for Gizzard. Even now he didn't know what had stopped him from following Tanya upstairs. All set up, on the point of having a fantasy fulfilled, he'd blown it.

And now Faith. She was obviously a very different species of girl from Tanya, but he'd managed to upset her as well. He couldn't imagine Faith going to boozy parties, let alone trying to drag boys into bedrooms – ludicrous thought! It wasn't easy to tell at first glance, though. He remembered Faith's clothes last week: the skirt short enough for him to glimpse her knickers, the skimpy vest top that clung to her small breasts. She had seemed then like any other teenage girl who wanted to look sexy. There was only the cross to give any sort of clue, and lots of people wore those quite meaninglessly.

He didn't want to argue with her, didn't want to leave it like this. He stood up. Damn! He'd forgotten how damp the grass was, and now he had a wet bum. He wondered where she'd gone. If she'd run to

Mummy or Daddy, well, that would be it. But if she were on her own, he could try to make up the argument.

He walked back towards the blackberry bushes, skirting the statue base where the two workers, a man and a woman, were piling cut brambles into a wheelbarrow. One of them smiled at him without speaking, and he wondered if they'd overheard his spat with Faith. Across the orchard, the three bags of blackberries lay on the grass; there was no sign of her. He stood for a moment, wondering what to do.

The grotto. That's where she'd be. With some difficulty he found the log path where it crept down from the open orchard. He made his descent to the lake shore and stood on the path in the open bowl of sky enclosed by trees, feeling the silence and seclusion. He heard the trickle of the spring that emerged from the grotto's interior, saw the crystal channel of its decanting into the lake, and a clear fan-shape where it funnelled into sandy water.

Faith was exactly where he'd found her last week, sitting on the bench inside. She looked up at him and away again quickly.

'Oh. You,' she sniffed.

He sat on the bench next to her. 'Look, I – I'm sorry.'

'Do you mean that?'

'Would I have trekked down here otherwise? I didn't mean to get at you.'

'But you did.' She turned her face away. 'Don't you like me or something?'

'Yes! I do like you,' he said uncertainly.

'You don't think I'm a snotty little St Ursula's girl?'

'No,' Greg lied. 'And you don't think I'm a vile loudmouthed yob?'

She looked at him and smiled, wiping a finger along the lower lashes of one eye. ' 'Course not. Why would I?'

'Been doing a good imitation.'

'Not really.' She hesitated. 'I'm sorry too.'

'For what?'

'For getting at you,' Faith said. 'I didn't really mean to either. We're all right now, aren't we?'

' 'Course we are.'

And to Greg's astonishment she turned and hugged him, leaning close. He smelled her hair, felt its silky length fall over his arm. Gingerly he put a hand to her back; at once she pulled away and stood up.

'That's all right then,' she said briskly. 'Shall we go and pick more blackberries?'

1916, late summer

When stand-to marked the dawn of dreary day,
When stretcher-parties bore their groaning load,
When boots were mired in wet and clinging clay,
When feet burned on a never-ending road,
When heaven was obscured by drifting smoke,
When reinforcements ~~were~~ came too few, too late,
When battle-plans were High Command's poor joke,
When God despaired and left us to our fate.

When nothing could protect us save barbed wire,
When flares and shells soared up as darkness fell,
When all the world seemed ~~lost~~ drowned in filth and mire,
When ~~High Wood~~ Tricourt was another name for Hell —
You were there where never love dared chance,
You were there to save me with your glance.

Edmund Pearson

Alternative ending:
   At these ~~and~~ other very trying times
Edmund sat and scowled and made up rhymes.

AC.

In an orchard in Picardy, Lieutenant Edmund Pearson was lying in uncut grass with his uniform jacket folded under his head as a pillow. Two peaked caps lay on the ground half-filled with damsons; a wasp hovered around the ripe fruit and Edmund raised a hand to swish it away. Beside him, cross-legged, sat Alex Culworth, reading from a small notebook. Edmund waited, watching his expression, and his eyes scanning the lines of handwriting – the lines Edmund had drafted and redrafted and copied out with such care.

Without comment, Alex turned a page and carried on reading intently. Whatever he did, he gave it the full blaze of his attention. Edmund liked that. Not for Alex the cursory reading, the polite response.

'Well, Lord Byron,' Alex said at last, 'never let an idle minute go to waste, I see.'

'If you think they're dreadful, please say so.'

'No need to raise your hackles. I haven't said anything yet.' Alex picked up the first page again. 'This one – the idea, and the opening – *Last night I saw the ghost of France / Rise from her grave to mourn* . . . Yes. And I like the last stanza. I'm not sure about *with wide-mouthed gashes torn*. It's a bit clumsy – not easy to say. And perhaps too obvious a rhyme.'

Edmund nodded.

'Hmm. The land as victim,' Alex said, and his voice took on a teasing tone. 'You would see it that way, as a bloated aristocrat, a member of the land-owning classes.'

'Of course. And the sonnet?' Edmund's words

came out hoarsened with doubt: Alex had not yet mentioned the second poem, the one addressed to him. He wished he had handed over the poems and left Alex alone to read them, not stayed here to register every eye-flicker, every compression of the lips. To offer his verses was to show Alex his thoughts and, he saw now, to expose himself to the possibility of hurt and rejection.

'The ending, of course. Thank you. I like the way the last two lines bring in something different entirely, something personal.' Alex looked back at the poem, at Edmund's neat handwriting. 'The rest, I don't know – maybe you've made it a little too easy for yourself?'

'Easy? If you knew how I struggled!'

'All the same, that structure, the repetition of *when*, and each line complete and self-contained – it means you can put them in any order to suit the rhyme-scheme.'

'Is that a criticism?'

'I'm being honest. Isn't that what you wanted? I love them, of course, because you wrote them. It's easy for me to criticize – I'm no poet myself.'

Edmund lay back and looked up at the sky, trying not to nurture a small and unreasonable disappointment. He had wanted Alex to say: *They're wonderful, they're brilliant, they're flawless.* Yet he knew that his poems were none of these things: they were competent at best. Did he want Alex to be a liar? Or to be so dazzled by emotion that he lost all critical awareness?

I must try harder, he told himself. One day I will write the best poem of my life, for him, and it will say everything I struggle to put into words. It will be dedicated *To A.C.* – cryptic, so that it can openly be a love poem, but only he will know who it's for. And into his mind slipped a picture of a slim, leather-bound volume, privately printed, with marbled end-papers and gilt lettering on its spine. Critics and scholars would speculate who A.C. might be, in the way they puzzled over Shakespeare's Dark Lady of the Sonnets.

'The thing about it, that sonnet,' Alex said, still considering, leaning back on braced arms, 'is that I don't think it's true.'

'You don't believe me?' Edmund was dismayed.

'I don't mean the ending.' Alex gave him a sidelong glance, a look that smoothed away misgivings. 'I mean the rest of it.'

'But—'

'Why don't you admit it? The war is the best thing that's happened to you.'

'Here, I might think so.' Edmund waved a hand to encompass the orchard, the slow-flowing river Lys that threaded through pollarded willows. His return to the 5th Epping Foresters had coincided with a period of rest behind the lines, which he had not deserved.

'Not just here,' Alex insisted. 'The front. The fighting. All of it. The things you wrote about. If you could choose now – this, or banish the whole war and go back to your old life – you'd choose this, wouldn't you?'

'Yes,' Edmund said after a moment's thought. 'It's changed everything. If it weren't for Kaiser Wilhelm, I'd be following my father's route. Cambridge, marriage, Graveney.' He lay back and looked up at the sky, wondering whether to tell Alex about Philippa Fitch being dangled in front of him like a baited hook.

'I'd despise you,' Alex said lightly, 'if we met, which of course we wouldn't.'

'I was quite sure at first that you did.'

'That was only testing. You know that. It wouldn't be fair of me to hold your upbringing against you.'

Without the war, Edmund knew that his path would not have crossed Alex's. A year older, Alex came from an East London family which had moved out to Woodford; he had won a scholarship to study Mathematics at London University. He was all that Edmund was not: cynical, sharp, socialist. When they had first met, at Officer Training Camp, they had disliked each other. Edmund saw Alex as a threat: clever and outspoken, with quick darting eyes that missed nothing. But attraction had grown between them against the odds. Where at first Edmund had seen only abrasiveness, he now found warmth, tenderness and humour. Alex was not handsome in any obvious way, but he had a powerful physical presence – tall, lanky, with fox-red hair that curled and kinked, intensely blue eyes and a smile of dazzling fierceness. There was something feral and dangerous about him, Edmund often thought, unable to take his eyes off him.

It was Alex, of course, who had dared to lead the way beyond friendship to intimacy. Edmund, who had always thought himself deeply conventional, reacted first with shock, then with joy and enthusiasm. He knew by now that Alex had had a previous lover; for Edmund it was Alex, only Alex. He had no interest in anyone else, male or female.

'Why? Why do you love me?' he had asked earlier, when dawn lightened their attic and house martins stirred in the eaves.

'You know why! I love your money, your wealth, your family fortune,' Alex said, rarely serious, 'your country seat, and the aristocratic blood that flows through your veins. And for condescending to notice a humble London boy like me.' He made a forelock-tugging gesture.

'Humble! I've never met anyone more sure of himself.'

Edmund thought that Alex would ask, 'And why do you love me?' in return, but he did not. Nevertheless, Edmund prepared his answer: because you're proud and strong, more vividly alive than anyone I know; because you have led me where I would never have thought of going; because you have taught me how to love.

Alex had taken out a stub of pencil and was writing in Edmund's notebook, his lips compressed in a secretive smile.

'When I was convalescing,' Edmund told him, 'I had the idea of writing verses about my home, as a way of showing it to you. The lake, the gardens, the summerhouse statues, the trees . . . but I hardly made a start. Perhaps I can do it more easily when I'm not there.'

'A poetic tour? Yes, I'd like that.'

'We could start at the grotto by the lake – that's my favourite place. My retreat.' Edmund closed his eyes to see the swirling patterns of tiles; he heard the trickle of spring water, smelled the dampness of earth and stone. 'My grandfather built it in memory of his first son, who died as a baby. Grandfather used to spend hours there, sitting by the lake, thinking and daydreaming. Now I do.'

'What do you daydream about?' Alex twirled a grass stem to tickle Edmund's nose.

Their eyes met; Edmund smiled. 'Every day, when I was at home, I went down there to read your letters and write mine.'

'While I wrote mine cramped in a dugout, with my feet in a puddle,' Alex said drily, 'and hid them quickly whenever Boyce came in with a mug of oily tea.' He picked a ripe damson out of his cap. 'I wish I could see you at your Graveney Hall. It would be amusing to see you as future lord of the manor, Little Lord Fauntleroy that you are.'

'I am *not* little Lord Fauntleroy, thank you!'

'I can just see you in your little velvet knickerbocker suit, with your perambulator and your nursemaid. Young Master Edmund. Here—'

He pinched the damson to make it split, flicked away the stone and held the fruit to Edmund's lips. Edmund opened his mouth, felt the brush of Alex's fingers, then the soft fleshy fruit, warm with sunshine. He ate, swallowed. 'Maybe you will see Graveney. Not yet, but maybe. When all this is over.'

'If?'

With the grass warm at his back Edmund looked up at the dazzle of blue sky, thinking that Alex was right: he really did want the war to go on for ever. 'My parents are planning for me to get married,' he said.

'Really? And who's the lucky girl?'

Edmund propped himself up on his jacket-pillow and looked at Alex for the pleasure of looking: at his sharp profile, his thin nose and well-defined cheekbones, and his hair the colour of autumn. His shirt collar was unfastened and his shirtsleeves rolled up, his jacket slung on the grass.

'I'm not *going* to,' Edmund answered. 'You don't seriously think I meant—'

'I hoped not. But is there a candidate?'

'Yes. Unfortunately. Her name's Philippa. Philippa Fitch. She's the daughter of my parents' closest friends, and they've all decided it would be the perfect match. She's pretty, educated, plays the piano, sings, rides to hounds, speaks fluent French, dresses elegantly, has perfect manners – oh, she has everything possible to commend her. I should imagine most young men in my position would think themselves very lucky.'

'And is Philippa herself one of those who think it the perfect match?'

'She'd be willing enough. I don't delude myself that it's on my account – the house and estate are fairly large enticements, wouldn't you say?'

90

'So she's a fortune hunter?' Alex plucked a stem of grass.

'Not exactly. We've known each other since we were children. It would be more a matter of convenience, of everyone knowing what they were getting from the bargain.' Edmund looked at Alex, reached a hand and laid it on his knee. '*Would* be, I said. I've no intention of complying, however much pressure Father puts on me. It's my duty to provide an heir for Graveney, and Philippa comes from good stock. That's how he sees it.'

Alex laughed and gently removed the hand from his knee. His glance said, *Careful – we might be seen from the windows*; it also said, *Later*. 'So it's all about breeding when it comes down to it. She might as well be a brood mare or a prize cow.'

'Exactly.'

'But if you don't do the decent thing and produce a son and heir . . .?'

'It will all go to some distant cousin, I think. It's the war that's made Father impatient. If he had his way I'd already have produced, and the son and heir would be safely at home in his nursery. Then, if I got blown to bits, at least the future would be assured.'

'That's a callous way of looking at it.'

'Yes. But that's how it is when there's property involved.' Edmund gazed across the orchard towards the alder-fringed bank of the river. 'I love the place, Graveney. Not the house so much as the land itself – the trees, the earth. Yes, I know, it's my landed gentry upbringing, before you say. I've never lived anywhere else, or wanted to. I've been brought up with the expectation of taking it over and living there till I die. But can you imagine me explaining? *I'm afraid I can't marry Philippa, Father, because I love someone else, and his name's Alex.*'

Alex pretended to consider this seriously. 'No, if you really want to be lord of the manor I'd say that was rather unwise.'

'I might never have known.'

'Well,' Alex said, 'a lot of people don't. Or don't let themselves admit it. After all, there are powerful incentives not to.'

'I'd give everything up, Graveney and all that goes with it – the land, the inheritance – to be with you.'

Alex looked at him steadily. 'I'd hate to be the one to make you do that.'

'You wouldn't make me. It would be what I chose for myself.' Edmund lay down again and stretched out both arms. 'Let's not go home! Let's stay here after the war. We could rent a small farmhouse, and keep chickens, and grow apples and plums and turnips.'

'Yes, this one will do nicely. I'm sure the present tenants won't mind giving it to us,' Alex said airily, turning this way and that to survey the orchard and its surroundings. 'We can go to the market, and speak French, and buy cheese and sausages, and sit smoking in the café. We can be two eccentric Englishmen.'

'No-one will bother us. Wouldn't that be perfect?'

'No-one will require us to produce sons and heirs, because there will be nothing to inherit.'

They were speaking flippantly, but as Edmund lay gazing at the cloud-flecked sky the idea began to take hold. If they survived the war they'd have the right, surely, to choose what future they wanted for themselves? Maybe he would choose to keep a few chickens, grow a few potatoes, instead of managing the great, sprawling, magnificent encumbrance that was Graveney. Choosing Alex as his partner was rather more contentious, but if they stayed here in rural France, where no-one would know them or expect anything of them, it would be far easier than in England.

'I'm not really joking,' he said, turning his head towards Alex. 'I mean it. I can't imagine a future without you.'

Alex looked down at him and said softly, 'Nor I.'

At moments like this, Edmund had the sense of everything settling into place. This, then, was love – not love as his father wanted it, all tied up with property and respectability and procreation. This was love that demanded nothing except itself.

If his father found out . . .

Perhaps, Edmund sometimes thought in his wilder moments, his father finding out would be the easiest solution. If he were disgraced, disinherited, turned out of Graveney without a penny to his name, he could live with Alex as he wanted. More immediately, they were occupied with making sure Captain Greenaway didn't find out. Here at the farm, the men slept in a cow-barn converted to makeshift dormitory; Edmund and Alex slept in the house with the other officers. As the two youngest lieutenants they shared a room in the attic and, secretly, a bed. Every morning, before Boyce, the orderly, knocked on the door with hot water for washing and shaving, one of them would get into his own unrumpled bed, roll around in it and feign deep sleep. For Alex the risk was part of the pleasure, but Edmund was convinced that one morning they'd oversleep, fail to hear Boyce's knocking and be discovered. With every detail of their lives so closely regulated, they found secret fulfilment in something that was theirs alone, up in the roof of the house, where martins twittered in the eaves and dawn came softly through threadbare curtains.

Lying in Alex's arms at night, listening to the boom and splutter of artillery to the east, Edmund thought that time behaved in peculiar ways. These days and nights at the farm seemed everlasting; he would remember them for ever. With Alex's breathing soft against his neck and the curtains stirring with cool night air, he could hardly believe that time was passing at all. And simultaneously the week was racing by, their week of rest and reprieve: four nights left, three nights, two. Alex always slept heavily – dreamlessly, he said. Edmund often lay awake.

In July, during his absence, the Foresters had been involved in the heavy fighting around Thiepval, farther south. Edmund, injured by a piece of shell embedded in his thigh a fortnight before the massed assault, had missed it all. On his return from convalescent leave he had found various changes in

C Company: Captain Massey had been killed in the second wave, and Major Evans, and three of the men in Edmund's own platoon, with four more wounded. Two of the dead privates had been boys younger than Edmund, and the third had been Georgie Baillie, eldest son of George Baillie senior, the head gardener at Graveney Hall.

As Alex would say little about the attacks other than that there had been 'a bit of a skirmish', most of Edmund's information came from Captain Greenaway. Edmund felt he had let them all down, but his conscience was particularly troubled by Georgie Baillie. At the time of Georgie's death, Edmund had been on his way back to France; news must have reached the Baillie parents shortly after. Georgie, quiet but sharp-witted, had once come unexpectedly upon Edmund and Alex in a candle-lit dug-out. They had only been talking, but Edmund had seen the look of startled revelation in Georgie's eyes. Since then, he had gone over and over what Georgie must have seen and heard: a hushed conversation, a hand raised to touch a sleeve, an exchange of glances. The thought that Georgie knew, and could take his knowledge home to Graveney to provide servants' gossip, brought Edmund out in a sweat of panic.

'He knows,' he fretted to Alex.

'No, he doesn't. He suspects, at most. Let him. How can he harm us even if he wanted to? And why should he?'

Now Georgie had been conveniently silenced. In Edmund's absence, Alex had had to write the letter home to the Baillie parents; Edmund had written to add his condolences, aware that his sadness was tinged with relief.

When they had moved into their room there was a gloomy painting on the wall facing both beds: the crucified Christ bleeding from his crown of thorns. The first time he got into Alex's bed, Edmund got out again to turn the picture to face the wall. 'I don't think He'd approve.'

'Superstitious nonsense,' Alex said. 'We're here to kill Germans. Is this more sinful than that?'

At the end of the week, the 5th Epping Foresters moved east to the front line.

Believed killed

Black-and-white photograph from the Graveney Hall booklet: 'A view of the Italian garden from the first floor terrace, 1912.' We are looking down the length of the walk towards the ha-ha and an elaborate wrought-iron gateway. The lawns are cut into geometric shapes by diagonal paths; in two places where they converge we see octagonal stone basins with elaborate fountains. The garden is punctuated by stone obelisks and statues, small standard trees and clipped cypress and yew, all in a complex symmetrical design. The twin summerhouses – one guarded by telamons, one by caryatids face each other across the width. As we can see no colour, the overall impression is of an extremely formal garden: clipped, ordered, meticulously maintained.

In bed on Monday morning, Greg was reading a booklet given him by Faith. It was rather dry: a few black-and-white photographs breaking up pages and pages of close print, listing unelaborated facts about earls and acreages. Greg skimmed through information about early buildings, extensions, feuding families and a hunting squire; about an earlier Tudor house on the site of Graveney Hall. The present mansion, he read, dated from the 1750s, going through a series of extensions and refinements in the late nineteenth century. The owner at that time, William Ernest Pearson, had added two new wings, a conservatory and a ballroom, and had hired an eminent architect to landscape the gardens and grounds. *The grotto by the lakeside is believed to have been commissioned by Pearson in memory of his first son, Edmund, who died in infancy,* Greg read. *It was Pearson himself who decorated the interior with its striking tile mosiac.* Faith must have known that. Why hadn't she told him when he asked?

Most of all, Greg wanted to find out about the fire, though the book gave little detail. *The fire which almost destroyed Graveney Hall is believed to have broken out during the morning of 6th April 1917,* he read. *Members of the household had set off for the Good Friday church service, and the fire was discovered by one of the servants. The local horse-drawn fire engine was summoned, but on arrival it was found that the water supply was inadequate. By this time the fire had taken hold, and servants set about removing items of value. It took several hours for the fire team to extinguish the blaze, and the building continued to smoulder for many days. Henry Pearson and his wife, Mary, later took up temporary residence in the Lodge by the eastern approach, apparently intending to attempt some restoration of the burnt-out shell, but this was never undertaken. The fire was attributed to a servant's carelessness. The Pearsons' only son, Edmund, aged twenty-one, who had been serving in the Epping Foresters Regiment since enlisting at the outbreak of war, is believed to have been killed at the time of the fire.*

Greg read that sentence three times, struck by the ambiguity of the phrasing. *Believed to have been killed* – that, presumably, meant he was never found. *At the time of the fire.* Did that mean *in* the fire? It sounded almost as if he had thrown himself into the flames – but the account mentioned no fatalities. And in 1917, a young army officer was unlikely to be at home. One of the hundreds of thousands killed in the First World War, then, whose death had happened to coincide with the destruction of his home? Still, it was an odd way to put it.

His interest in Graveney Hall was quickened by the mention of Edmund Pearson: it gave the place an inhabitant he could begin to identify with, unlike the fox-hunting squires and squabbling earls. Another doomed young soldier, like Wilfred Owen. In 1914 he'd have been eighteen, only a year older than Greg. The photograph of Owen slipped into Greg's mind: serious, shy, guarding his intelligence, his talent with words. He had died young, but he had outlived Edmund Pearson by more than a year. Greg flicked through the booklet to see if there was a photograph of Edmund, but there was none.

Believed to have been killed. Did no-one know for sure?

Had Edmund, at eighteen, joined up voluntarily, or was he pushed into it by family or school? He'd have been at Eton or Rugby or somewhere like that, Greg supposed – one of those schools that supplied huge numbers of young officers for the lists of Glorious Dead. Had he fallen for all that Rupert Brooke patriotism Greg had been reading about – expecting laurels, nobility and picturesque sacrifice? And what had he found?

He would ask Faith what she knew about Edmund Pearson, Greg decided, glancing at his watch, realizing that he'd ignored his mother's post-alarm shout and should have been up fifteen minutes ago. He showered and dressed quickly. Katy and their father were in the kitchen, Katy shovelling cornflakes and reading *Mizz*, their dad with his tie hanging loose round his neck, making coffee.

'Is there a boy in your form called Dean Brampton?' Greg asked, pushing past Katy on his way to the bread-bin.

'*Rrrucchh!*'

'Here we have an example of the young female of the species,' said their dad, in David Attenborough mode. 'Whilst feeding she emits a series of grunts, apparently a primitive form of communication. Coffee, Greg?'

'Ta. Well, is there?'

'Yeah, more's the pity,' Katy said with her mouth full. 'Nerd. Thinks he's hard. Always looking for trouble. What d'you want to know about *him* for?'

'Does he know me?'

'Everyone knows you.' Katy made it into a sneer.
'How?'

She scraped her bowl with the spoon. 'Because half the girls in my form fancy you, nerd-features. The sad half, that is. Haven't you noticed all these sick-cow faces in the corridor whenever you walk past? Makes me want to throw up. Can't see what the big deal is, personally, but there's no accounting for taste.'

Their father's eyebrows had shot up into his hair. He passed Greg a mug of coffee and nodded at him, impressed. 'Takes after his dad, obviously,' he remarked, knotting his tie. 'Good looks and sheer animal magnetism.'

'You wish! Both of you.' Katy dumped her cereal bowl in the sink for someone else to wash up. 'That Jordan you go round with now,' she added over her shoulder to Greg, 'he *is* lush.'

'Oh? I suppose you want me to tell him you said so?'

Katy stuck out her tongue.

'So this boy – Dean whatever,' their dad said, 'you're not telling me *he's* making sick-cow faces at Greg as well?'

'Sick, yes,' Greg said.

Katy looked at him closely. 'What's he done?'

'Oh, nothing much. He wrote something about me on – on a wall,' Greg said.

'What, in the boys' bogs? How d'you know it was him? And what did he write?'

'*Greg H is a tosspot*, if you really want to know,' Greg said, ignoring her first question.

Katy laughed delightedly. Their father went back into David Attenborough, addressing an invisible camera. 'Rivalry is frequently observed among young males. This distinctive marking of walls may indicate an outbreak of jealousy from a thwarted juvenile—'

'Juvenile delinquent, more like,' Greg said.

'Shut up, Dad,' Katy said. 'Where's Mum? She's going to make me late if she doesn't get a move on.'

'Good weekend?' Greg asked Jordan at registration. 'How was the swimming?'

'OK, thanks. Yours?'

'Fine,' Greg said; then, seeing Jordan's secretive, rather smug expression, 'Well, did you win?'

Jordan nodded.

'What, the butterfly?'

'And the freestyle. And got my best times for both.'

'Brilliant!'

'Er . . .' Jordan looked embarrassed. 'I was wondering if – we're having a special meal at home next Saturday night, for Michelle's birthday, and I thought you might come.'

'What, a party?'

'Not really, just family and a couple of friends of Michelle's.'

'OK. Er . . . thanks,' Greg said, simply because he could think of no way of refusing. He was wary of occasions that might demand his best behaviour. And there would be Michelle. Jordan had told him that Michelle had started off at Radway, but since her illness their parents had decided to fork out the necessary fees for St Ursula's, because she was too frail for the boisterousness of comprehensive life and missed so much school that she needed individual tuition. Greg pictured a wan, drooping invalid. What would he say to her? If something better came up he'd make an excuse not to go. On the other hand, it might be a handy way to fend off whatever Gizzardry might await him next weekend.

The weather turned cold and autumnal during the day, the wind coming from the north. At the end of school Greg collected his bike and cycled down the main driveway. A girl in navy-blue uniform stood at the entrance, conspicuous among the indifferent greys and unofficial variations of the Radway pupils. A group of Year Nine boys were calling out to her, jeering – Greg couldn't hear what, but she turned aside, chin high.

Her hair was pulled back in a neat French plait, not loose round her face as he'd seen it before, but he recognized the turn of her head. Faith. Braking, he pulled over to the kerb next to her.

'What are you doing here?' It was almost a mile from St Ursula's.

'Waiting for you.'

'Me? Why?'

'I wanted to see you,' Faith said. 'To talk. You'd better give me your mobile number, then I can text you next time.'

Greg registered the *next time*. 'Has something happened?' He was aware of being seen by everyone coming down the driveway – him and a St Ursula's girl.

'No. Why? Does something have to happen for me to want to see you?'

He felt self-conscious, annoyed, pleased. 'Come on, then. We can't stand here. Let's go somewhere.'

Where? Not home. Katy would be there, all eyes and ears and snipey remarks.

'We could go into town. Get a coffee,' Faith said.

In the burger bar at the far end, he thought she meant. They set off, Greg pushing his bike, Faith walking beside him, accompanied by wolf-whistles from some tedious kids behind. When they reached the High Street, Faith stopped outside Casa Veronese, the Italian restaurant near the church.

'You mean here? Will they let us in?'

'Why wouldn't they?' Faith said. 'We're customers, same as everyone else.'

'I know that. I meant can we have just coffee?'

'Don't see why not. I'll ask.'

Greg secured his bike and Faith led the way inside. The Italian waiter recognized her and showed them to a table by the window, bringing menus. The decor was minimalist – elegant black tables and chairs, white walls hung with paintings of skewed red squares. There were no other customers; the tables were set for dinner.

Faith handed back the menu without looking at it. 'Just cappuccino, please. No flaked chocolate. Greg?'

'The same. With chocolate,' Greg said. When the waiter had gone, he asked jokily, 'Do you come here often?'

'I've eaten here a few times with my parents. We love Italian food.'

Greg was silent. One glance at the menu had shown him that Casa Veronese was out of his parents' price range. They rarely ate out as a family, and when they did it was a bar meal at the pub. Surreptitiously he checked the coins in his pocket, hoping he had enough for a cappuccino. It was another reminder of the difference between Faith's background and his own; it made him uncomfortable. He would have felt happier in the burger bar, drinking from a styrofoam cup. But at least here there were no gawpers from school.

'What do you want to talk about?'

Faith fiddled with her napkin, losing the composure she had shown to the waiter. 'I hope you didn't mind me turning up like that.' She looked at him, awaiting his response.

He gave a shrug, non-committal. In a way he *did* mind: she had put him on the spot, obliging him to make a public spectacle of his friendship – if that was what this was – with a St Ursula's girl. 'It was a surprise.'

'A nice one?'

He gave a faint nod, unsmiling.

'I just wanted—' She looked away from him, gazing through the window as though her attention was caught by something. 'I wanted to say sorry for being so prickly – you know, when we argued. I've been thinking about it all the time since. I shouldn't have got annoyed like that.'

'Doesn't matter. Anyway, you said you were sorry on Sunday.'

The cappuccino arrived, in heavy white cups, with chunks of brown sugar in the saucers. Greg sipped at his, grateful for the diversion, tasting creamy foam through the sweetness of sprinkled chocolate. Was that all? She'd stood outside school, exposing herself to the taunts of Radway loudmouths, just to say that? Why not leave it till next weekend? She really was a very odd girl – intense, brooding. What he mainly remembered about their argument was the way she'd flung herself at him, then just as suddenly pulled away. With any other girl he'd have thought he was well in, but with Faith it seemed to be more a matter of being true to herself, of setting things straight in a way that satisfied her sense of honour, or truth, or whatever it was.

'But it does matter.' Her dark eyebrows were drawn together in a frown. 'I ought to be more sure of what I believe in – no, I *am* sure. So if you want to discuss it properly, we can.'

Greg dropped the chunks of sugar into his coffee, stirred it, and tapped the side of the cup irritably with his spoon. 'You've brought me here to have another discussion about God?'

'If you want.'

'It's up to you what you believe in. Nothing to do with me.' He couldn't, at present, think of a single thing he wanted to say on the subject; in fact he was bored by it. He said, instead, 'You know that booklet you gave me? I was reading it this morning. Saw the photos of the gardens as they used to be, and your caryatid.'

'Mm?'

'And I read about the fire. You know Edmund Pearson?'

She nodded. 'The son who was killed in the war?'

'How do you know he was killed in the war? The booklet doesn't say that. It says *Believed to have been killed at the time of the fire.*'

'I know, but surely—'

'If he'd died in the war, wouldn't it have said? *Died in action*, or *Died at – at Passchendaele*, say? Whatever.'

'What are you suggesting, then?'

'I don't know. It's odd, though, isn't it? Does it mean *in* the fire? But then why not say so?'

Faith shook her head firmly. 'No. Definitely not. There'd have been . . .' she made a face '. . . bones, a charred body. And he'd be buried somewhere.'

'Well, he must be buried *some*where, either way.'

'Yes, but if he died at home he'd be in the churchyard next door.' Faith made a gesture with her head. 'Lots of his relations are there. We'll go and have a look if you like. But I'm sure we won't find him. I don't really see why you're bothering about it. There would have been plenty of chances for him to get killed in 1917. There's nothing specially odd about that. And we're not likely to find out now, are we?'

'*Believed to have been killed*. That's not the same as *was* killed. That must mean his body was never found. His parents outlived him, didn't they? Didn't they know any more than it says in the book?'

107

'I expect his name's on the monument at Thiepval,' Faith said. 'Or that other one at the place beginning with Y – what is it? – Ypres, in Belgium. You know, those huge Memorials to the Missing, with thousands of names engraved on them? I've been to Thiepval, on the school battlefields trip. If I'd known about Edmund then, I could have looked for him.'

'But perhaps he didn't die at all,' Greg said, thinking aloud.

'You mean—?' Faith lowered her cup carefully to its saucer, staring at him. 'You're not thinking he could still be alive? That's impossible! He'd be over a hundred years old if he was twenty-one in nineteen seventeen.'

'Don't be daft. What I mean is, supposing he survived the war? He could have married, had children. There might be descendants.'

'If he'd survived the war he'd have come back to Graveney,' Faith pointed out. 'Obviously. The book doesn't mention him after the war. *Or* any descendants of his. Surely he, or they, would have taken over what was left of the house and the estate? It all went to some second cousin, the book says.'

'What if he survived, came home, found Graveney burned out and decided to start again somewhere else?' Greg was struck by a new idea. 'Who wrote the book? Maybe we could ask him.'

'I don't know if we can. It was written ages ago, before the Friends took over – you can see how old-fashioned it looks, all that tiny print. It's going to be re-done, with colour photos, when the work's finished, if it ever *is* finished.'

'I suppose you're right,' Greg conceded. 'The most likely explanation is that he *did* die in the trenches. Poor sod. Only twenty-one. That's only four years older than me, and he enlisted at eighteen. I bet he swallowed all that Rupert Brooke stuff about honour and glory.'

Faith nodded. *'If I should die, think only this of me –* that's the famous one, isn't it? We read that.'

'If he died in nineteen seventeen – that was after the Battle of the Somme – he'd have seen enough to change his mind,' Greg said. 'Can I have your sugar if you don't want it?'

Faith nodded; he reached over for the two brown chunks, put them in his mouth and crunched them.

'There were two Edmund Pearsons,' he said, thinking, his mouth full of sweetness, 'and they both died young.'

Faith gave him a quizzical look.

'The first one died as a baby,' Greg explained. 'If he'd lived, he'd have been our Edmund's uncle. Your grotto was made for him.'

'Oh, that one. Yes, I know. You can see E and P in the mosaic patterns if you look hard.'

'Why didn't you tell me when we were down there?'

She smiled at him. 'Didn't know you well enough then, did I? It's not the sort of thing I tell just anyone. The grotto's my special place, remember? I'll show you next time.' She finished her coffee and scooped up the remaining foam with her spoon, scraping for every last smear. Greg watched her, bemused. That didn't quite go with the air of sophistication she'd tried to convey when they came in. 'I'll ask my parents if they know anything else about Edmund Pearson the Second,' she said, glancing up.

'Are they very strict, your parents?' he asked. *Being Christians*, he meant, but he didn't want to spark another argument.

'In some ways. They wouldn't let me go to all-night parties or anything like that. They always have to know where I'm going and who I'm with.'

'Like now?'

'No. Well, I didn't know about it myself. Only thought of coming to look for you when I came out of school.'

'Would they mind?'

'I shouldn't think so. I mean, they've met you. They'd prefer it if I was going out with a boy from the church, but those are as rare as hens' teeth. That's one of my dad's weird sayings. Not enough to pick and choose from.'

Greg shifted in his seat. Wait a minute! Who said anything about *going out*?

'They don't mind me having boyfriends,' Faith went on. 'They trust me to know what I'm doing and what I won't do. I mean, I'd never have sex before marriage. They don't have to warn me about pregnancy and contraceptives and diseases, because I just wouldn't. I don't think you should throw yourself away on the first person you fancy, or who fancies you. It's more special than that.'

Oh. Right. Greg was silent. Was this her way of

telling him not to expect sex? Or just an assumption that he wanted it? He felt himself being pushed farther than was comfortable. He sneaked a look at her. In her school uniform she looked rather . . . classy was the word that came into his mind. She was at least passably good-looking, especially when she smiled. Her skirt wasn't particularly short, nowhere near as short as Katy's – they were probably a lot stricter at St Ursula's – but she sat turned towards him with one leg crossed over the other, giving him a good view of her knees and thighs, shapely in black tights. School governors might think they could put girls into white shirts and navy-striped ties and blazers to make them look demure and respectable: it only made them look sexy. As before with Faith, he felt that the words coming out of her mouth were at odds with her body language. What was she saying? *You can go out with me but I'll set the rules.* Or was it Mummy and Daddy who set the rules?

Having one cup of coffee didn't mean they were *going out*. He could get up and cycle home whenever he chose.

'I'm going to have another coffee before we go and look in the graveyard.' Faith looked round for the waiter. 'Do you want one?'

'Yeah, all right.'

Gizzard phoned while Greg was starting his homework. 'What got into you Saturday night, slugbait?'

'Nothing. I'd had enough of that party, that was all.'

'Thought I'd fixed you up nicely with Tanya. You must be well demented.'

'What did she say?' Greg asked cautiously.

'One minute you were all over her, the next out the door.' An abrupt hoot of laughter made Greg hold the receiver away from his ear. 'Says she's going to stop playing around with schoolboys. She'll stick to men from now on.'

'I didn't fancy her, that's all. And I don't like being set up.'

'Thought you'd be grateful,' Gizzard said, aggrieved.

'Well, I'm not. The fact is,' Greg improvised, 'I'm going out with someone else.'

'Yeah? Why didn't you say so, moron? Could have brought her along. Anyone I know?'

'No. She goes to St Ursula's.'

'An All Saint, eh? You want to watch those. If you thought Tanya was a man-eater—'

'I can manage, thanks,' Greg said.

He went back to his homework. For English tomorrow he had four poems to read and think about. Greg sat on his bed, reading a sonnet Mr O'Donnell had given them to compare with Rupert Brooke's *The Soldier*. It began, '*When you see millions of the mouthless dead . . .*' and was by another soldier-poet, Charles Hamilton Sorley. His was another lost voice: only twenty when he was killed in October 1915. This poem, Mr O'Donnell had said, was found in his kit after his death, so was never published in his lifetime. Were they all at it, the generation of young officers, Greg wondered – working away at their sonnets as if it were obligatory, the only way of recording experience? But he liked this one better than Rupert Brooke's rather smug patriotism. *'Say only this. "They are dead"*,*'* Sorley had written.

The First World War was back in the last century, and soon it would have happened a hundred years ago, but for some reason Greg felt closer to it than to other conflicts since. He had studied it in GCSE History; he had read *All Quiet on the Western Front* and seen the film; he had watched documentaries, with first-hand accounts from elderly survivors. It was hard to see these doddery, watery-eyed old men as the unsuspecting young soldiers they had been at the time; easier to imagine himself as one of them, like Edmund. Or like Paul Bäumer in *All Quiet on the Western Front*, going straight from school to the army in a fervour of patriotism no-one would feel today, seeing his friends maimed and killed, himself doomed to survive. He and Gizzard would be privates – Gizzard the born survivor, the crafty scrounger who always knew where to get fags and booze – but Jordan would be an officer: handsome and correct in a peaked cap, every button-badge polished, his face taut in the guarded expression Greg knew well. *'Like swimmers into cleanness leaping . . .'* They would leap not into cleanness but into the squalor of the Western Front, so familiar from photographs that it was hard to believe the war had not actually been fought in black and white. Jordan would be horribly injured in an attack, and Greg would glimpse his white, sweating face as he was carried away on a stretcher. Michelle at home would open the telegram . . . except that Michelle would surely be dead too, because there would be no kidney dialysis back then . . .

'Greg! Dinner's ready!' Katy yelled from the bottom of the stairs.

Greg came back to the present: his rumpled duvet, a thump of bass from his cassette player, and the Sorley poem still in his hand. He'd been staring at it sightlessly.

'Coming!' he yelled back. He stood up and yanked his T-shirt straight, glared at himself in the mirror and examined a potential spot on his chin. Deep in his chest there was an ache of loss for the imagined death of Jordan.

Yobs

Greg's photograph (colour): a corner of a partially demolished wall. On the brickwork, the words DEAN WOZ ERE are sprayed in acidic yellow, and GREG H IS A TOSSPOT in green. The letters are fuzzy and uneven. There is a litter of Coke cans, fag-ends and sweet wrappers, scattered around the blackened remains of a fire.

'Heard you had an assignation yesterday,' Jordan said. He and Greg stood by the drinks machine in the common room, sifting coins.

It took Greg a couple of seconds to realize what he meant.

'It wasn't an assignation. I hadn't arranged anything. Here.' He handed Jordan the ten-pence piece he was short of.

'Thanks.' Jordan fed it into the slot and pressed *Coffee White No Sugar*. 'Girlfriend?' he asked casually.

'No, just someone I know. A friend – well, hardly even that, really.'

Was he imagining it, or did Jordan seem relieved?

Jordan took his coffee and sipped it carefully; it was always too hot. Greg put his own coins in and pressed *Coffee White With Sugar.* 'What about you?' He matched Jordan's offhand tone. 'Going out with anyone?'

Jordan shook his head. Greg, on the point of asking whether he'd ever had a proper girlfriend, was trying to find the wording when Bonnie came up to the machine, dumping her rucksack at their feet. 'Hi, Greg. Hi, Jordy. Got any change? Need to wake myself up before double Maths. God, English was dire, wasn't it?' She looked at Greg, then at Jordan. 'What's up with you two? Am I interrupting something?'

'No,' Jordan said.

'Done your Maths?' Greg asked, knowing she wouldn't have. Bonnie simpered at him. 'Mind-reader! That's just what I was going to ask. Let me copy yours!' she pleaded. 'You know what Sourface Simpson told me last time I forgot.' To get her out of the way, Greg gave her his file, and swapped her pound coin for change. She flashed her insincere smile: 'Thanks, Greg, you're a star,' got her coffee and took it and his Maths file to one of the corner tables, getting to work with more eagerness than she ever showed in class.

Jordan gave Greg a wry look. 'What were you going to say?'

'Oh . . .' They took their coffee and sat down at the table farthest away from Bonnie.

'Christ, it's like a morgue in here!' A jostling group

had come in; the cassette player was turned on, filling the room with something electronic and repetitive. It screened conversation very usefully.

'About girls,' Greg said. 'I was going to ask if you've ever had – you know – a real girlfriend?'

'Girl *friends*, yes,' Jordan said. 'Girlfriend, no. Only if you count when I was at junior school and a girl called Rosie decided I was going to marry her.'

'So you've never – I mean, have you ever just been with a girl at a party or something, and actually got to the point of . . .' Greg made a *You know what I mean* gesture.

'Have I ever done it? Is that what you're getting at?' Jordan was sitting back in his chair, looking at Greg with calm amusement. 'No. Why d'you ask?'

'Well, you know. Some blokes talk about nothing else. Gizzard, for example. He thinks I'm retarded because I haven't—' Greg lowered his voice, although there was no-one close enough to hear – 'you know. He tried to set me up on Saturday night, at a party. There was this girl, Tanya – gorgeous, really – all over me, practically dragging me upstairs. When it came to it, I blew it. No, I didn't want to – I just cleared off. What would you have done?'

'Same as you, I expect. I don't like being pushed into things. I'd rather decide for myself.'

'Gizzard and this girl Tanya have got me down as a pathetic wimp. Didn't have the bottle.'

'Let them. Doesn't matter, does it? We're not sex machines. May not want to be, either. It's more important than that.'

117

Greg looked at him suspiciously. 'Are you religious?'

'No. Why?'

'What you said. It reminded me of someone else – of that St Ursula girl. No sex before marriage, that's what she says. Not that I was asking. She's just a friend, like I said.'

'That's not what I meant,' Jordan said. 'More a matter of being . . . careful, I suppose.'

Memories of Social and Personal Skills lessons floated into Greg's mind – warnings about AIDS and herpes and teenage pregnancies, statistics and role-plays and even excruciating demonstrations involving carrots. A complete waste of time, according to some of the louder girls like Bonnie – everyone knew it all already apart from those who didn't, and they were the ones who had no need to know.

'I don't mean AIDS and that sort of thing,' Jordan continued. 'I mean careful of how you feel. And how the other person feels. But the main thing is, there's no need to rush. There's plenty of time.'

'Hey, you two!' It was Ben Cousins, with a clip-board. 'I'm getting names for the cricket. Staff v. Sixth Form, Friday week after school. Can I put you both down?'

'OK.'

'Yeah, go on.'

Ben sat down to add their names to his list and stayed, chatting, till the bell went. Greg half-listened to the conversation about which teachers were the sneakiest spin-bowlers and which were most likely to hit sixes, watching Jordan. He was so different from Gizzard. What you saw was what you got with Gizzard; but with Jordan, what you were allowed to see was only a fraction of what might be there to find. Or was that just because of the way his features happened to be arranged? His dark, finely-shaped eyebrows gave him a brooding look; but Greg knew that Jordan could be pondering nothing more profound than whether to have cheese or tuna in his lunchtime sandwich and still have that air of intense preoccupation. Thinking of Jordan's invitation for Saturday, Greg found that he was pleased. Gizzard was friendly with everyone; friendship with Jordan would be deeper, and would have to be better deserved.

On Thursday, in the cool of early evening, Greg cycled out to Graveney Hall.

'What's the fascination with that place?' Mr Teale had asked in Art, last lesson of the afternoon, looking at Greg's prints. Greg was still trying to work out the answer.

His response in the Art room, after a moment's thought, was: 'It wouldn't have the same appeal at all if the house was still intact and lived-in – you know, like any other stately home. As it is, it's a kind of symbol of something.'

'Of what?' Mr Teale asked, inevitably.

'It reminds me of the *Titanic*,' Greg said after another pause. 'Except that we can see the wreckage.'

'Think about it,' said the teacher.

Now, pedalling down the track, Greg thought it was lucky he didn't have to express his thoughts in the form of a poem, the way Sorley and Owen had. Pictures were easier; they didn't need explaining. You could make a point just by putting one thing next to another. The placing of an old photo copied from the guidebook next to one showing the litter and the *Keep Out* signs would make its own impact, without words. He had decided now that his project would include drawings as well as photographs: line drawings, ink and a greenish wash, to show mould and moss growing over stone. He intended to copy some of the stone edgings and fragments of ruined columns and statues. The damaged summerhouses, he thought, could be shown as architectural drawings, the way a designer might have envisaged them more than two hundred years ago, pristine and new. The decorative details would be good to draw: the vines and fruit, and something Mr Teale had said was acanthus – large leaves in bold, sculptural shapes.

Whatever the place's fascination, it was strong enough to pull him there now, when he could have spent the evening in front of the TV or pretending to do homework. Graveney Hall was more than a handy stimulus for his Art project – it had got into his mind and installed itself there. He had arranged to meet Faith on Sunday morning at the grotto, but had suddenly felt unwilling to wait that long; he wanted to spend time alone with his sketchbook and camera. It would be good to have the place to himself, with no-one peering over his shoulder or asking questions, and not even Faith as a distraction.

The ruined mansion was not so much *Titanic* as *Mary Celeste*, he thought, pedalling close enough to see the blanks of the windows, the twining ivy, the hollow inside: like the ghost ship it was abandoned, enticing the passer-by with its secrets. He left his bike by the steps at the front and walked slowly inside. Echoey space rose above him like the inside of a cathedral. Some time he'd see if Jordan felt like coming here for a look round. Jordan had seen the prints, expressed an interest; Greg wanted to show him the grounds and the lake, watching his reactions, or rather his characteristic, thoughtful non-reaction.

On the garden side, greenness and light opened in front of him. He stepped out to the grass and looked down the length of the garden. It was not difficult to imagine Edmund Pearson standing here, on what would have been the terrace – a slim young man in army uniform, taking his leave before returning to Flanders. The back of Greg's neck tingled. With no-one about, he almost had the sense that Edmund might appear, summoned by the power of thought. Had this been his last view of Graveney Hall? What miserable death had awaited him at the front?

It took him a few seconds to register shouts from the lower garden. Resentment bristled inside him. Those bloody kids again! If that slimeball Dean Brampton was among them . . .

He couldn't see the boys at first, his eyes scanning the ruined garden. Then a movement caught his eye:

an upraised arm, a thrown brick. He heard the crack of stone on stone, followed by a yell of encouragement. The boys – Dean and a dark-skinned boy, and a third smaller one – were hurling bricks at the caryatid on the summerhouse, aiming for its head.

'Oi!' Greg yelled, propelled by anger across the grass.

The Asian boy was first to see him; he skittered off sideways and grabbed Dean Brampton by the arm. Dean dropped the brick he was aiming and all three faced Greg as if he was a figure of authority; then, realizing who it was, Dean laughed.

'What the hell d'you think you're doing?' Greg shouted.

It was all too obvious what they were doing: trying to smash the beautiful stone face of the caryatid, the perfect one. Already Greg could see splintered fresh stone where a piece had been chipped off the fruit garland.

'Are you completely moronic or what? God!'

He couldn't find words to express his outrage. Dean yelled, 'What's your problem, saddo? Own the place, do you?'

The sneering expression on his face made Greg's knuckles tighten. He stepped closer.

'If you damage that – if I ever see you here again, I'll—'

'Yeah, what'll you do, tosser? 'S only an old statue, not worth anything!'

'Prat! Poofter!' The Asian boy joined in the jeering; the small one, more fearful, kept a cautious distance.

Greg made a grab for Dean Brampton, whose face contorted into a snarl. Not sure what he intended to do, Greg found himself with a double handful of anorak. With a grunt of indignation, the boy wriggled out of his grasp. Greg both felt and heard the tearing of the anorak sleeve.

'Get off him, pervert!' the Asian boy yelled.

Dean Brampton, wriggling free of the garment, kicked out, catching Greg on the shin. Greg seized him hard by the arm, taken over by single-minded fury. The boy looked back at him, chin jutting. There was a flicker of fear in his eyes that belied the practised toughness.

Greg made his own face hard. 'If I find you here again – ,' his voice came out low and menacing, ' – I'll smash your stupid face in.' He gave a hard shake and flung the boy away. Dean stumbled and picked himself up, glaring his hatred. The other two came closer, circling, looking at Dean for guidance.

This was stupid – three against one if it came to a real fight. They might be younger and smaller, but Dean Brampton had the look of a dangerous wild animal. Anger surged through Greg's body. He picked up the anorak and threw it to the ground by the boy's feet. 'Fuck off out of here. Go on. *Now.*'

'Run, Yusuf!' yelled the smaller boy, who was already well on his way towards the ruined conservatory.

The boy called Yusuf did, leaving Dean Brampton confronting Greg. Realizing that he was alone, the boy's confidence wavered. 'Wanker!' He thrust two fingers at Greg's face, then ran after his friends, leaping a chunk of masonry. With baboon-like whoops, the three disappeared towards the main steps, quick and agile.

Greg stayed where he was. He wasn't going to run after them, inviting more abuse or thrown bricks. Carefully, he examined the caryatid. Her beautiful face stared impassively over his head, undamaged. He could see only the small chip he had already noticed, from her garland. If he'd come along ten minutes later . . . what were they trying to do, reduce her face to broken stone, destroy it the way time and weather had destroyed her twin?

He didn't feel like drawing now. He sat on the steps of the summerhouse and stared across at the bearded telamons. This was stupid – it needed a high wire fence to keep those morons out. He could understand them coming here to muck about, to climb in the buildings, but this—! He was breathing hard, disturbed by the incident in more ways than one. Dean Brampton's mocking face had fired him into not just anger, but violent rage. If he'd given way to impulse, he could have smashed the boy's head against the stone of the summerhouse. He could still feel the itch of wanting to grab and hurt, flowing down his arms into his fingers and fists. He had made the first grab, even though the insolent little git had been asking for it. But what else could he have done? You couldn't reason with someone like Dean Brampton.

Wearily, he got up and went to find his bike. It was

lying on its side halfway up the steps, with the rear-shift mechanism wedged in the spokes.

'Oh, bloody hell!'

It took him nearly an hour to get it home, with only the front wheel usable, by which time – ravenous, tired, fed-up and with his arms aching from lifting the back wheel clear of the ground – he had thought of a range of fitting torments for Dean Brampton and associates.

EP

Greg's photograph (colour): close-up, part of the mosaic design inside the lakeside grotto at Graveney Hall. The mosaic is made of broken pieces of Delft tiles, white and shades of blue. Each fragment is embedded in plaster in what appears at first to be a random pattern, but when you look again you can see the initials E and P among the swirls.

'Thanks for coming,' Jordan said, standing in the rain. 'I don't suppose it was top choice for a Saturday night, someone else's family do.'

Greg zipped up his jacket and reached into his pocket for his bike keys. 'It was fine, thanks. Different. Don't get soaked – go on in!' He pushed the bike out from its resting place by the wheelie bin. 'You swimming tomorrow?'

' 'Course, first thing. You?'

'No – I don't work Sundays.'

'I know. You could come and swim though,' Jordan said. 'Just swim.'

Greg shook his head. 'What, miss my Sunday lie-in?' Besides, he was going to Graveney Hall. 'How about—'

'What?'

On the point of asking if Jordan wanted to come too, after the training, Greg thought better of it. 'No, nothing.' Faith would be there, and something made him uneasy about the idea of Faith and Jordan meeting. He wanted to keep them in separate compartments. 'How did you get so hooked on swimming, anyway?'

'Dad started me off when I was quite little – he liked it. And, don't laugh—'

'No, go on.'

'I used to have this dream of being rescued by a dolphin. There were stories I'd heard, or read. I'd be in the sea, drowning, going under, then just when my lungs were bursting for air the dolphin would race up and push me to the surface and carry me all the way to the shore. And after that I wanted to *be* a dolphin. Used to pretend to be one in the pool. See, I told you it was stupid.'

But you *are* like a dolphin, Greg thought, when you swim butterfly, and nearly said so. Instead, he surprised himself by coming out with: 'Was it sexy?'

'Sexy?'

'The dream. The dolphin.'

Jordan thought for a moment, then laughed. 'Yes. Yes, it was.'

Greg pushed the bike out of the driveway, brushed rainwater off the saddle and mounted. 'See you

Monday,' he called, wheeling away. He didn't hear the door close, and when he looked back Jordan was still standing by the garden fence, in the slanting rain.

Greg raised a hand in farewell, then ducked his head and concentrated on managing the unfamiliar gear system on his dad's old bike. With his own in the repair shop he was having to make do with this; it had drop handlebars and an old downtube changer that had to be juggled, and whenever he got it wrong the chain came off. Head down, he pushed hard up the hill. The McAuliffes' house was fifteen minutes' bike ride out of town, in a village off the Chelmsford road – not so much village as a cluster of houses round a crossroads. 'You could easily have stayed the night if we'd thought about it,' Jordan's mother had said when Greg was leaving. 'You'll get soaked, biking.'

Michelle's party had been the sort of family occasion that Greg's mother occasionally tried to orchestrate at home. It never quite worked, mainly, Greg suspected, because his mum was too anxious to gild the proceedings with a fabricated happy-family gloss. Katy would get into a strop, or the meal would be an ambitious failure, or Nan would get one of her migraines and have to lie in a darkened room. Greg would sooner have sat ten Maths exams than risk inviting any friend to share such an ordeal with his lot, but the McAuliffes seemed better at it, as if they practised more often. Delicious food, lots of it, appeared on the table; no-one took umbrage with anyone else; the quiz games after the meal were conducted with enthusiasm rather than animosity.

The house, one of a pair of former farm cottages, was rather shabbily furnished, but there were shelves and shelves of books and CDs; food, music and books were all taken seriously here, it seemed to Greg. The McAuliffe parents, a good few years older than his own, struck him as intellectual. Jordan's dad, tall, spare and greying, could have appeared formidable if he hadn't been compering party games and handing out chocolate prizes; Mrs McAuliffe was quietly watchful. The two boys, Jordan and the much younger Mark, got their looks from their father, while Michelle had her mother's fair hair and sharp, intelligent face. There were three other girls present, her friends; one of them, Greg noticed with amusement, kept gazing at Jordan with undisguised adoration. He also saw that Jordan hadn't registered this, though the girl couldn't conceal her delight when she was teamed with him in one of the quizzes. Didn't Jordan ever look in a mirror, and see the girl-pulling potential of what was reflected? It was one of the likeable things about him that he seemed oblivious.

Nearing town, Greg changed gear at the summit of the long, gradual hill and found that he'd dislodged the chain again. Blast! He dismounted to sort it out, feeling the cold trickle of rain down the back of his neck. 'It's a matter of touch and delicacy,' his dad had said when Greg complained about the bike's temperamental habits. 'You'll soon get a feel for it.' So far, Greg hadn't. Touch and delicacy weren't his strong points, obviously.

*

He met Faith by the Coach House. 'They're boxing up the caryatids!' she told him. 'Isn't it awful? The telamons too.' Irregular hammering could be heard from the direction of the garden.

'Boxing them up?' Greg thought of coffins. 'But how did they get them off the walls?'

'They didn't, stupid! They're making boxes to fit over them, on the summerhouses, for protection. It's because of those awful vandals in the week. And they're putting up barbed wire and padlocking the entrance to stop people trespassing. But Dad says if vandals are determined enough they'll get in somehow.'

'They did my bike in as well, those cretins,' Greg told her. 'Knackered the rear-shift mechanism. A hundred quid, it's costing, to have it repaired! My dad's putting in fifty but I've got to find the rest myself. That's a big chunk out of my earnings.'

'Dad says you know them from school. They sound like animals,' Faith said with distaste.

As usual she was getting under his skin, needling him. 'Yeah, well, you do get all sorts at a comprehensive. I don't suppose you get much vandalism at St Ursula's. But I don't do a lot of socializing with Year Nine yobs, myself.'

If Faith registered his sarcasm, she made no comment. 'Can't you make them pay for your bike?'

'The head of Year Nine had a go – their parents wouldn't pay. And it was nothing to do with school really, so he said if I wanted to pursue it I'd have to go to the police.'

'Why don't you?'

'Not worth it. They're not going to budge, are they?' Greg didn't tell her the rest of what the year head had said: that Dean Brampton's mother had fired off a torrent of abuse about Greg hitting and threatening her blameless boy. 'But that's—' Greg had protested to Mr Rackham, then stopped. What was the point? It was one person's word against three others, and anyway, it was true. The police, if they bothered to take up the matter, would get the same story from Mrs Brampton, with embellishments. 'I can't do any more, sorry,' Mr Rackham said, ushering Greg out of his office. 'It's not a school thing, is it? If it had happened while your bike was on the school premises, things would be different. As it is I'll have a word with the lads and give them a warning.' And that was that: Greg labelled as a dubious character, a bullier of young kids. He felt sore about that, sorer still about the hundred quid.

'I can't bear to think of my caryatid!' Faith said, though they were heading slowly in that direction. 'All nailed up in a wooden box. When will I see her again? Not till all the restoration's done, Dad says, and there's a proper security fence. Oh, why can't those idiots go somewhere else?'

Her caryatid! Greg had begun to think of it as his, since the Art project. His main concern now was that he wouldn't be able to take any more photographs, and would have to make do with the ones he'd taken last Sunday. He resented the whole incident, especially Faith's implication that he'd practically

131

invited Dean Brampton and friends to chuck bricks at the statuary. When he phoned Faith's father to tell him of the damage, he'd omitted to mention the skirmish. Whichever way you looked at it, he hadn't come out of it well – neither behaving with much dignity nor seeing the boys off effectively.

'My mum doesn't want me going down to the grotto on my own any more,' Faith grumbled. 'Only when I'm with you.'

'What, because of those morons? They haven't been down to the lake, have they?'

'Who knows where they'll go?'

They had reached the summerhouse. One of the Friends, a man called Phil, was poised on a stepladder by the caryatids, while Michael Tarrant, by a heap of planks on the grass, steadied the ladder and passed up nails. The box being nailed into place was indeed shaped like a coffin; the caryatid was already hidden from view. Greg thought of her beautiful face, the face that had gazed impassively across the garden for two hundred years, boxed up in darkness. It seemed symbolic: beauty hidden by ugliness. Art too fragile for the brutish gaze of the twenty-first century. Youth and grace masked by a crude emblem of death.

'Will you take all that off again for Open Day?' Faith asked.

The man called Phil looked down at her, laughing. 'I don't think this lot's coming off very easily. This should stop your friends' little game,' he added to Greg.

'They're not my friends!' Greg was getting fed up with this.

'It's so *awful*,' Faith wailed. 'Like she's being punished for something she hasn't done. Like a medieval torture – they used to brick people up in walls, didn't they?'

'Go and help your mum in the Coach House if you don't want to watch,' her father said.

'Shall we?' Faith turned to Greg. 'She's repairing the display stands, ready for Open Day. I said I might help.'

Greg stalled. Once he got into Mummy's clutches, she'd have him running errands all day. He'd met her the week before; she was an RE teacher at Faith's school, and treated everyone as if they were ten years old. 'You were going to show me the initials in the grotto,' he reminded her. 'Let's go down there.'

The lake was silent, away from the activity around the house; faint mist hung over the water. A mountain ash tree at the edge of the wood was bright with berries. Summer was over; it felt like autumn now, the air tinged with coldness to come. Faith was wearing a cable sweater, Greg his zip-up fleece.

'Here.' Faith pointed, inside the grotto. Following her in, Greg looked closely, seeing that what he had taken to be an abstract design of swirls was in fact made up of twining capital Es and Ps. The whole tile pattern was a memorial to Edmund Pearson, the short-lived baby. He thought of the distraught father smashing tiles, sorting the pieces, dedicating himself to his task. The grotto was as vulnerable as the caryatids, just as easily damaged by spray-paint or lobbed bricks, but Greg hoped the Friends wouldn't think of boxing it in for protection. Had Dean & Co. come down this far? If they had, they surely would have left evidence, but there was none – no litter of cans or crisp packets, no spray-paint graffiti. Greg thought of it as Faith's special place; she was the only person he had ever seen here.

'Did you find out any more about our one?' he asked her.

'Our what?'

'Our Edmund. The other Edmund Pearson.'

She shook her head. 'I asked Dad, but he only knows what's in the book. He agreed with me – most likely Missing in Action. He said the Commonwealth War Graves might be able to help. They could tell us if he's got an official war grave somewhere, or if he's on one of the Memorials to the Missing.'

'But then why only *Believed to have been killed*?'

'Missing means just that, doesn't it? *Missing believed killed*. Those memorials are for people who have no known grave.'

'I want to find him,' Greg said. 'I want to *know*.'

Faith looked at him. 'Why does he interest you so much? He's only one of the people who lived here.'

'It doesn't seen properly finished, left vague like this. There must be something for us to find out.'

'But why us?'

'Because we're the ones asking the questions.'

'*You* are. I don't think there's much of a mystery. He died somewhere in France or Belgium and his name'll be on a memorial there.'

Greg thrust his hands into the pockets of his fleece

and turned away to look out over the water. Again he felt that prickling at the back of his neck, a sense that if he kept quiet and concentrated, Edmund might appear on the lakeside path, strolling, his uniform jacket slung over one shoulder. Greg could identify with Edmund, the young officer thrown into the cauldron of the First World War, far more than with the wealthy squires and fox-hunting gentlemen who had lived at Graveney. Odd, really, because if Edmund Pearson had survived the war, he would have become a wealthy estate-owner in his turn, and would be no more interesting than the others. Did he come down here, home on leave, to sit in the grotto with his own initials entwined on the walls, a ready-made memorial, and look out at the water and ponder? What did he think about? Surviving until 1917, he must have known how high the chances were of being killed or maimed. What must that be like, at the age of twenty-one?

'It's one of the things that makes me not believe in God,' he said to Faith.

'What is?'

'The First World War. How could that happen if God was in charge?'

Faith had settled on the marble bench, taking out her bottle of water. 'The war was made by man, not by God.' Her answer came ready-made.

'The other day you said you wanted a discussion – a proper discussion.' Greg sat on the other half of the curve, with the gargoyle spouting its arc of water between them. 'I've thought about this. It seems to me you want it all ways. Not just you – I mean Christians do.'

Faith looked at him, interested, not prickly this time. 'I don't see what you mean.'

'You want to believe in your God, so you've got easy excuses for all the things he makes a bodge of.' He paused to marshal his argument. 'Listen. You'd say, God knows everything, right?'

'Yes, He's omniscient.'

'Right. And he can do everything, as well, because he's God.'

'Omnipotent.'

'OK. Omniscient and omnipotent. And the third thing, God is good.'

She nodded.

'Well, it doesn't add up, does it? You can have any two of those things, but not all three – it doesn't make sense. Because as it is – as you believe it, I mean – your omniscient God knew hundreds of thousands of people were dying in that war, were *going* to die. They were going to be shelled to bits or get gassed or get gangrene or drown in shell-holes or die in agony in hospitals or go mad with fright. And he didn't lift a finger to stop it. Even though he could have, if he's omnipotent. So those two things rule out the third – if he exists at all, he can't be good. And that's only one example. Same applies even more to earthquakes or floods or avalanches. Acts of God, they're called, aren't they? What sort of God would deliberately act like that?'

'Wars are made by men,' Faith said. 'And even

floods and tornadoes might be, because of global warming. God chooses not to interfere.'

'So he's not good!'

'No. Not because He's not good. Because it's in our best interests not to interfere.'

'How can you say that? How could it be better to let the First World War happen than not? And the Holocaust – how could that be in *any*one's interests? And famines, and land-mines and the Twin Towers?'

'We can't know the reason for things like that. But God *must* have a reason.'

'What, like you said he has for Michelle McAuliffe – for keeping her tied to a dialysis machine at the age of fifteen? Don't tell me – it's a punishment for something she did in a previous existence, right? Or what about *him*?' Greg touched the EP initials above his head. 'The baby, I mean, not our Edmund. Dying as a baby – what was that, a punishment for him, or for his parents, or for all of them?'

'We can't know. I don't believe in that punishment-for-a-previous existence line. But there may be some good to come out of it. Michelle, say – she must be a different person because of her illness. She must affect people around her.'

'But where's the logic in that? If illness is so good for everyone, why aren't we *all* ill?'

'That's stupid. If we were all ill, how would we appreciate health?'

Greg threw out his hands in frustration. 'That's what gets me. It's a circular argument, isn't it? We don't know why things happen, so we invent an omniscient God who does know, and because according to you he must be a good God, there must be a good reason for everything, however terrible. It's an easy answer, *too* easy.'

'We don't invent God. He exists,' Faith said passionately. 'He exists. He sent His son to prove it. He's in everything. In you and in me.'

'Leave me out of it. I'm just a collection of cells. Think about it! The Earth is a tiny planet in a solar system somewhere in an immense universe that's been here for billions of years. Jesus didn't turn up till two thousand years ago. That's a bit of a late entrance, the way I see it.'

'So you do believe in Jesus?'

'I suppose so. But only as far as there must have been someone by that name, who lived and died. But I also know there's a couple of hundred billion stars in the Milky Way, and that's only our own galaxy – it's mind-boggling! What's so special about this planet? It's just a – a chunk of rock hurtling round a minor sun that'll fizzle itself out in a few billion years. Why should God decide to send his son *here*?'

'At least you're prepared to have your mind boggled! That's a start.'

'OK, but it's not a start in your direction. Why should God, if there was a God, think I'm important enough to bother with? I'm an insignificant speck – so are you.'

'But don't you see?' Faith turned to him with missionary zeal. 'You're asking questions – you're thinking about the reason for your existence! It's a first step to faith. Doesn't it occur to you that God has brought you to me, a believer, for that purpose? I don't believe anything happens by chance.'

'Oh. Right. God sees me wandering about aimlessly, and he thinks: "I know! I'll introduce him to Faith. That'll soon put him right." What is he – a heavenly dating agency?'

Faith laughed. 'If you like.'

He immediately wished he hadn't said that, *dating*. It was all too obvious, wasn't it? Faith thought she was going to turn him into a God-squaddie, so that he'd be an acceptable boyfriend – acceptable to her parents as well. No thanks.

'You see yourself as my saviour, do you?' he said, flippantly.

'No.' Her face became serious. 'There's only one Saviour.' She touched the crucifix at her throat. 'If you open your heart to him, He will show you His love and His truth. And that's the only way it can happen. You can't get there by reason, or logic, or arguing.'

'But reason and logic are all there is. How can I know what I think otherwise?' He got up and stood by the lakeside, looking out at the wind-ruffled water. It was hopeless, trying to have a sensible discussion with her. She twisted and turned everything to suit herself.

'Reason and logic can get in the way,' she insisted. 'Trust your instinct. Your instinct is leading you towards God's love. You can turn your back on me, but don't turn it on God.'

He wished she'd stop talking like Thought for the

139

Day on the radio in the mornings. Any minute now she'd be inviting him to Sunday school. Why was it that the more scorn he poured on her arguments, the more she thought she was succeeding?

'My instinct,' he said, 'is leading me towards the loo and a cup of coffee. And that's all. I'm going back up.'

1917, February

On the road from Bailleul

The road is strewn with war's appalling waste –
~~Spent shells, smashed wood, a cart with wheels away~~
And corpses left to grimace at the sky –
We turn our heads, and march on by in haste.

But
~~Now~~ here's a tableau that draws all men's eyes –
A horse and soldier, felled together, dead.
The ground beneath them soaked and stained dull red.
The horse's wide eye stares as if surprised

To find itself so far from England's fields.
The soldier's hand still holds a length of rein.
His fingers tangled in the horse's mane –
A parting clutch, and simple love revealed.

I seem to hear the soldier's dying thought –
'Forgive me for my part in this, dear friend.
Your grace and spirit earned a nobler end
Than falling thus, by random shellburst caught.'

~~Heaped shells, and roofs caved in~~
~~Heaped shells, and ruined huts and~~

141

And looking down on this embrace of death
A roadside Calvary - a Christ of wood,
Who surely would have wept, if image could,
To see them parted at their dying breath.

But Christ himself might cease with one more shell,
And who would notice, in this time of war?
The column marches by, and I'm heart-sore,
For there's no Heaven, only man-made Hell.

Edmund Pearson

"Religion is the opium of the people" — Karl Marx.
It's taken you long enough to realize...

Approaching the front, Edmund thought whimsically, was like reaching the seaside. The front line was a barrier more effective than coastline or cliffs. No-Man's-Land was a dangerous channel; sentries were like coastguards, scanning the sea for invaders. The land beyond, German-held, was alien country. The analogy was reflected in C Company's nicknames for the area: the irregular trench that fronted their sector was called the Golden Mile, a night show of Very lights or star shells was Blackpool Illuminations, and a sap that stretched out into No-Man's-Land was known as Morecambe Pier.

For now, the sector was fairly quiet. The 5th Epping Foresters were occupying a front-line position close to the Belgian border. It was rumoured that the next offensive would take place farther up, around the town of Ypres, where the bulge of the salient was surrounded on all sides by German-held ridges.

'I want *action*,' Alex grumbled. 'All this waiting about is driving me mad.'

'You'll get action soon enough,' said one of the other officers.

Alex had been promoted to captain. Edmund watched him going about his duties with a mixture of admiration and envy. He was energetic, meticulous, leaving no detail unchecked; he was far more popular with the men than Edmund ever managed. As Alex moved among them, making sure their food had been served before eating his own meal, or checking sentry positions along the Golden Mile, he had the knack of making an easy joke or asking about a sweetheart or baby in a way the men obviously appreciated. Trying to copy, Edmund was unable to shake off his reserve, or a suspicion that the men laughed at him behind his back. It seemed to come naturally to Alex. When Wadey, a young lance-corporal, went into a shivering funk during a burst of shelling, Alex soothed and comforted him with a kindness that surprised Edmund; he could just as typically have reacted with scorn or impatience. Edmund was almost jealous.

If Alex ever felt afraid, he did not show it. Edmund saw the gleam in his eye as he planned a forthcoming trench raid with Captain Greenaway in the officers' dug-out over the remains of their supper. Talk of gun emplacements, sniper cover, box-barrages; games of tactics and daring; the company of other men – what more could Alex want? This was what he was good at; the war brought out his finest qualities.

'If you were sent home on leave for a fortnight, this very minute,' Edmund teased him when the discussion was over, 'I believe you'd refuse to go.'

'Home?' Alex had hardly slept; he rubbed a hand across his eyes. 'What is there for me to do at home other than fret to be back here? I haven't got your rolling acres to wander in, or country house-parties for amusement.'

Mid-February, and winter showed no sign of yielding to spring. The frost turned soil to concrete and breath to steam; it numbed fingers and noses and threatened toes with its bite. This was a mining area, bleak and industrial, the landscape pimpled with slag heaps and pocked with quarries. The scenery held little to attract the eye. Efforts were concentrated on strengthening the line: attempting to dig sumps, and carrying supplies of wire, duckboards and sandbags through the poorly-marked communication trenches. Through nights of intense cold this work progressed, not without casualties. It was said that the Germans knew the position not only of every road, but of every duckboard and walkway; they picked out occasional victims with surgical accuracy.

Almost nightly, patrols were going out into No-Man's-Land to check the flanks of the sector and to find out whether a clump of bushes or a remnant of brickwork might conceal a machine-gun post. The barbed wire must be regularly repaired, a dangerous and time-consuming task. To his own surprise, Edmund was acquiring a reputation for recklessness; he was catching bravery from Alex. They volunteered for patrols, and sometimes made unauthorized forays beyond the wire. There was a thrill of bravado in leaving the cover of the trench, in being exposed to the night; in creeping, sometimes, close enough to the German trenches to hear snatches of conversations of which they might understand an occasional word. Once, as they returned from patrol, a rifle bullet passed so close that Edmund felt the rush of air on his cheek and heard it slam into the sandbags behind him. He felt light-headed, invulnerable. Hissing the password to the sentry, he slithered down into their trench, pulled Alex after him and helped him to his feet, laughing. Both of them were coal streaked and filthy in the early grey light. For a wild moment Edmund thought: I have never been happier in my whole life. This is living in a way I have never dreamed.

'Do you *want* to get yourselves killed?' said the new junior officer, Paterson's replacement.

'Both or neither.' Alex spoke into Edmund's ear. 'Both live or both die.'

In daylight, all life was conducted below ground. The furtive creeping, head kept carefully below the dripping parapet, felt to Edmund like a literal enactment of the secrecy of his personal life. In the back-to-front

145

world of the trenches, day was night and night was day. Daytime was for rest and sleeping, for brewing mugs of tea, for distributing mail and for writing letters. Night-time was for working-parties, and for vigilance, when the two armies, dug into opposing trenches, revealed their presence through desultory shelling, a sniper's rifle, the rise and flare of Very lights. Humans needed to be as alert and cunning as foxes or rats.

Edmund was in the officers' dug-out, trying to sleep. Captain Greenaway was snoring, with a rasping intake of breath that strained Edmund's nerves; Barnes, the other subaltern, was reading. Turning uncomfortably to face the shored-up wall, Edmund pulled his blanket over his ears. Alex was a few feet away on his own bunk, already unconscious, one arm flung loosely aside. Every time they settled to sleep, Edmund lay in a frustration of longing and desire. If Barnes as well as Greenaway had been soundly snoring, he would have risked crossing the few feet of clinker floor just to touch Alex's trailing hand or gaze at his sleeping face. As it was, he had to make do with imagining. Closing his eyes, he thought of his lover's body warm and close, the smell of his skin, the way his blue eyes looked vague when he woke, then sharpened into alertness. Edmund put the trodden coal-dust and the gas-curtain out of his mind to see instead the light-filled window of the Picardy farmhouse, the long dusks and dawns, the bare floorboards and simple furniture of their attic refuge. Here he was driven to distraction – they were so close and so apart. Is this love, he wondered, or is it madness? I am obsessed with him to a pitch of delirium. And then Alex would look at him in that fleeting, intimate way, or touch his hand, and he would be momentarily soothed until next time the fever burned him.

Fully awake now, Edmund propped himself up, wound his scarf around his neck and pulled on woollen gloves. The dug-out was so cold that his breath clouded the air. He took a sheet of lined paper from his pocket and unfolded it to read the lines he had laboured over, peering in dim light. As this poem contained no declaration, it had been safe enough to show it to Alex while there were other officers nearby. Alex had read it carefully, twice, then nodded and smiled. 'Yes, I like it. The second line's a bit of a tongue-twister, but the whole thing – the horse, the man, the Christ-figure – it's like a photograph.'

Alex was never extravagant with praise, but Edmund knew that he would always be honest. Clutching a stub of pencil in his gloved hand, resting the page against his pocket notebook, he tried out variations of the awkward second line: *Heaped shells* perhaps . . . *Heaped shells, and roofs caved in, and scattered tiles* . . . that would keep the iambic rhythm, but would mean changing the next line, which would be a pity, as the grimness of the scene was in the littering of corpses along with other waste. Perhaps *left* wasn't right: *corpses strewn to grimace at the sky . . . corpses leer defiance at the sky* . . . no, defiance wasn't right at all . . . he muttered the phrases aloud, scribbled out, amended, and finally rewrote the line as it had been to start with.

Barnes turned a page of his book; he had moved aside discreetly, hunching his shoulder. Hearing Edmund's muttering, he probably thought he was praying aloud. Barnes always said the Lord's Prayer to himself before sleeping, sometimes adding a few requests of his own. Touchingly simple-minded, Edmund thought.

For A.C., he wrote on the back of the paper, then stopped. Always, he came up against the gulf between thought and expression, the unwillingness of words to group themselves for his purpose.

'What's wrong?' Edmund asked, seeing Alex's wincing expression as he got to his feet.

'Galloping gut-rot. I've already been three times in the last hour – excuse me—' Alex ducked through the gas-curtain; Edmund heard his feet hurrying away on the boards. He could sympathize, having suffered from diarrhoea himself more than once, as everyone did – it was an inevitable consequence of tainted water, dubious meat and the generally unhygienic conditions under which meals were prepared. The remedy was kaolin and morphine, a thick, chalky-tasting medicine.

When Alex returned from the latrine trench, some ten minutes later, Edmund said: 'You ought to go along to the MO. He'll soon sort you out.'

'With that foul kaolin stuff? I'd rather put up with it, thanks.' Alex sat at the dug-out table and looked at the heap of papers that awaited his attention. Now that he was captain, he had endless reports to write and memos to send – on subjects ranging from casualty figures to the numbers of spare socks possessed by his company.

It was only on a whim that Edmund went out on patrol that night.

He did not have enough to do: merely giving cover to a wiring party that had gone off without incident. He stood motionless by the loophole, eyes straining, rifle aimed at the German lines, while Faulkner and his party fiddled with barbed wire. Afterwards, when they had crept back in, he felt restless. There was a thorny bush out in No-Man's-Land, near a miners' railway track, that he felt sure was used as a sniper's post. There had been no sniper fire tonight – yet – but he wanted to investigate.

Finding Alex on his way to battalion headquarters, Edmund told him he was going out.

'I'll wait,' Alex said. 'Take care. Don't take risks.'

As if he never took risks himself! Edmund thought. He crept forward along Morecambe Pier with Boyce behind. 'Patrol going out,' he told the sergeant on sentry duty, then led the way through the narrow, concealed gap. Spreadeagled, he and Boyce made their way across the treacherous expanse towards a huddle of bushes, negotiating an ice-glazed ditch, noting every dip that might offer cover. The ground was rough with shale under his hands and knees; a flare soared and flickered, momentarily lighting the bush Edmund had come out to investigate. His whole attention was focused on the line of rough grass that showed the position of the light railway track. It crossed his mind that a German patrol might be doing exactly the same thing; they could, all unknowing, be creeping towards each other in the darkness. Heart pumping, pistol at the ready, he crawled closer, discovering the bushes to be harmless, a gnarled cluster, smaller than they had looked through the periscope. No crouched figure, no rifle barrel.

'Bit farther along,' he whispered to Boyce. 'There's a ditch along the track—'

At that moment the shelling started. Not only here – something was happening to the north, towards Ypres. Flares and alarm lights performed their eerie dance in the sky, with greenish flickers. The British guns were answering, raking the German front line. Looking to his left, Edmund pressed himself close to the ground as a shell whined over to thud and splatter well behind their own front line. Time to get back in, he gestured to Boyce; the ditch could wait. Running in the darkness, then flattening themselves in the light of a new flare, they made their way, zigzagging shell-holes. He slithered into Morecambe Pier, and turned to make sure Boyce was behind him. 'Well done, sir,' said the sentry, ducking as earth and coal-dust showered them. 'That was our back trench got hit just now.'

Edmund nodded. Staring into the half-light he made his way along the sap to where he knew Alex would be waiting for him. The air was full of dust and the acrid smell of cordite. He wondered if anyone had the stove lit, for coffee.

'Stretcher-bearer! Stretcher-bearer!' someone was yelling.

Alex was there by the periscope, still looking out to the German lines. Edmund touched his arm. 'Alex? Nothing there, but we couldn't stay around for a close look once the shelling started—'

The head turned, and Edmund stepped back. It was not Alex but Willerby, a young lance-corporal – tall, skinny, hardly old enough to shave. 'No, sir, it's me. Captain Culworth wasn't well – bad stomach cramp, he said. Told me to wait here in his place.'

Edmund stared, heard the yell: 'Stretcher-bearer! Now!' and heavy footfalls. The latrine trench! He turned on his heel, slithering on the iced duckboard, and met Faulkner coming from the next bay.

'Sorry, sir. Culworth's been hit. Bad. I've sent a runner to Captain Greenaway.'

But Alex is here. Where I left him. He said he'd wait. Blindly, Edmund followed Faulkner into the communication trench; saw the stretcher-party bent over their load. The man they were lifting to the stretcher was making terrible sounds – rasping moans, no strength to cry out. *It can't be Alex. I left him waiting for me. He must be there, waiting still—*

'Let me—' Edmund's voice was hoarse; he dropped to his knees. He saw Alex's eyes wide open, unrecognizing; head arched back in a rictus of pain. 'Alex! Alex! Where are you hurt?' Alex opened his mouth but did not speak; he was breathing in short, painful gasps.

'What terrible bad luck,' Faulkner said. 'He was in our firing-bay not five minutes ago.'

151

'Alex!' Edmund pleaded. The icy air could not overcome the stench from the latrines. Tenderly, he touched Alex's face, and felt it clammed with sweat.

'Stand back, sir.'

The bearers lifted the stretcher, tilting it. Alex's face contorted, but it was Edmund who cried out – a long, keening wail that he had not known himself capable of making, that seemed to come from some desperately wounded animal. He saw astonished eyes looking at him. And now Captain Greenaway was here – too many bodies cluttering the space. He took Edmund firmly by the arm.

'Go back to your post. Culworth is being taken care of.'

'But I've got to go with—'

'I've given you an order – we're not having a discussion about it.' He leaned closer and spoke in an undertone. 'Pull yourself together. Think of the example you're giving the men.'

Edmund stared back at him, tears burning his eyes, then managed a ragged salute. 'Yes, sir.'

'That's better.' Greenaway patted his shoulder. 'I'll keep you posted.'

Faulkner steered Edmund back to the fire-step. 'I'm sorry, sir, really I am,' he said softly.

Did he know? Did they all know?

'Go and take over from Willerby,' Edmund said coldly.

Galloping gut-rot! Edmund could not get it into his head, what had happened: the arbitrariness of those two events coinciding so cruelly – a stray shell and a dash to the latrines. Alex! Brave Alex who was never afraid, who never thought of his own safety, who could have been injured twenty times over in a trench raid, in an assault, in a feat of daring . . . Edmund, supposedly checking the sentries along C Company's front, made his way unseeing. Again and again he saw Alex waiting where he had left him by the periscope; saw the bent shoulders and the head turning to him, the face that was not Alex's. *Wait – wait there! Don't go back—*

As soon as he was relieved, an interminable two hours later, Edmund went to look for him. An ambulance stood outside the casualty clearing station, a small collection of tents. Dismay tugged at Edmund as he realized that Alex would most likely have been taken away to the base hospital in Boulogne, but the news was worse.

'He's too ill to be moved,' a Red Cross nurse told Edmund. 'You can come in for a few minutes, that's all.'

Alex was the only patient; the other beds stood empty. This, Edmund knew, did not indicate a lack of wounded, but meant that an attack was expected shortly and everyone fit enough to be moved had been sent on. Alex lay alone in the bitterly cold tent. His skin, always pale, had a strange waxy look, glossed with sweat. He shivered under several blankets. Edmund gazed, desperate and useless, unsure whether Alex recognized him. Alex's head turned restlessly from side to side, his eyes unfocused; he made a small, painful sound with each breath. The nurse straightened his bedclothes and felt his pulse, frowning. Edmund wished she would go away, or do something more likely to ease Alex's suffering.

'It's me – Edmund!' He knelt by the bed, touched Alex's face and felt first cold clamminess, then pulsing heat. Alex twitched his head as if shaking off a fly; he had retreated to somewhere deep inside himself. 'Can't you give him something?' Edmund demanded of the nurse.

'He's had morphine.' She was a kind-faced woman of perhaps thirty. 'I can't give him any more.'

'How badly injured is he?' Edmund asked bleakly.

The nurse indicated that they should move away from the bed. He got to his feet and followed her; she spoke in an undertone.

'It's very bad, the doctor said – extensive damage to internal organs. He's not likely to survive the night. I'm sorry.'

Edmund clenched his fists in his greatcoat pockets and bit his lip. Absently he felt the trickle of blood, tasted it, swallowed hard.

'I'm sorry,' the nurse said again. She paused. 'You're not related?'

'Friend,' Edmund said. The inadequate word sounded like a flat lie. *We are lovers – we are linked body and soul*, he wanted to tell her, as if such a declaration would save Alex. *I am him and he is me. If he dies, I will die too.* He stood in the tent opening. It was sharply cold, and a sprinkling of frost lay over the grass at his feet, outlining every blade. He saw his breath as clouds in the air – it was so easy, breathing, taken for granted until you saw someone struggling with every inhalation. The sky was lightening over the dull landscape and the heaped hills of slag. Alex must not die here. Alex must not die anywhere.

'God – please God – let him live,' Edmund muttered, taking a few steps out into the open. He was not used to praying, not any more. As a boy he had attended church every Sunday and taken part in daily prayers either at home or at school, hardly questioning what he was taught, thinking of God as a benign, watchful presence in his life. Alex had changed that; he had challenged Edmund's belief as he challenged everything conventional. 'Belief in a heavenly after-life keeps people docile and undemanding in this one. I don't intend to be docile; neither need you.'

And Edmund, unable to reconcile his Church of England upbringing with what he had discovered about his sexual leanings, had been glad to discard God. Now, though, in his desperation, he yearned for the comfort of a father-figure who would listen and heed and intervene. He closed his eyes and tried to pray as he had never prayed before. 'God – dear God. Let him live. He must live.'

But Alex alive was reduced to an incoherent mass of pain, unable to speak, or hear words of comfort. Edmund looked towards the German lines, seeing the dawn sky flushed pink, rising to clearest deep blue, with a crescent moon fading in the light. He saw the beauty of the dawn, and resented it; of all things he did not want beauty to mock him. Not now, while Alex was dying. And how could he ask God for help, a God he had rejected and defied?

The idea slipped into his mind and lodged there. Alex's suffering was a punishment for his homosexuality. And his own punishment was this: to be forced to stand by, helplessly, while his lover passed through torment and out of his reach. Alex had tried to demolish God, but maybe God, the God of love and forgiveness, would still save Alex.

'Lord,' he prayed again, silently, 'forgive me, please forgive me. And him. If you let him live, I'll believe properly again. I'll break off with him – I will. I'll go home after the war and marry Philippa and produce an heir for Graveney.'

Footsteps crunched towards him. 'Bit parky for standing around.' It was a Red Cross orderly, making his way to the tent. 'You all right, sir?'

'Yes, thank you – good morning,' Edmund said, and waited for the man to go on his way before continuing his silent conversation. 'Are you listening? Let me tell you again. I swear it solemnly.' He closed his eyes and felt the pain of loss sharpen inside him with a new twist. 'If you do as I ask, if you spare him, I will give him up. I will end it with him.' His fingernails dug hard into his palms. 'I promise. That's my bargain.'

Inside his head he heard a phrase from one of the Reverend Tilley's sermons: *Thou shalt not tempt the Lord thy God.* Edmund had never quite understood what it meant – *could* God be tempted? But God could not lose, though the crazy logic of the bargain was compelling.

Alex and I are the ones who'll lose, Edmund thought. Either way.

Website

Image downloaded from the Commonwealth War Graves website: a slab of smooth, greyish-white stone, the base of a war memorial. In close-up, we read in carved lettering: THEIR NAME LIVETH FOR EVERMORE. At the base of the slab are propped two circular wreaths studded with artificial poppies. A handwritten label is attached to each wreath.

Late on Tuesday evening, when everyone else had gone to bed, Greg sat at the computer, dialling up the internet connection.

A simple search took him to the Commonwealth War Graves website. The home page showed a list of contents, and a caption *Their Name Liveth for Evermore.* At the bottom, *To search the register click here.*

The click took him to a picture of a memorial slab, and *This Register provides personal and service details of commemoration for the 1.7 million of the Commonwealth forces who died in the First or Second World Wars.* This was more comprehensive than Greg had hoped for. If

Edmund Pearson had died in the army, he would be here. A few clicks of the mouse could reveal what had happened to him, and where. Greg's senses quickened with a hunter's excitement as he followed the instructions to *search the register*.

Surname: Pearson

Initial(s):   E

War or Year of Death: 1917

Force: Army

Nationality: UK

The search brought up a list of ten E. Pearsons, each with his rank, regiment and date of death. Greg scanned them eagerly. Not one of them was from the Epping Foresters, and only one was an officer, Second Lieutenant E. J. Pearson. Another click identified him as Edward John Pearson of Northampton, a second lieutenant in the Royal Field Artillery, who had died on 2 August 1917 aged twenty-five and was buried in the Huts Cemetery at Ypres in Belgium.

Greg checked the other nine just in case, then tried 1918, but found nothing that could possibly be Edmund Pearson of Graveney Hall. A blank. Edmund had slipped away again.

He stared at the screen in frustration. Now what? On an impulse he typed in his own name. G. Hobbs, Army, First World War yielded twenty-six names. There would be twenty-six gravestones with his name on them. Thinking of the fictional selves he had invented for himself, Jordan and Gizzard, he tried the other two names. Of J. McAuliffes there were eight, of G. Guisboroughs none, which seemed to confirm his view of Gizzard as a natural survivor. He wondered about the real men who had worn his name and Jordan's into battle and into death. But not, it seemed, accompanied by Edmund Pearson.

He called Faith on her mobile.

'What?' Her voice was thick and blurry. 'I'm in bed!'

In his urgency to tell her, he'd forgotten how late it was. He explained about the website, then: 'He's not listed, Edmund I mean, not in all the 1.7 million! That means he *can't* have died in the war.'

'What, then? We know he's not in the graveyard with his relations. We know he's not in a Commonwealth War Grave. So where is he?'

'And why didn't he come back to Graveney Hall?'

'I know!' Faith said, sounding properly awake. 'I'll ask Dad to help me check the *Births, Marriages and Deaths* in the church records. Even if he didn't live at Graveney he'd be in there if he got married or had children, and when he died. If he came back to the area at all.'

'What if—?' Greg was thinking aloud.

'What if what?'

'What if he was a deserter?'

There was a pause while they both thought about this. Then Faith said, 'They shot them, didn't they?'

'If they were caught. What if he got away with it?'

'But why should you think he was a deserter?'

160

'Because I can't think of anything else that makes sense,' Greg said.

At the pool early next morning, perched on his high seat, he watched the training session. There were plenty of accomplished swimmers, female as well as male, Jordan the unassuming star. Greg watched as he stood poised to dive, then the deep, clean swoop. In the water he was streamlined and powerful, somersaulting into a tumble-turn, swimming length after length of crawl, back crawl, and – his speciality – butterfly.

'You ought to join the club,' he had told Greg. 'We could do with more people in the team. What's your best stroke?'

'Front crawl. But by *best* I mean least bad. You've seen me – I can swim for miles but I'm never going to win races. You'd leave me standing.'

Jordan was preparing now for county trials. When the other swimmers finished their session, the coach kept him a little longer to work on the butterfly. It looked so easy, done properly: as if the water itself were gathering its forces to hurl the swimmer along the surface. Humped back, head tucked in, water showering from arrowed arms, water gleaming on skin; then the darting precision of the turn, the thrust underwater, the renewed power of the stroke. Wonder if I could photograph that? Greg thought. Would the digital camera have a fast enough shutter-speed? Keeping in mind David Bailey's comment about noticing the ordinary, he was building up a second sequence of pictures, taken at the pool. Watery images: the unbroken surface when the pool was empty; the steps dropping into turquoise clearness; the clean-ploughed wash from a strong swimmer. He wanted underwater shots too, if he could find a way of getting them.

Paul, one of the staff, came to take over at the poolside. 'Fantastic, that.' He jerked his head towards Jordan in the pool. 'Our Olympic hope.'

'You're joking!'

'Probably. Pretty damn good though. Wish I could do butterfly. All I do is make tidal waves and half-drown myself.'

'Same here.'

Greg went into the changing room to get out of his shorts and T-shirt and into school uniform, taking his time. When he came away from the locker, bag slung over his shoulder, most of the swimmers had gone. Jordan was standing under the shower, his back to Greg; his trunks, towel and goggles hung on a hook. He was rinsing his hair, arms upraised, head tilted back, foam sliding between his shoulder-blades. Greg stopped, looked, took in what struck him as beautifully photographable: the light, the spray, the lovely curves and angles. *Frame, click* went his mental camera. Jordan turned; saw him, and smiled.

'Hi. Are you biking in? Ready in a couple of minutes if you don't mind hanging on.'

'OK,' Greg said. He went to the mirror and tidied his hair. It was tidy already, but he needed to hide his confusion. Jordan had seen him standing there, looking, looking, a little more intently than was permissible, and did not know it was with photographic intent.

After History, Greg stayed behind on the pretext of explaining to Mrs Hampson that his homework wasn't in because the computer's ink cartridge had run out. She waved aside his excuses, picking up her pile of books. 'Tomorrow will do. Such is my faith in human nature that I'm prepared to believe you.'

'Actually, I wanted to ask you something. You know the First World War?'

'Greg, I'm a History teacher.' She dumped her pile back on the desk. 'I may have heard it mentioned once or twice.'

He ignored the sarcasm. 'You know how people got shot by firing squad for deserting? If that happened, would they still be buried in the proper war cemeteries?'

'Oh yes,' Mrs Hampson said. 'In fact there's been a lot of controversy recently – you may have heard about it. Whether the records should be put straight now that we know about shell-shock and war neuroses. I've got a book if you'd like to borrow it.'

'Thanks. The gravestone inscriptions wouldn't say anything, would they – about the men being executed?'

'No. They'd have exactly the same style of wording as all the others. Just the regimental details and date. Hang on – I'll get that book from my office.'

It took her a few minutes to find it. Jordan was

waiting outside in the corridor; they'd be a little late for their next lesson. Greg shoved the book into his rucksack, and they walked together to the Maths block on the opposite side of the campus. This took them past the staff car park and through the area behind the kitchens where the recycling bins were kept, a couple of storage sheds blocking the view from the main building. A group of Year Nines loitered there, smoking. Most younger boys would have scarpered if two sixth-formers came along, but not these: with a sense of inevitability Greg recognized Dean Brampton and friends. Dean stood firm, eyeballing Greg. Yusuf, who had made a move towards the recycling bin, saw that Dean wasn't giving way and put on a tough pose.

'Oooh, look who it isn't! Hobb-Knobb! Thinks he's hard,' Dean said loudly, then spat at the ground.

'Hard Knob!' Yusuf gave Dean a shove and lurched about with exaggerated laughter.

'If you want to carry on walking about in one piece,' Greg said, 'you won't touch my bike again. Go anywhere near it and I'm calling the police.'

'Who says we touched your poxy bike?' Dean jutted his chin at Greg. 'You grassed us up to Rackley. We'll get you back, don't worry.'

'Have you got all day to stand round being unpleasant?' Jordan asked. 'No lesson to go to?'

'What's it to you, tosser?' Dean flicked his cigarette end at him. Jordan, not used to getting into arguments with mouthy Year Nines, sidestepped neatly and made to walk on.

'You grassed us up,' Dean repeated, thrusting his face at Greg. 'You'll be paying for that. And soon.'

'What d'you expect if you do criminal damage for kicks?'

The smaller boy, the least aggressive of the three, was looking towards the gym. 'Mad Mitch,' he warned. 'Coming this way.'

Mr Mitchell, one of the PE teachers, was merely standing outside the building waiting for the Year Nine footballers, but the sighting was enough to make Yusuf fling down his fag and for even Dean to amble off.

'Better run along,' Greg said to Dean.

He waited for the parting taunt and it came, hurled at him over Dean's shoulder: 'You're gay!'

Greg looked at Jordan. 'As if!' It came out too loudly.

Jordan made no response. He swivelled the toe of his boot on the glowing fag end and asked, 'Why've they got it in for you?'

'Morons like them don't need a reason.' Greg was more angered by the incident than he felt was dignified. Dean Brampton got to him every time. Yusuf was a pain, the fair boy was just a sidekick, but that Dean – the way he stared with utter contempt – brought out aggressive instincts Greg didn't know he had. And this latest tactic – *you're gay* . . . Kids threw that about all the time as an insult, Greg knew that. 'You've nicked my pencil case! You're gay' – it was meaningless. All the same, he didn't like it. 'Forget them,' he said to Jordan. 'They're not worth it.'

'But they did your bike in! We could shop them for smoking?'

Greg shook his head. 'They'd have to knife someone before the Head would get off his backside. Anyway, it'd only make them worse.'

'Be careful, though,' Jordan said. 'Trouble waiting to happen, they are.'

Mrs Hampson's book *Shot at Dawn* had an index listing all the First World War soldiers executed for cowardice or desertion. E. Pearson was not among them. Indeed, Greg would have been surprised to find him; if he'd been there, he'd also have been on the Commonwealth War Graves website. Some of the tales were appalling – men with nerves shot to pieces being dragged before firing squads, and even one account of a boy being executed while he was still too young to have legally enlisted. Greg was relieved that Edmund Pearson had been spared such a fate. Perhaps Faith's researches had been more fruitful.

She rang him that evening. 'Meet me after school tomorrow?'

Greg didn't want her turning up at the gates again. 'Where?'

'Where we went last time? The Casa Veronese?'

'OK. See you there then, at the CV, round four.'

The following day he parked his bike and stood outside the Italian restaurant to wait for her. A brisk tapping on the glass surprised him, and he turned to see her already seated inside, chatting to the waiter. As soon as Greg went in, the waiter went back to the kitchens, as if they were young lovers desperate for privacy. But they weren't alone this time; there were two other customers, women with carrier bags full of shopping, who sat at the table nearest the back.

'Well?' Greg said. 'Did you find something?'

Faith gave him a reproving look. 'Hello, Faith, how lovely to see you, and have you had a good day?'

He grinned. 'Yeah, yeah, that as well.'

'You're really into this hunt for Edmund Pearson, aren't you?'

'Thought you were as well.' If she was going to start being difficult, he might as well order something. He was ravenous; he snatched up the menu to see if he could afford anything to eat.

'Well, yes,' Faith conceded. 'I am, now. You've got me intrigued. I've already ordered, by the way. Cappuccino, OK?'

Greg nodded. 'Are you going to tell me, then?'

She took a notebook from her school bag. 'We didn't find much. Births, yes. Edmund Henry Gibbs Pearson, eighteenth of March eighteen ninety-six, Graveney Hall, son of Henry Gibbs Maynard Pearson and Elizabeth Mary Pearson. Baptized thirtieth April. No wedding. No death.'

'Oh.' Greg felt flattened with disappointment. 'So where does that leave us?'

'We found the deaths of both parents. It took us ages.' Faith turned a page. 'His father, April nineteen thirty-seven; mother, January forty-eight. She was seventy-three when she died – lived right through the second war. And we looked carefully for any

167

other Pearsons, but the ones we found obviously weren't anything to do with our lot – not at the right time, anyway. The Pearsons seem to have died out with Edmund.'

'With his mother, you mean?'

'Well, yes. But Edmund would have been the one expected to produce the next generation. That's what I meant. And there wasn't a next generation, not at Graveney. But we didn't stop there. Dad had the idea of going along to the local newspaper offices, to check the story about the fire. They've got microfiche going back donkeys' years.'

'Good thinking. And?'

'Here's what it said. Basically the same as the guidebook – and look.' She pointed to her notes. '*It was extremely fortunate that, the fire having broken out during daylight hours, no-one was injured. "If the fire had occurred at night there would surely have been fatalities," said the Chief Fire Officer.*'

'So he couldn't have died in the fire,' said Greg. 'Can I have a copy of that?'

'No problem. I'm going to type it up on my computer, for the exhibition. I'll do a print-out for you.'

The waiter brought the cappuccinos; Greg explained about the *Shot at Dawn* book, and what Mrs Hampson had said about gravestones. 'Another dead end.'

'And here's another one – I nearly forgot.' Faith leaned forward, elbows on the table. 'You know you were asking about the chap who wrote the book? I asked Dad. He died six months ago – he was in his nineties.'

'Only six months ago? If only we'd got onto this sooner! We could have talked to him. If he was ninety-something, he might even have been around when the house burned down and when Edmund disappeared—'

'But the book doesn't make it sound like he ever lived there or worked there. Anyway, he was a bit gaga towards the end, Dad said. Alzheimer's.'

Greg rapped an impatient drum-roll on the table. 'Oh, this is hopeless! We're getting nowhere.'

'But we're eliminating things as well. We know Edmund's not listed as dead in the war. We know he wasn't executed for desertion. We know he didn't come back here.'

'We *think* he didn't. Or if he did, he didn't die here. So what are we left with? *Believed killed*, that's what we're left with. Where we started.'

After a moment of silence, Faith pushed back her chair. 'Shall we go for a walk?'

'Where?'

'On the common. Just for half an hour. You could leave your bike here.'

Well, all right. He wasn't in a hurry, it was a warm afternoon, and he hadn't got much homework.

The common was the farthest end of Epping Forest, Green Belt land that saved the Essex countryside from being swallowed up in the sprawl of Greater London. From here, rides and paths led off into thickets of ancient woodland, where the ground was strewn with beech leaves and threaded with streams. Greg and Faith walked past the old timbered cottages at the town end and along to where the common widened, by the cricket pitch. If they carried on, alongside the main road to London, they'd see Graveney Hall facing them on its shoulder of higher ground.

'I've been thinking again,' Greg said, 'about why I can't believe in God.'

Why had he opened his mouth? He'd told himself not to get into this kind of pointless discussion. She looked at him. 'OK, let's hear it.'

'It's the heaven and hell business. Not just that I don't believe in hell – all those medieval pictures of people being pitchforked into fires and tormented by devils. I don't believe in heaven either. It doesn't make any sense to me.'

'But those pictures only show human ideas, human fears. I don't believe in hell that way either. Hell to me is being cut off from God's love. But that wouldn't be a punishment so much as my own choice – my own chosen punishment – because I can have God's love if I choose it. Heaven – you don't believe in it because you can't begin to imagine it, but that doesn't mean it isn't there. You might as well say you don't believe in black holes because you can't see them. They'd have been unimaginable a hundred years ago. There are things we just can't know.'

'Yes, but it's not logical to put it the other way round – it's beyond us to imagine something, therefore it must exist. And why *should* heaven exist? What's the point of having an imaginary world that's better than this one? Surely the point is that we ought to do a better job of looking after the world we've got, because it's *all* we've got – not kid ourselves there's going to be something better afterwards.'

'But Jesus talked about heaven,' Faith objected. 'And Jesus doesn't lie.'

'Perhaps he didn't deliberately lie, but who was Jesus anyway?'

'He was the Son of God,' Faith said in a tone that admitted no doubt.

'He said he was.'

'He *was*. Would he have said so otherwise? Are you calling Jesus a liar?'

'How can I know if he was a liar or not?'

'He said, *Before Abraham was, I am*. I think those are the most beautiful words in the Gospels. Not I *was* – I *am*. Am always, for ever.'

'How can you prove he was telling the truth?'

'Because He always told the truth. He said *I am the way, the truth and the life*. His resurrection proved it – He rose from the dead, He ascended to heaven.'

'I don't believe that. Everything has to obey the laws of Physics.'

'According to you. Materialist!'

'According to physicists. I don't know nearly as much about Jesus as you do—'

'You can find out!'

'– but obviously he did exist – at least someone called Jesus existed, who was a wise and clever man, a good leader, and obviously very charismatic. But just a man.'

'Yes, just a man because that's what God chose for him! But not *just* a man.' Faith stopped walking.

'What you don't understand is that I'm not only talking about someone I've read about in the Bible. I *know* Him. And He knows me.'

'OK, then – what does he look like?'

Faith gave him a look of exasperation. 'Does it matter what He looks like?'

'It might. You tell me. Could he be the same Jesus to you if he was ugly or disfigured?'

'Yes, of course, but He isn't.'

'You don't know that! And I don't believe you.'

'I know I don't know. But I know what I believe. There was that computer-generated thing in the papers – it looked nothing like Jesus in paintings, but that's been rubbished. Is it coincidence that so many painters have given Him the same sort of look, the *Light of the World* look? – you know what I mean, the famous painting?'

'It's not likely, though, is it, that he'd have looked like that? The real Jesus was a Middle-Eastern Jew. Why would he have white skin? What we get is Jesus made to look European, because we think the son of God would have to look like us.'

'It doesn't matter,' Faith insisted.

'But think about it! The son of God we get from artists is young and usually good-looking. There's this painting by Salvador Dali, *The Crucifixion*, and it's almost sexy. I mean, it would be from a female point of view. This real body stretched on the Cross. It's like a bondage photo or something. There's a kind of masochism about it. *Hey, I'll get up here and die for you, and you can have a good look and get a thrill.*'

Faith grimaced. 'Oh, don't! That's a horrible way of putting it! Crucifixion was the most horrible torture.'

'I know. But you look at the painting, then tell me if the Crucifixion would mean the same to you if Jesus was old and ugly.'

'So? That's Salvador Dali. People can do what they like with the image of the Crucifixion. It doesn't change the truth of it.'

'The truth is that a man was crucified the way hundreds and thousands of criminals were crucified by the Romans. People get what they want to believe. Jesus is a myth. The real Jesus, whoever he was, has been *made* into a myth.'

'No. To you He is,' Faith insisted. 'That's because you're putting up barriers. You're closing your mind.'

'That's what you always say when I don't think the same as you.'

'You're entitled to think whatever you want, because God has given you free will.'

'That's another whole argument,' Greg said. 'Let's not get into that.'

'Some other time, then. We'll put Free Will on the agenda.' Faith linked her arm through his. 'I like talking to you.'

'Why?' Greg asked, rather startled by the arm-linking; it seemed out of character.

'Because.'

Relieved that she hadn't taken offence this time, he made no move to detach himself. 'I didn't mean to get into all that again.'

Faith smiled but said nothing. He knew what her

interpretation would be: she saw herself as missionary, him as the reluctant convert. She was welcome to carry on believing that if it avoided conflict. She didn't seem to understand that sometimes he enjoyed arguing for its own sake. They had reached the farthest end of the common, where the open plain met the shrubby edge of the forest. The long grasses were end-of-summer bleached and there were ripe blackberries in the bramble bushes beside the path they had chosen. 'Nothing to collect them in today,' Faith said, looking. 'Anyway, Mum's had her blackberry binge.'

'When is it, this Open Day?' Greg asked.

'Sunday week. You will come, won't you?'

'What would I have to do?' he stalled.

'You could help me sell stuff. The jam, and postcards and guidebooks. It'd be fun.'

'I might,' Greg said, wary of her idea of fun.

'When I say *fun*, I mean it'll be a lot more interesting for me if you're there. Greg . . .' She stopped walking, pulling him to a halt.

'Mm?'

'You know what I was saying the other day about boyfriends?'

'What? Have you met someone?'

She laughed nervously. 'I've met *you*, stupid! Do you . . .' She looked away; he saw the rush of blood to her cheeks. 'Greg, you do like me, don't you – a bit?'

''Course I do. Would I spend all this time arguing with you otherwise?'

She flashed him a sidelong, almost coquettish look. 'You don't show it.'

'Show it how? What do you want me to do?'

'What do you think?' She dropped her school bag, turned to face him, looked up at him; he felt her fingers curling round his hand.

'Are you kidding? What about your rules?' he said lightly. 'No sex before marriage, that's what you told me.'

She stepped back, eyes wide, appalled. 'I didn't mean *that*! Is that what you thought? It doesn't have to be all or nothing, does it?'

'I thought we were just friends!'

'Why? I never said so.'

'Thought you preferred it that way.'

'Because I'm a Christian?'

'OK, because of that. And because I'm not.'

'That doesn't mean I have to go into a nunnery! Couldn't we . . .' She came close again, touching his arm. Awkwardly, because it was easier than talking, he put both arms round her. He bent his head; her face turned up to him eagerly. Their mouths met. He could tell she wasn't used to being kissed, not like tarty Tanya, who had been all probing tongue and thrusting chest. Faith held herself quite still, as if she didn't know how to carry on breathing. He held her gently, aware of the slenderness and strength of her body, and the clean fragrance of hair and skin. Inhibited by her innocence, he made the kiss a rather perfunctory one. What if someone from school was watching? What if her mum came along in search of fruit for jam? He stood looking over Faith's head to where the broad forest track, marked and churned by hoofprints, dipped away from the common between holly thickets. She stood close and silent as if expecting something more. He released her, giving her shoulder a little pat as he might pat a well-behaved dog: dismissive.

'What's wrong?' She looked up at him in dismay. 'Aren't I – aren't I any good?'

'It's not your fault. I don't know – it feels weird.'

'How do you mean?'

'It doesn't feel right, kissing you.'

With a small sound of exasperation, Faith turned away. Greg stayed put, hands thrust into his pockets, looking down at the depths of trees behind trees that dipped and rose with the fall and swell of ground, and at the first leaves turning toast-coloured, as if scorched. He had messed this up, as he seemed to be messing up everything. He hadn't wanted to hurt or upset her – again – but he had.

Into his mind, vivid and disturbing, slipped the moment yesterday morning in the changing room when Jordan had turned and looked at him. It had only taken an instant, but there had been a sort of connection. An exchange, an unspoken understanding. He had stared openly at Jordan as he stood there naked; he had gazed for too long, and Jordan had seen and not minded. Jordan's glance had seemed to say: *I know. It's all right.*

God, what am I thinking? Is he – am I – does he think – do I—

He swung round. Faith had gone: she was striding away round the edge of the cricket pitch, back towards the town. He thought of yelling, running after her, but stayed where he was and watched her go.

Gaia

Greg's mental snapshot: In the swimming-pool changing room, Jordan stands beneath the shower, his back to the viewer. Water bounces off his head, shoulders and upraised arms. His body is slender and strong; his wet skin gleams in the artificial light. He is washing himself unselfconsciously, not knowing he is being watched.

Greg watched Faith stomping along the edge of the common and out of sight.

It was her fault, wasn't it? She'd started this. They were becoming good friends till she'd spoiled it. Let her go off in a huff if she wanted to. If he ran after her and said he was sorry, she'd get the wrong idea again.

Wrong? Right? Which was which? How could you tell?

Greg heard Dean's taunt: *'You're gay!'* Well, I'm not, Greg thought. Definitely not. I could have kissed her properly if I'd wanted to.

Kids said that quite meaninglessly. Unless Dean could read Greg's mind better than Greg could read it

177

himself, and sort out the muddle, he couldn't possibly know.

Know what? What is there to know?

Greg walked back slowly, kicking at leaves, thinking about Jordan. I am *not* gay, he told himself. Not even remotely. Just because I—

Just because he's always on my mind. Just because I'd rather be with him than with anyone else. Just because it's enough to be together, not even talking. Just because he obviously likes me the same way.

Again Greg thought of that glance, of what had seemed like a current running between them. But what had Jordan actually said? *Hi. Ready in a couple of minutes, if you don't mind hanging on.* Definitely not the words of someone who had just experienced a blinding revelation. Male bonding, Greg decided, that's all. He picked up a conker that gleamed among fallen leaves, and put it in his pocket for the cats at home.

All this seemed so utterly stupid by the next day, that Greg couldn't believe he'd given it brain-space. After lunch, when they both had a study period in the library before Physics last thing, Jordan said: 'How about this evening?'

'What?'

'Shall we go up to that ruined house you're always on about? I'd like to see it.'

'OK, why not?'

They arranged to meet later on bikes at the church.

At home, making himself a ham sandwich in the kitchen, Greg found himself the centre of attention.

'Oh, you're not honouring us with your presence later, then?' Katy observed.

'No, I'm going out.'

'Who with?'

'Who's the lucky girl?' asked their father, home early and rummaging in the bottom of the fridge for a beer can.

'It's not a girl. I'm meeting Jordan.' Greg looked for mustard in the larder, mentally kicking himself as he waited for Katy to swipe back with the jibe he'd set up for her; but instead she made her eyes round and said, 'Jordan, *mmmm*. Bring him home if you want.'

'I wouldn't subject him to that.'

'I'd like to meet this Jordan myself,' said their mother; 'he seems to be mentioned quite a lot. Why don't you invite him round some time, Greg?'

'I might,' Greg said cautiously. 'But only if you can guarantee Katy'll be somewhere else.'

By the time they reached Graveney Hall, Greg felt almost nervous. The place was deserted, the way he liked it best: nothing but birds and rabbits to disturb the lingering presence of the past. He and Jordan hid their bikes in the place Faith had shown him – well out of sight round the farthest side of the stables, behind the brick ice house. There was no-one else around. Since the vandalism, the front entrance was padlocked, and there were barbed-wire strands all along the fence that separated the front of the house from the gardens, but it was easy enough to get in for anyone with a mind to. They walked slowly around the main house, Jordan asking questions, Greg taking photographs: one with Jordan in it, just one. 'Could you stand over there for a second, by the entrance?' All very low-key. Friday evening, unwinding from school, thinking about the weekend; maybe a couple of beers at the pub later.

They wandered away from the house, their feet brushing the grass. Greg explained about the ha-ha; they stood there looking out over the curve of hillside, towards the woods. A pheasant screeched from the cover of the trees. It was a perfectly still evening. Jordan climbed down over the fragments of the steps that had marked the western entrance, where the magnificent gates had once been, and followed the ha-ha where it contoured round. Watching him walk, the way he placed his feet, the shape of his shoulder-blades through a thin sweatshirt, Greg caught himself deliberately lagging behind for the pleasure of looking, and felt newly disturbed. He'd speed up: have a quick look round, then suggest biking to the Forest Tavern, where they might find some of the girls from school and things would be more normal.

But Jordan wouldn't be hurried. He walked on slowly, looking at everything. At the farthest end of the yew hedge that had once marked the boundary of the formal garden, there was a large hexagonal slab of concrete, about a metre high, with steps up. He stopped, seeing this.

'What is it? A bandstand?' He turned and waited for Greg to catch up.

'There used to be a statue here. There were statues all over the garden, all gone now. This one was of Pan – I've seen a photo.'

'Must have been a huge statue, then, going by the size of this base.'

'It was. Larger than life.'

'You've seen Pan in real life?' Jordan said, so seriously that Greg didn't immediately realize he was teasing. 'He was the one with goat legs and horns, wasn't he? Liked music and a lot of noise? I wonder which way he'd have been facing. Down towards those woods would have been best. He was always capering about through the woods, wasn't he? I don't think he was a tame god.'

'But are any gods tame?' Greg blathered. 'I don't think there can be such a thing as a tame god. God – capital-G God – isn't tame.'

Jordan looked at him, puzzled. 'I only meant I didn't think he'd belong up here, near the house, where it was all smart and manicured from what you say. If I had a stately home and a Pan statue, I'd put Pan in a clearing, in the wildest part of the woods. I don't know about capital-G God. As far as I'm concerned, he's fictional, like Pan – a bit prone to sending down plagues of locusts and afflicting people with boils, wasn't he?'

'If God is fictional, then what? Do you believe in something else?'

Jordan gave him another quizzical look, paused, and said: 'Really it's odd we don't spend the whole time wondering. Why don't we wake up every morning and think, Hey! Here's daylight again! And there's oxygen for me to breathe! And I'm alive! And who's arranged all this, and what's it all for? We ought to be more *surprised*. But we get so used to it, we stop wondering how it happens, and clutter up our brains with what's happening in *Brookside* or whether we've got the right kind of trainers. This is a good place to ask, really – Pan's place. Because if I had to say I was anything – atheist, agnostic or whatever – I'd have to say pantheist.'

Greg raised his eyebrows. 'You believe in Pan?'

'It means *all*. God-in-everything. Only I wouldn't call it God. A kind of spirit of the earth might be another way to put it. Gaia. It makes more sense to me than anything else. Have you heard of it?'

'Yes,' Greg said. 'Only I thought it was a rock group.'

Jordan laughed. 'Gaia means earth spirit. It's a kind of energy, a will to live or to survive. It's what keeps the planet going in spite of humans molesting it. Or *has* kept it going. Perhaps eventually Gaia will give up and the earth will suffocate in a cloud of green-house gases.'

'Yeah, so where do humans fit in?'

'Gaia must be in us, but only as in all animals – all creatures and all plants. Everything has the same will to live. But we're not that important – no more than slugs or snails, only we're a million times more harmful collectively. Gaia could manage a lot better without us. The problem is we can't just *be*. We want more than we ought to have – we want cars and cinemas and swimming pools and continental holidays, and we don't just want them, we take it for granted we're entitled to them. If we could just *be*, just live off what the earth can give us, not by taking and taking, the rainforests would grow and the atmosphere would clear and the earth would find its own balance.'

'So a catastrophic disease – a plague or something that killed off the whole human race – would be a good thing on the whole?'

Jordan considered. 'Yes, for Gaia, for the earth and its survival – if we haven't damaged it too much already. But it's impossible to think on that sort of scale, isn't it? We're too wrapped up in ourselves, thinking we're so important. We're here and now.'

'Yeah,' Greg said. The hereness and nowness were very much on his mind.

'And of course I want all those things too – the cars and holidays. Especially the swimming pools. I'm not really planning to live in a cave in the Outer Hebrides.' Jordan sat on the statue plinth, elbows resting on his knees. 'We can't link up the two – the two scales we think in, or on. The us and the whole. They're so vastly apart that we don't even see the connection. Everyday stuff gets in the way.'

'You've never said any of this before,' Greg said, sitting too, a careful distance apart. In fact, he'd never heard Jordan talk so much about anything.

'No. Well, you asked. I don't think about this all the time because – well, what I said about everyday stuff. Anyway, most people would think I was a complete nutter. You know that Wordsworth poem we read, *Tintern Abbey*? He would have known what I'm on about. And I know what he was on about. *The spirit that moves all things*. Bit of a pantheist, Wordsworth was. O'Donnell was having a job convincing everyone in the classroom on a Monday morning. Should have brought us up here.' He turned towards the house. 'This whole place is a kind of symbol of Gaia, really. Humans came and built on it, tamed it, made straight lines and put down concrete. Now the humans have gone and Gaia is taking it back. Things grow wherever they can. These blackberry bushes and tree saplings are full of the will to live. I like it like this.'

'Me too,' Greg said. He picked up a stone and chucked it over the ha-ha, then another. They sat in silence for a few moments. About to suggest they went down to the lake, Greg began getting to his feet when Jordan, absorbed in his own thoughts, said, 'If I had to find the equivalent of praying, it would be swimming. That's when I'm most me – do you know what I mean? – when I can *be* the most I can be. It's a sort of pure, concentrated *being* – no room for anything else. *I swim, therefore I am.* No, perhaps what I mean is *I am, therefore I swim.* What would it be for you? The best way of being?'

Greg thought. 'A physical thing? Riding down a steep hill on my bike – I don't know – scoring a goal. Diving.'

'Sex, I suppose, must be like that as well,' Jordan said, 'if you do it properly.'

'Properly?'

'With your whole self.' Jordan leaned forward and plucked a grass stem.

The quietness hummed in Greg's ears, blurring his thoughts.

Jordan looked at him. 'Maybe that's why you didn't go with that girl at that party. You didn't want it to be just a quick grope. It ought to be more than that. It ought to mean something.'

A burning silence. Greg fiddled with his bootlace. Where was this leading? Did he want to go where it might lead? He had to *know*, even if he didn't want—

'I have a dream – a fantasy,' Jordan said, 'of spending a night in the open, by the sea, with another person, on a warm, still night when the sky's really clear. We'd lie all night looking up at the stars and listening to the waves, and then when the dawn came we'd wade into the sea and swim. That would be perfect enough to last my whole life. Stars and darkness and space and sand and waves and water and light.'

Another person? You mean a girl? Greg wanted to ask, though he was almost certain by now that Jordan did not.

But Jordan was off in another direction. 'You know I told you Michelle was waiting for a transplant?'

'Mm?' Greg was startled, half-disappointed.

'My mum's going to donate a kidney. Isn't that incredibly brave? I think so.'

'Yes, it is.' Greg could barely make himself sound interested. 'Is it risky, then? For your mum, I mean?'

'Yes – well, there's the small risk of something going wrong with the kidney she's left with. And there's no guarantee of the transplant being successful. Either way, it'll take Mum two or three months to get over the operation. But it's better for Michelle, not just because she won't have to wait, but because the chances are higher than if she got one from someone not related. And she won't have to live with the knowledge of someone dying before she can have their kidney. When you're on the transplant list, you're waiting – hoping – for a kidney to become available. And the most likely source is someone who dies in intensive care after a car accident or something like that.'

'Mm, difficult. When will this happen?'

'Soon, when they've finished all the tests to make sure it's a perfect match, and the counselling.' Jordan paused. Greg, sensing that he wanted to say more, looked at him encouragingly; he went on, 'I did offer to give her one of mine when we first talked about it, but I only did it because I knew they'd all say no. My parents, the doctors, Michelle herself. And that let me off the hook. I'm not brave enough, or generous enough, when it comes down to it. I feel bad about that. It was cheating. I got the credit for offering when I knew I wasn't really risking anything by opening my mouth.'

'I don't think you need beat your brains about it! It would be an awful lot to ask of you. Going through a big operation – losing fitness, when you're in the middle of training – when it could turn out to be useless. Put on the line like that, I don't think I'd volunteer for my pain of a sister—'

'But no-one *has* asked it of me. I thought I should be able to ask it of myself, so that Michelle can have a normal life. Imagine what it's like for her – tied to a machine she can't live without, always having to watch her diet, never being able to go on holiday unless it's near a hospital with a dialysis unit.'

'She hasn't got the choice. You have.'

'But that's what I mean. It's only when you're faced with a difficult choice that you find out things about yourself.'

For a second their eyes met; Greg looked away. Another silence. A wagtail landed on the stone facing of the ha-ha, flicking its tail.

'See, that's a big difference between your family and mine,' Greg said gruffly. 'Your lot talk about things. Mine don't. We're just people who happen to live in the same house and don't always get on specially well. It's a logistics thing, really – getting everyone in and out of the bathroom and out of the house on time, and out of each other's hair. That's how my lot function.'

'We've always talked about things,' Jordan said. 'Especially since Michelle's been ill. It makes you . . . stop being petty, I suppose. You realize how important your family is. And my parents have always been pretty good at listening and helping with problems. I wouldn't be afraid to tell them anything.'

Greg huffed a laugh, thinking of his own parents. His dad's attempts at man-to-son frankness were an embarrassment to both of them, making Greg want to wriggle away.

'What?' Jordan said.

The wagtail was startled off, with a *chizzick* call and a fanning of white tail feathers. Close at hand, war whoops and cackles shredded the quietness. Something looped through the air: a chunk of dead wood, narrowly missing Jordan's head, thudded on the edge of the ha-ha then rolled over. Voices jeered from behind the hedge.

'Faggots!'

'Gay boys! Pooftaaahs!'

'Bum bandits!'

Greg was on his feet at once, turning, defensive. Dean Brampton stood in the gap in the yew hedge, leering, tongue rolling obscenely, hand pumping in an unmistakable gesture; then he ran after the other two towards the house, thrusting two fingers at the sky.

'Bastards!' Greg spat out the word.

'Those yobs from school? Why do they keep coming here?'

'Because they're mindless morons.' Greg was more angry than he wanted Jordan to see: he was hot with frustrated aggression. Furious with Dean & Co. for stalking him and Jordan, for being here at all. Furious with himself for letting it happen.

'Don't take any notice,' Jordan said. 'It'll only make them worse if we go after them.'

'What they said—'

'They'd yell that at any two blokes,' Jordan said calmly.

'They spoil everything.' Greg's fists tightened. What now? To go down to the lake would be to risk the boys following, to invite them to trash the place with abuse and stone-throwing and spray-cans. 'We'll have to get them out of here. They'll start damaging the house, throwing bricks.' He saw Jordan's hesitation. 'I don't mean fight them. Chase them off the place. They've always cleared off quickly enough before, even when I was on my own.'

They crossed the grass. The shell of the house seemed as deserted now as it had been when they arrived. It was eerie in its emptiness, facing the waning sun.

'I bet they're inside.'

Jordan looked at the DANGER KEEP OUT signs. 'I thought it was all boarded up?'

'You can still get in round this side. That's where they'll be.' Greg pushed aside trailing ivy and led the way below the steps and inside to the towering central area. Their footfalls echoed off the walls. Jordan made a sound of amazement, looking up at the staircase to nowhere, the vast first-floor fireplace, the sapling trees clinging to brickwork toeholds, and on up to sky and clouds.

'No sign of them.'

'No,' Greg said, 'but they've climbed around in here before. With a bit of luck they'll break their stupid necks.'

Above their heads, a whistle: then a shower of brick-dust.

'Come and get us, Hobb-Knob! Tosser! If you're not chicken.'

Greg looked up – unwisely, as a whole brick hurtled down this time, ricocheting off the wall behind him and splatting close to his feet, breaking into three jagged pieces.

'Are you brain-dead or what?' he yelled up. 'Don't you know this whole building could come down?'

He glimpsed a figure clambering close to the crumbled edge of the staircase, another darting through a doorway on the upper floor. Baboon-calls echoed through the shell of the house. A renewed volley of brick-dust and brick-pieces showered them, a renewed torrent of insults. Jordan began to move back the way they'd come in; Greg made to follow him. No point in this. They'd walked into an ambush, presenting themselves as targets. Faith's dad had said that if the boys committed any more vandalism, he'd phone the police. Jordan's mobile phone was in his bike-bag . . .

But now there was a scuffling sound above, a frightened yell, a grumble and scrape of dislodged brickwork, and Greg's upturned eyes blinking dust saw a toppling shape, an arm-waving rag-doll of a body, in slow-motion drop from the edge of the staircase. Awkward fall and slither against a jutting edge of chimney-breast – the body upended, tilted, dropped at a new angle. Greg's dash – an attempt to break the fall – brought him flat-footed to the wrong place. All in a heartstopping, throat-grabbing moment, he heard freefalling body strike concrete: a soft, cracking flump. Breath slammed out of a bird-fragile body. Then silence. Jordan standing frozen, horrified. Greg first numb, then trembling. Now both moving at once.

Dean on the ground. Dean the Mouth, quiet now. Blood trickling from the side of his mouth, limbs limp, like a drowned spider. Greg, trained life-saver, was first to act.

Is he dead?

Check he's breathing. Check airways clear. Don't move him more than I have to.

With any luck they'll break their moronic necks—

Jordan: 'Is he—?'

The boy's eyes were closed, his mouth open. A convulsive twist of his neck, then the smallest of wheezing sounds, painful, as air re-entered his shocked body.

'He's breathing. Trying to,' Greg said to Jordan. 'Your mobile—'

'You've killed him!' Yusuf shrieked from above, hysterical. 'It's your fault! You made him do it!' The other boy, the third one, was a pale, frightened face, looking from the place in the stairway with a gap missing like a bite, where Dean had fallen.

Jordan craned up. 'Get yourselves down here! Is there another way?' The faces dodged out of sight; Greg heard the scrape of brick on brick, farther over.

'Leave them,' he shouted at Jordan. 'Get the phone!' He bent over the boy, checking for breathing again. 'Dean! *Dean!* Can you hear me?' The visible hand felt cold to the touch, the other was bent under the body.

Greg pulled his sweatshirt over his head and covered the boy with it. Got to keep him warm. Dean gave a small whimper, his eyelids twitching. He looked pitifully thin – sprawled and twisted on the ground he was just a scrawny kid, with God knew what injuries to bones and internal organs . . .

Endless, endless minutes. Jordan reappeared, having made the 999 call – thank God, thank whoever, for mobile phones. Yusuf and the other boy appeared at ground level, having slithered down some way Greg was glad not to have seen. Yusuf was aggressive, restrained by Jordan; the blonde one, huge-eyed and timid, hung back, only worried about the trouble he was going to get into. Greg resolutely stopped anyone from touching or moving the injured boy. Waiting, waiting. Wasn't anyone coming?

'You did tell them urgent?'

'Yes, 'course. I'll go and wait at the front, show them how to get in.'

'You two, go with Jordan,' Greg said.

They went, Yusuf subdued at last, the blonde boy tearful, leaving Greg with Dean Brampton, the broken puppet, the fallen far-from-angel.

What if he stops breathing? – what if he dies? – I said it – I wished it – with a bit of luck they'll break their stupid necks—!

At last, hurrying footsteps. Voices. Uniformed men – ambulance crew and police. Hands reaching, taking over, taking charge. All attention on the small figure on the ground.

Intensive care

Greg's mental snapshot: a deserted corridor in the hospital. The strip of polished lino leads to a seating area furnished with red plastic chairs. Signs point to X-Ray, Out-Patients, All Wards, Operating Theatre.

By the time he went to bed, very late, Greg had gone over and over the incident for the police and for Faith's father, till the words began to sound like a rehearsed script, somehow losing the essence of what had happened. Finally, in the shower and in bed, the fall came back to him with all its shocking realness: he couldn't get out of his mind that body-jarring, bonecracking flump that had been a human body hitting rough floor and strewn bricks. Again and again the boy whirled through the spaces of Greg's mind. Again and again he saw the body unanchored and dropping, its fall arrested by the slam of concrete.

They had ended up at Jordan's house: a detective constable and a WPC, Jordan and Greg, and then Faith's father (not Faith herself, to Greg's relief), summoned by one of the police officers. There were a lot of formal introductions, hand-shakings, explanations. Jordan's parents supplied cups of tea. Faith's dad, very agitated, was questioned about the previous vandalism and the new security arrangements to the front of the house, then Greg and Jordan had to make separate statements. The words Greg shaped into a coherent account hid what he could not explain rationally: the jaw-clenching anger that gripped him when he saw Dean Brampton's leering face. He had wanted to smash, to injure, to grab where it hurt. How could the police be expected to match that power to enrage with the pale, unconscious, stick-thin boy carried away on a padded stretcher?

The WPC phoned the hospital, and came back into the room very serious-faced. 'He's in Intensive Care. Still semi-conscious. They're afraid he's got serious injuries to his spine.'

Everyone was silent for a moment, then Faith's father said: 'We must pray for him.'

For a wild moment Greg thought he was suggesting they should all get down on their knees that very minute, but the detective constable glossed over the remark. 'Yes, indeed. Poor young lad. Well, we'll find out first thing tomorrow if there's any change.'

Jordan looked as exhausted as Greg felt, and he had to be up early next day for training. 'Are you all right to get home, Greg?' Mrs McAuliffe asked. 'I'll drive you, if you like.'

'Thanks, I've got my bike.'

Jordan came outside with him. Greg stood by the bikes, loath to part.

'See you tomorrow?' Jordan said.

'Yeah. I'll phone.'

And a brief touch: Jordan's hand on Greg's arm, Greg's hand on Jordan's shoulder. A manly acknowledgement of the ordeal they'd shared, that was what it was.

As soon as Greg got in, Faith phoned, very agitated. 'Isn't it awful? I'll see you on Sunday, won't I? Greg, look, I'm really sorry about the other day. I made an idiot of myself. Can we forget about it?'

And now, having had to go through yet another explanation for his own parents, Greg was at last in bed, wide-awake and restless.

With a bit of luck they'll break their moronic necks.

My fault, my fault. Don't be stupid, of course it's not my fault. I didn't make him climb the building. But all the same . . .

I wanted him hurt, and now he is hurt.

But I couldn't have made it happen, just by wishing . . .

I didn't mean—

Greg turned on his bedside light, sat up, lay down again, stared at the ceiling. Jordan. He needed to talk to Jordan, and now. He dialled Jordan's mobile number, but got only voice-mail. 'Call me,' Greg said, 'soon as you can.' He turned off the light and rolled over in a huddle of frustration.

We must pray for him.

We. All of us. If the power of thought could send Dean Brampton plummeting, then the power of

195

thought might make him recover. Not praying: Greg couldn't. But he could *wish* . . .

'Get better, you horrible little oik,' he muttered aloud. 'Get yourself out of there.'

Why? Why do I want that? Just so I can let myself off the hook? Oh, this is stupid . . .

He turned over, thumped his pillow and tried grimly to sleep. Eventually he was jolted from a dream in the early hours, with a hoarse yell of alarm that brought his father to his room. It was like being a little kid again: his dad tousled and concerned, Greg sitting up in bed, dizzy with shock, his heart pounding. 'I'm OK, Dad. Sorry. Just a bad dream.' In sleep he had seen Dean Brampton falling, arms and legs flailing, endlessly falling. In sleep he had waited for the crash-landing he was powerless to stop.

At last he slept heavily, right through his alarm, waking only twenty minutes before he was due at the pool. Katy, up early for once on a Saturday, waylaid him excitedly in the kitchen: 'Is Dean Brampton going to die?'

'Katy!' their mother warned. 'You're a callous little blood-sucker!'

'Serves him right if you ask me,' Katy said. 'Has he got brain-damage? And how would anyone be able to tell?'

'Katy—'

'And why were the police questioning you last night, Greg? Was it your fault?'

About to grab a croissant to eat on the way to work, Greg decided not to bother. His mother looked at him anxiously. 'Are you sure you ought to be going today? Can't you say you're not well?'

'I'm fine. Just tired.'

'Want me to drive you there?'

'*No!* I'm not an invalid, for Christ's sake. See you later.'

He just about made it; Paul was looking pointedly at his watch as the automatic doors sighed open to let Greg in. 'I was about to phone, check you were coming.'

'Sorry. Bit of a rush this morning.'

Greg was down for a stint at Reception. Everything around him looked too bright, too brash, everyone too cheerful; it was like having a hangover. The phone rang: Jordan. 'Got your message. How's things?'

'Bad,' Greg said.

'You've phoned the hospital?'

'No.'

'I thought that's what you meant. 'Cos it *is* bad. They think he may be paralysed from the waist down.'

'How d'you know?'

'That bloke Michael – Tarrant, is it? – went round to the hospital himself. He phoned us after.'

Silence. Impossible to talk properly in Reception; there was already a woman with two kids standing there, loaded with bags of kit, holding out her membership card and pointedly waiting for Greg to put the phone down.

'I looked for you, earlier,' Jordan said.

'Overslept. You made it to training, same as usual?'

'Yes. There's a club meet tonight at Ravenscroft,'

197

Jordan said. 'I'm doing 'fly and four-by-hundred freestyle and medley. Come and watch? It'll take your mind off it.'

'Show-off. You just want me to see you win.'

'With a bit of luck and a following wind.'

'You don't need luck. Or wind. Must get boring, winning all the time.'

'There'll be room in the minibus. Sandy's picking me up at the bus stop near the church. See you there six-thirty, if you feel like coming.'

Given the choice between watching Jordan swim or going off his head sorting out a tangle of worries, Greg went. At twenty-five past six the minibus was already parked in one of the bays near the church. Jordan was waiting. Sandy, the wiry-haired man Greg had seen at the Wednesday coaching sessions, was in the driver's seat.

'All right if Greg comes with us?' Jordan asked him.

Sandy nodded, taking Jordan's sports bag and stowing it in the back. 'Plenty of room.'

'He's a strong swimmer,' Jordan said. 'Front crawl.'

'Oh, aye?' The coach eyed Greg with speculative interest. 'We could do with another good freestyle swimmer for the relays. Fancy giving it a go?'

'I'm not fast enough.'

'We can help you improve on that. You've got the physique. I'm at the pool every morning, Monday to Saturday, six-thirty sharp. Come along next week if you're interested.'

'Sneaky!' Greg said as he and Jordan got into the back of the minibus. Other team members were arriving, stowing their bags, laughing and chatting.

Jordan smiled. 'I knew he'd snap you up.'

There were few spectators at the Ravenscroft pool: just a dotting of family supporters. Greg went into the small gallery, next to a couple sharing coffee from a flask. He watched the first few races with mild interest, waiting for Jordan and the hundred metres butterfly, his speciality. If Jordan did well in the trials next month, and of course he would, he'd be swimming for the county, then the England trials . . .

Eight swimmers were competing in Jordan's race. They filed out to the starting blocks, stripping off tracksuits, putting on goggles. Greg had watched this at the Olympics and the Commonwealth Games: the almost gladiatorial build-up, the revealing of fantastically-toned bodies, the salutes to the crowd. Here there was none of the showiness, because there was no crowd to speak of. Greg's eyes were on Jordan, who looked unfamiliar in a white cap. He had the physique, all right: slender but strong, long-limbed, less sturdy than Greg. He was in lane 4, in the centre of the pool, where he preferred to be. Next to him was the bald-headed guy he'd pointed out to Jordan as they arrived, his main rival from the Ravenscroft team. The bald man looked tough and hard, a few years older – but Ian Thorpe had won Olympic gold medals at seventeen, and Jordan had beaten this man many times before.

They stood waiting, shaking out their legs,

swinging their arms. Jordan looked nervous, Greg thought. He glanced across; Greg gave him a thumbs-up and an encouraging grin.

'Take your marks.'

Tense concentration, bodies doubled over, a neat row of them. The water, unruffled, shimmering, was so clear that every tile on the bottom of the pool was sharply outlined. The buzz of the starter sent the swimmers airborne like a hail of arrows, into the kink and plunge, the crucial few seconds underwater that could win or lose a race; nothing on view but the streaking torpedo shapes below the surface. Then, bursting through like leaping dolphins in a welter of spray, the leaders were into their strokes. Already the swimmer in lane 8 was badly behind, having spent too long underwater. Jordan swam as easily and fluently as Greg had seen many a time in practice, riding the water: humped back, the trail and overarching fling of arms that was so beautiful to watch; two strokes to a breath, hips undulating in the rhythmic sway and push Greg could never master. After the first turn, the dip and thrust from the poolside, the red-capped swimmer in lane 3 was edging ahead. Jordan wouldn't be worried by that, with three lengths to go; he knew how to judge pace, saving himself for the final burst of speed. For the next two lengths the red cap was ahead, then Jordan, the bald man and one other keeping pace, the rest straggling behind, and the slowest beginning to tire and flail. And now the final leg: red-cap was flagging now as Jordan and the bald guy battled it out. 'Go,

Jordan!' Greg was on his feet; the bald man, less fluent and graceful, was pulling ahead by sheer dogged strength. Jordan, with renewed energy, made a final surge, diving for the rail, but the other man was there a fraction ahead.

Greg saw Jordan turn round with sheer, shocked disbelief on his face, used only to winning. Never beaten at butterfly since he was fifteen, he was beaten now. Greg knew that the time shown on the clock didn't match the best he'd produced in training.

Recovering, Jordan saluted the other man and turned to face the gallery, pulling a wry face at Greg. He vaulted out of the pool and tugged off his cap and goggles. Sandy came up and gave him a disappointed, perfunctory pat, then they exchanged a few words, the coach shaking his head. There was a brief huddle, members of the team coming up to find out what had gone wrong. One of them, Carly, the girl who had won the breast-stroke, gave Jordan a consoling hug and a kiss: Greg saw Jordan's hand rest briefly on her waist, saw the girl smiling up at him, saw her shapely body in a racer-back suit, her long hair down her back. He felt something twist over in his stomach.

Yesterday he had been almost sure, but in that second he was not. What if, even now, he'd got it wrong?

Jordan had not swum his best, but still Greg thought of what he said yesterday: *'I swim, therefore I am.* No, perhaps what I mean is *I am, therefore I swim.'* That time in the changing room – maybe what Greg had seen was not what he thought, nothing personal at all, but the afterglow of the almost spiritual experience that swimming was for Jordan.

Now Jordan, beaten, threw a towel round his shoulders. He came over to Greg in the gallery and leaned on the rail. 'Sorry.'

'What happened?'

Jordan smiled ruefully. 'Mind not on the job.'

'Yeah? What was it on?'

'You know. Everything.'

What did that mean? Greg glanced away and saw Carly staring across at them. What did *that* mean? He felt as if the air around him was sparking with electric currents.

'Now what?' he asked, trying to sound normal.

'Relays – girls first, then us.'

Jordan's team won both the relays, medley and freestyle (why did they need another member?) and then it was over. Having turned in better performances, Jordan seemed cheerful as they went back to the minibus, whereas Greg felt deflated, exhausted, even though all he'd done was watch. Carly, with her long hair roughly towel-dried, sat in the seat in front of them, turning to Jordan. 'Coming to the pub?' She had a pert, pretty face – a scatter of freckles over her nose, a wide smile.

'Sorry,' Jordan said. 'Going somewhere else.'

Visibly, Carly tried to cover her disappointment. 'Some other time.' She looked at Greg. 'You're joining the team, then? We could do with some more male talent.'

'I might.'

'And she's not talking about swimming talent,' said the girl next to her.

'Oh! You—'

'Carly,' called Sandy from the driver's seat, 'did you say your parents could help out with transport next Saturday?'

Greg took advantage of the diversion to ask Jordan, 'Where you off to, then?'

'Hospital. Coming?'

For a confused second Greg thought Jordan must have injured himself, and that was why he'd lost his race. 'What for?'

Jordan looked at him. 'See that little git Dean Brampton.'

'You serious?'

''Course. Come with me?'

Greg shrugged. 'OK. If we must.'

Jordan called out, 'Sandy, can you drop us at the Green Man?'

Sandy nodded. He pulled up at the lights beside the pub, where a road forked off to the hospital. 'Remember you're in training,' he said sternly to Jordan. 'See you Monday.'

'He thinks we're heading for a boozy night,' Jordan said, as the red tail-lights pulled away. He shouldered his sports bag. 'He'll give me a hard time next week. But it's all relative.'

'Meaning?'

'Me getting stressed about a few seconds off my race time. Dean lying there paralysed.'

They were in the hospital drive, road noise fading

behind them. The air was cool and soothing. Greg felt the tensions of the evening slide away, the tension he had felt keenly as an onlooker; but relief was laced with expectancy. Now it was just him and Jordan. And after this there would be Afterwards. Afterwards he would have to talk to Jordan or stay knotted up in this doubt and confusion that was scrambling his brain.

'You know I . . .' He kicked a stone.

'What?'

'Yesterday I said to you, *With a bit of luck they'll break their moronic necks.* You're a witness. And within a few minutes he practically did.'

'And I said how handy it would be if someone died and left a nice pair of kidneys hanging round spare.'

'You don't seriously think—'

'We made it happen?' Jordan said, with a sideways look. 'Don't be stupid! 'Course not.'

'*Is* it stupid? He's a horrible little oik but I wouldn't wish that on him. Paralysed from the waist down – that puts some fairly important organs out of action, let alone being stuck in a wheelchair for life. But I *did* wish it. Why are we here, then, if you don't think there's some power in thinking – in wishing? We were talking about Gaia and God and stuff. Are you telling me you're here out of sheer brotherly love for the whole human race? No. Guilt, that's what's brought us here.'

'That's rubbish! It's not our fault. We didn't tell him to go clambering round a dangerous building, did we? Didn't even think it. But you can't seriously believe it's so easy to wish things into happening. You don't believe in God, let alone one who sits up there with the world's wish-list, ticking things off. I'm not beating my brains about that.'

'Yes, you are. That's why you lost your race.'

'OK, I thought of someone dying, because of Michelle and her kidney. But I didn't specify Dean Brampton, and anyway it hasn't happened yet, 'cos he isn't dead. You're not suggesting he picked up my thought-waves and kindly flung himself at our feet as a sacrifice? He's not dead, and nobody's said he's likely to die. He's not about to snuff it with a signed donor card in his hand, is he?'

'So, now you've said all that, why are we here? You saying it *is* brotherly love? In that case why aren't we here every night, visiting anyone who happens to be in hospital? There's no shortage.'

'Look,' Jordan said, 'there's two things. One, it's an awful thing that's happened to him. Two, he's an obnoxious arrogant little turd. Am I really, genuinely sorry for him? Or is it really *He got what was coming to him, might knock some sense into him*? I'd be a lot sorrier if it was someone else – practically *any*one else. What it comes down to is, I feel responsible. That's why I'm here. OK, so it's for me, to make myself feel better. That's why we do most things when it comes down to it.'

'Responsible, though – you're contradicting your-self!'

'Yeah, I know. Responsible's not the right word. It's

more like his life has got kind of tangled up with ours, and like it or not we've got to care about it.'

Ours. What did that mean?

They had reached the hospital entrance now, an ambulance pulling up at the doors of A and E, the crew leaping out to fling the back doors open. Someone else's life in ruins. Greg stopped and looked in bewilderment at the signboard, which had arrows pointing in all directions, but Jordan didn't need to stop and look. He knew where Intensive Care was.

Greg caught up. 'Do you think they'll let us see him?'

'Probably not. We can try.'

Hospitals. Greg hated them. He'd been here twice: once with a suspected fractured wrist in a football accident, once when his gran had been ill. He hated the miles of corridors, the clinical smells, the anonymity of everything. Come in here as a patient and you were on a conveyer belt. Dean Brampton, Dean the Mouth, would have become an item for processing. Jordan led the way through a maze of corridors, past the Operating Theatre and Radiology, to the Intensive Care ward. Inside, Greg glimpsed a room divided into bays, one of them screened by curtains. He saw drips, monitors, a nurse doing something to a motionless figure in the nearest bed. Another nurse looked up from a medication trolley as they entered, and came over quickly.

'We've come to see Dean Brampton,' Jordan explained.

'I'm sorry, he's not well enough for visitors.' The nurse spoke in a hushed voice. 'You're not family, are you?' She gave Jordan a second look. 'You were here a couple of weeks ago, weren't you?'

'Michelle McAuliffe's brother,' Jordan said. 'And friends of Dean.'

Stretching the point, Greg thought, but the nurse nodded. 'Oh yes. Well, it's not really allowed, but if you wait here a minute I'll just see if . . .' She ushered them into a separate waiting area with cushions and magazines.

Greg looked at Jordan; Jordan made a don't-ask-me expression. A few moments later a different nurse appeared, accompanied by a tall woman with bottle-blonde hair. 'Here we are, Mrs Brampton. Friends of Dean's. I'll leave you to chat.'

The woman looked surprised, then gave a taut smile. As soon as the nurse had gone, she looked at each of the boys narrowly.

'Thought she meant Yusuf and Lee. Who're you, then?'

'We were at the house when Dean had his accident,' Jordan explained. 'It was Greg who looked after him till the ambulance came.'

'Oh, it was, was it? I've heard all about you two.' Mrs Brampton jutted her chin at Greg. 'You in particular. Ought to be ashamed of yourself, picking on younger kids! I'm going to be up that school first thing Monday.'

'No, wait! You've—' Jordan tried.

'*Picking* on?' Greg repeated. 'If anyone's done that it's been Dean, making himself a pain.' But he hadn't come here to make accusations.

207

'I know what I know,' Mrs Brampton said. She squared up to Greg, looking ready for a fight herself – so close that he smelled a waft of perfume and stale cigarette smoke. 'My boy's stuck in here with spine damage, might spend the rest of his life in a wheelchair, and you're walking round like Jack the Lad! Come here to gloat, I s'pose.' She glanced at Jordan with a Dean-like sneer. 'And bringing your boyfriend as well! Ought to be ashamed of yourselves, you pair of poofters. Going up that house to do God knows what!'

Greg didn't dare look at Jordan. Mrs Brampton was having exactly the same effect as her son – sending a powerful charge of anger through him, as if she had flicked a switch. He tried to control his voice. 'Wait a minute. Dean and his friends went to the house to chuck stones and damage things—'

'So you say. That's not what I've heard.'

'I've seen him! I've seen the graffiti, seen him lobbing stones, deliberately trying to damage a statue—'

'Don't you try to put him in the wrong!' Mrs Brampton's voice became shrill. 'I know who's to blame, and I'm going to make sure everyone else knows. Why were they climbing up the walls? To get away from you and your bullying!'

'That's rubbish!' Jordan said.

She rounded on him. 'You calling me a liar now? My Dean's lying there and you've come here to call me a liar?'

Her shouting brought the nurse hurrying back, the

one who knew Jordan. 'Oh, come now, Mrs Brampton – don't get yourself worked up again. That's not going to help anyone.'

Mrs Brampton's shoulders started to quiver. She pulled a tissue from her sleeve. 'Get them out of here! Coming here to stir up more trouble!'

The nurse, one arm round her, gestured to Jordan and Greg to go outside. Mrs Brampton sat down on one of the sofas, sniffing, wiping her eyes with the tissue. 'Christ, I need a fag,' Greg heard her saying as he and Jordan went back into the ward. He glanced round again, looking for Dean, wondering which of the shrouded fingers linked to tubes and dials could be him.

Out in the corridor, walking away, Jordan puffed out his breath. 'Vile woman! Poor old Dean – what chance has he got with a mother like that?'

Greg had something more urgent on his mind. 'What she said—'

'About bullying? Yeah – how can she get it so twisted?'

'Not about bullying,' Greg said. 'About poofters.'

A pause, then: 'Don't worry about it. She doesn't know, any more than Dean does.'

'Know?'

'Greg.' Jordan stopped and looked at him. 'Don't *you* know?'

Greg hesitated, struggled for words, said nothing.

'Poofter isn't the word I'd actually use,' Jordan said, with not quite his usual calm. 'I wondered if you'd realized. Sometimes I thought you had –

yesterday, I thought – and then I wasn't sure how you—'

Greg didn't answer. They were walking side by side – he had no idea where, or which way was out – past an empty reception desk and a sign for Gynaecology and Out-Patients. Everything, he thought, was going to stay imprinted on his mind for ever. Then the corridor opened up into a seating area with red plastic seats arranged round three sides of a square, and a small refreshment stall, unattended.

'Do you mind?' Jordan asked. Greg heard the tremor in his voice that belied the lightness.

'Let's sit down here for a minute.' Greg felt too dazed to carry on walking. They sat. Neither spoke for a few seconds, then Greg said: 'Did you think—' at the same moment as Jordan said: 'A few times I—'

'Go on. You first.'

'A few times I was going to say something,' Jordan said, 'but then I didn't.'

Heels clicked along the corridor; an off-duty nurse in a navy coat came round the corner and looked at them in surprise. 'There's no-one in Out-Patients, not at this time of night. Can I help you?'

'We're just talking, thanks,' Jordan said. 'We've been visiting someone.' The nurse gave them a final, doubtful look and walked on. Greg, still fazed, gave a nervous laugh. 'She probably thinks we're waiting to nick drugs and stuff.'

'Or else we're homeless, looking for beds for the night,' Jordan said. 'You didn't answer just now when I asked if you minded.'

'No. No, I don't mind. But if you're asking if I'm gay—'

Jordan nodded, waiting.

Greg shook his head. 'I've never thought so. But it's doing my head in. I mean, I fancy girls. I don't know any more – it's weird, all this—'

'All this what? *What's* doing your head in?'

'This is. You are. I think about you all the time.' Greg's mouth wrenched itself into a grimacing smile; he shook his head, looking down at his clasped hands.

'What's funny?'

'Can't believe what I just said.'

'But you did say it. If it helps,' Jordan said, 'I think about you all the time as well. It's all right, isn't it?'

'So you *know* you're – since when? How long have you known?'

'Two years, three.'

'So have you ever—?'

'I've never had a real relationship, no,' Jordan said, though that was not quite what Greg had meant. 'There was someone I sort of hero-worshipped, someone in the year above us. He never knew. I've forgotten about him now.'

There was something about the way Jordan said *he* and *him* that told Greg he had not quite forgotten.

'Why don't we go home?' Jordan said. 'We could talk there.'

'Go round yours?'

'Mm.'

'Hang on a bit.' At Jordan's house there would be people: friendly, concerned people, but still people.

They would want to know about the swimming meet, about Dean. Greg needed to get his head straight before he could cope with other people. 'That girl, Carly,' he said, remembering the hug, the smile, the twinge of jealousy he had felt, watching, and surely *that* proved something – 'she likes you.'

'I like her too, but not that way. She's a team mate, that's all. You didn't think—'

'Didn't know what to think.'

'But you minded?'

Greg nodded.

'You don't need to,' Jordan said. 'It's you I want to be with. No-one else.'

There was a silence. Greg thought: *What next? This is mad!* They were sitting within touching distance, but separate. What if Jordan reached out to stroke his hand, or his hair? Greg felt the air prickling his skin. For all his looking and looking and wondering, he could not meet Jordan's eye. His gaze was fixed on a poster on the wall opposite that instructed him to eat five portions of fruit and vegetables every day.

Jordan shifted in his seat. 'My parents know.'

'Know?'

'That I'm gay,' Jordan said. 'I thought it best if they knew.'

Greg puffed out his cheeks. 'Christ! I'd die rather than have mine know – if I *was* gay, I mean. You *told* yours?'

'We talk about things,' Jordan said. 'I told you that. So I've come out, but only at home. Everywhere else, school especially, I'm firmly still in. Not quite brave enough for that yet. School is the worst place there is – well, you don't need me to tell you that. A couple of years on, at college or whatever, I won't mind.'

'But your parents – you tell them *everything*? I mean, how did that come up? When?'

'About a year ago. I wanted them to know.'

'What, just like that? Round the tea-table? *By the way, folks, I'm gay?*'

'No. Dad first. We've talked about it . . . a few times. He thought it might be just a phase, I might turn out to like girls after all – I think that's what he hoped. But, well, it isn't. So Dad helped me to realize how it's got to be. You know how you see gay blokes on TV all the time, picking each other up, doing stuff in men's bogs – well, I don't want it like that, sordid. It's got to be real, worth something. The other person's got to be someone I can trust, someone I can be with. Everything.'

'Someone you can look at the stars with and swim in the sea with at dawn?'

'Yes,' Jordan said. There was a pause, then: 'That's why I told you. To see if you like stargazing.'

Another expectant silence; Greg's vocal cords felt numbed. He cleared his throat, stalled: 'So it's only your dad who knows, then?'

'Oh no,' Jordan said, matter-of-factly. 'We decided it was best to tell Mum and Michelle as well.'

'*Michelle* knows?' For one squirming second, the idea of telling Katy floated into Greg's head.

'Why not?'

Greg threw out both hands – *It's obvious*. But it was not obvious to Jordan.

'It's like – when someone nearly dies, when Michelle nearly did, it puts things into perspective,' Jordan explained. 'What does anything else matter, as long as we're all alive and together? What's the point of hiding things? I didn't want Michelle asking me about girlfriends – didn't want to pretend. It's better that she knows. And she's mature enough to be fine about it.'

'Hang on a minute. Do you mean to say – that time I came round for Michelle's birthday, and last night – they were all looking at me as your *boyfriend*? A candidate for your Special Someone?'

'If you want to put it like that. They like you.'

Greg huffed out his breath. 'Oh, great!'

'Why does that annoy you?'

'You really need me to spell it out? Your mum said I could say the *night*, for Christ's sake! Is that what you meant just now, about going round yours? Come and stay the night? What, share your bed, with everyone's approval? I suppose even your little brother knows? You wouldn't want to leave anyone out of confession time—'

'Not Mark, of course not, he's much too young to understand. And Mum didn't mean share my bed. They're open-minded, but not *that* open-minded.' Jordan was starting to assume the closed-off look he often wore at school: *Private, keep out*. 'Why are you annoyed? I'm not putting any pressure on you. I don't want anything unless you want it too.'

214

'It's obvious, isn't it? Everyone knowing. Everyone watching. *Christ*—'

'You don't believe in him.'

'No, and you know what?' Greg shifted his feet. 'I don't believe this, either. Any of it.' Abruptly he stood up. 'Forget it – just forget it, this whole conversation!'

Jordan looked up at him: reproachful, dismayed. 'You know that's impossible.'

'Not for me it isn't.' Greg shook his head, thrusting his hands into his jeans pockets. 'See you.'

'Greg—'

'Leave me alone!'

Greg turned and walked away fast, slamming through double doors, hearing them clack shut behind him in the emptiness of the corridor. He did not look back.

The Intensive Care sign loomed in front of him; he was back in the maze. He pushed open the door and marched in. By the far window, he saw Dean Brampton's mother slumped in a chair with her back to him, beside the farthest bed. Dean lay on his back, his face still, so young – just a desperately injured boy, not the mouthy yob Greg knew.

A nurse came towards him, both hands held up: *Stop.* She shepherded Greg back into the waiting area, out of sight.

'What do you want? I can't let you into the ward. Mrs Brampton's very upset.'

'I want to know how he is. Dean.' Greg's voice came out gruffly.

'You're not family—'

'No.' Greg couldn't bring himself to say *friend* either, repeating Jordan's lie. 'But I want to know.'

'Well, he's very poorly. As comfortable as can be expected. Not much change. That's all I can tell you.'

Nothing, in other words. Nothing, wrapped up in hospital euphemisms.

'He's not paralysed, is he? Will he be able to walk?'

'I'm sorry, it's too early to tell.'

'OK. Thanks.'

'Go straight back to Reception and out that way,' the nurse told him. 'You shouldn't be wandering round the hospital at this time of night.'

The ward doors opened to his shove. He half-wanted Jordan to have followed him, and was both relieved and disappointed that he had not. The corridor stretched both ways, polished and blank. Greg grimaced, clenching his fists till his nails dug into his palms; he bit his lip hard, wanting to hurt someone. Himself, most of all.

'Jesus *Christ!*'

He had to get out of here. He walked fast, blindly, hardly noticing where the signs led him, till he found himself back at Accident and Emergency, with double doors leading out. The cool air welcomed him. He started to jog up the long entrance drive, then settled into a steady run, the rhythm of his feet pushing all thought from his head. A blur of lights from the streetlamps danced in his head, traffic noise snarled at his heels; he ran till his teeth ached and his lungs were sore. He had to keep running.

1917, April

Caryatid

Your beauty is as clear today as when
My boyish eyes drank in your nakedness.
~~Deep Great~~ sorrow has befallen me since then;
My tear-stained cheek receives your cold caress.
You could have looked on Pharaohs or proud Kings;
Instead you gaze above my troubled head.
Now war has blighted vain imaginings:
I've only this to tell you: <u>He is dead.</u>

Your heavy-lidded eyes look sad; your hand
Forever offers me your gift of vines.
Your mouth might speak — but what grief have you
known?
Your soul can never feel the woes of man.
I've come to you for comfort, but I find
No pity in your ageless heart of stone.

Edmund Pearson

217

'I'm recommending you for a week's home leave,' Captain Greenaway had told Edmund, 'during which time I expect you – in fact I order you – to put this behind you, and come back with your mind properly on the job.'

Edmund stood in the garden at Graveney Hall, looking over the ha-ha. It was April; the air smelled of spring and new growth; the trees were bursting into leaf. A mockery.

Alex was dead.

Alex was a name on a Casualty list.

Alex had Died of Wounds.

Alex was buried in a shallow grave near mine-workings.

Alex was nowhere.

Alex had gone, and God had not kept his bargain.

God, if he had listened at all, had shown Edmund that he would not be bargained with. He had taken revenge on Alex – not just by letting him die, but by making him suffer a protracted, agonized death. Reducing him, at the end, to something less than human: a tormented animal, twisted and distorted with pain. Surviving the first night against all expectations, Alex had lasted two more, merely to give Edmund false hope and to endure two days and nights of torture from his internal injuries. Unable to bear it, Edmund had begged the nurse for morphine until at last Alex, never once recognizing him, had slipped away to wherever he was now.

'His suffering's over now,' the nurse had said, soft-voiced, drawing the sheet over Alex's face.

Somehow, in that squalid front-line hospital that reeked of pus and excrement and disinfectant, she managed to keep herself neat, her apron and cuffs shining white. Edmund looked at her through a dazzle of tears. She might as well have been speaking Chinese for all the sense her words made to him.

At the burial service he stood rigid and cold, unable to let himself think or feel. Six others were buried at the same time: two officers, three privates and a sergeant. A brief, impersonal prayer did for all. When it was finished Edmund was overcome by a fit of shuddering, feverish and violent. Back in the dug-out, Faulkner brought him hot coffee laced with whisky. Afterwards he drank the best part of a bottle of whisky, seeking oblivion, and found it temporarily in a drunken sleep.

For the next interminable days he was half-mad with grief. People spoke to him and he did not hear. He felt his eyes rolling in their sockets like marbles, his brain was a scrambled mess of disconnected wires. He couldn't eat, couldn't sleep. He courted death: he took risks, stuck his head above the parapet, waiting for a German sniper to despatch him, sending him after Alex. No rifle-crack obliged. He was sentenced to live, if this could be called life. He must continue to fight a war whose outcome meant nothing to him. He would gladly have welcomed the chance to accompany his unit into some hopeless, doomed attack that would obliterate the lot of them. A futile death would be the fitting end to his futile life.

After a few days of this, Captain Greenaway called Edmund into his dug-out and told him to remember his responsibilities. 'I know you've taken Culworth's death very hard, as indeed we all have. He was one of our best officers, and I liked him immensely. But you can't let yourself dwell on it. You've become slack in your duties – you're letting your men down. They need leadership, not this mawkish lingering on something that can't be changed.'

Put this behind you. Be a man. Smarten up. Easy commands; impossible to obey. The stark fact of Alex's death was constantly before him; there was nothing else. After Alex, an empty void, an airless vacuum. What was the point of going on breathing? Yet he must, because his body stubbornly insisted on taking in oxygen, circulating blood, repairing damaged cells. Was it possible simply to will yourself to die, tell your body to stop functioning? On the front line he had seen how vulnerable human flesh was: how blood, brains, intestines could be spilled and scattered, how fit young bodies could quickly become festering flyblown gobbets for rats to feed on. A shell-blast, a bullet, a bayonet wound could do that. How could his own body remain healthy, oblivious to his reeling brain?

Since God had let him down, Edmund would believe in Alex. Cling to him. Remember every word he had said, every look, every touch. God had not agreed to the bargain and Edmund was freed from his part in it. If God had obliged, he would be faced with the impossibility of keeping his promise. He now had no choice to make, and permission to love Alex for ever. He felt ashamed of how easily he had been tricked into betrayal in a moment of blind repentance. It was another instance of God's cruelty.

Here at Graveney it was as painful to remember Alex alive as it was to think of his miserable death. The greening fields and trees reminded Edmund of the week they had spent at the farmhouse in Picardy, talking of their future. He wandered along to the Pan statue. Pan, on his pedestal, raised his pipes to his lips; around him cavorted three naked infants carrying a garland of leaves. As a child Edmund had liked Pan, with his dancing goat legs and the two small horns sticking out of his hair. He had pretended to hear Pan's flutey music, had looked out of his bedroom window in summer dusks, imagining he might see the god and his cherubic attendants leap off their pedestal to cavort round the fountains and flower-beds. Pan had been more interesting than God; he had more fun, and made no demands. Now he was frozen in a dance of pointless merriment, mocking Edmund and his sorrow, as everything seemed to.

His parents, inevitably, had decided to add to his torment by arranging a dinner party for this evening. He closed his eyes, thinking of the ordeal awaiting him. The Fitches, of course, were the principal guests. Philippa would be coiffed and simpering, her parents watching avidly for any symptom of concealed passion on Edmund's part. His own mother had already hinted that this leave, coming unexpectedly, would be the ideal time to *put things on a proper footing*, as she expressed it. She meant that he should propose to Philippa, engage himself to her. It would give everyone something nice to look forward to as a change from this horrid war, she said. Not that the horrid war made much impression that Edmund could see on Graveney Hall. Dinner parties were a little less frequent, the range of dishes less extensive, and the table-talk was likely to refer to the latest *Times* headlines, with deferential nods towards Edmund, representative of England's brave soldiers; but otherwise daily life went on as normal, fixed in its routines. Other big houses had been transformed into convalescent hospitals, but Graveney Hall kept itself aloof, isolated on the edge of the forest like a remnant of a past age. The century was moving on, the war taking place out of Graveney's sphere.

Edmund would not marry Philippa, would not sire an heir for Graveney. He had been released from his duty, and Alex had been the price. But only he and God knew that.

Slowly, reluctantly, he walked across the garden and up the steps, indoors and upstairs, though he could hear the voices of guests in the drawing room, where they had gathered to drink sherry. In his room he looked at himself in the cheval mirror, straightened his tie, gazed into the frightening blanks of his own eyes. Then he lay on his bed and took out his pocket-book, unwrapping it from the scrap of oilskin he used to protect it from dampness. Tucked inside the notebook he kept the letters Alex had written him. There were not many, as for most of their time they had been together with no need to write letters, though sometimes in the front line, cramped and constrained by the presence of others, they had written notes and slipped them into each other's hands or pockets. Alex's crumpled notes, too, were in the notebook. It had occurred to Edmund that if he were killed, these letters and notes, plainly love-letters, would be sent home along with his other belongings, and his secret would be known; but he could not bear to part with them, and that meant always carrying them on his person, since there was nowhere safe to hide them. Now they were his most precious possessions.

He knew their contents almost by heart. Alex was there in the sweep of black ink, in the splaying of fountain-pen nib, in the characteristic letter *g*s, in the swoop-tailed capital *A* with which he signed himself. Among the letters there was a poem, closely-written on a sheet of lined paper, which Alex had copied out and given him last Christmas Eve.

'I read this in *The Times* last year, before I knew you,' Alex had told him. 'I think you will like it.'

The poem was entitled *The Oxen*, and was by the novelist Mr Thomas Hardy:

Christmas Eve, and twelve of the clock.
'Now they are all on their knees,'
An elder said as we sat in a flock
By the embers at hearthside ease.

223

We pictured the meek mild creatures where
They dwelt in their strawy pen,
Nor did it occur to one of us there
To doubt they were kneeling then.

So fair a fancy few would weave
In these years! Yet, I feel,
If someone said, on Christmas Eve,
'Come; see the oxen kneel

In the lonely barton in yonder coomb
Our childhood used to know,'
I should go with him into the gloom,
Hoping it might be so.

When he had first unfolded it, conscious of Alex's eyes on him, waiting for a response, Edmund read the poem three times: for himself, for Alex, for Alex wanting to share it with him. He tried not to notice a small twinge of resentment: Alex was giving him Mr Hardy's poem to show him the work of a real poet, to point out the inadequacies of his own verses.

'Yes, it's very fine,' he agreed. 'Why do you like it so much?'

They were in the reserve trench, leaning against the parapet in the chilly grey dawn. Somewhere bacon was frying.

'Because Thomas Hardy obviously thinks as I used to about God.' Alex was banging his arms against his sides to keep warm. 'He can't really believe in him, but would willingly accept proof if it were offered. Do you know, the first time I read those last lines they sent a shiver down my spine.'

Edmund looked at him. 'Of fear?'

'No. Of wanting.'

'You want to believe, like he does? What does Karl Marx have to say about that?'

'I did at the time I first read the poem. Not now. *So fair a fancy few would weave, in these years . . .* Thomas Hardy must have meant all this –' Alex waved a gloved hand in the direction of No-Man's-Land'– as well as advances in scientific knowledge. The war makes it impossible to believe, even for those who did before. There's no God. There's only humans and what they do to each other.'

'Unless you come across oxen kneeling at midnight. Perhaps we could go and look for some tonight. Would that convince you?'

'Front-line duties don't stop for Christmas, unfortunately.'

'But if—?'

'If we trooped off to some cowshed and found oxen kneeling in the straw? No. It wouldn't convince me. I'd just think they were chewing the cud. It's a fairy-tale, as Hardy implies. A nice one, but still a fairy-tale. I'd need better proof than that.'

Alone in his bedroom Edmund closed his eyes, hearing Alex's voice, seeing the warmth of his smile, the dazzle of his glance, then opened them to the renewed shock of his absence. Every time the same punch of loss, the same return to emptiness. He refolded the paper, then looked at his own *Caryatid* poem, which Alex would never see. He spent a few moments frowning at the troublesome third line, then gave up with a gesture of frustration. What did it matter?

What did anything matter?

He had asked for proof and none had been given. Had Mr Hardy made a similar bargain with God – show me kneeling oxen on Christmas Eve and I'll believe? And had God obliged, though he had failed to oblige now? It made a better poem with the question unanswered, but now Edmund could only remember what Alex had said: *There's no God*. No proof. No reason. No logic. No justice. No love. God was a fairy-tale: father-figure, guardian, all-potent giant, watcher, creator, delusion, fictional character in an age-old story, filler of a gap. Imagined answerer of questions that had no answers. All man's needs rolled into one. But no more real than Pan, or Venus, or Apollo. Edmund thought: I tried to bargain with a non-entity. Alex died. Oxen do not kneel except for reasons of their own.

He felt oddly detached from himself. He watched himself, neatly dressed, hair combed, going down for dinner: down to the panelled drawing room, where drinks were set out on a polished table. He watched himself submit to being greeted, admired and fussed over. It was better this way, too painful to be properly in his body.

'And of course Philippa's been so looking forward to seeing you,' Mrs Fitch gushed.

Philippa came forward, smiling shyly. She had on a

green dress with a V-neck that showed a lot of creamy skin, and wore an apricot-coloured hothouse flower in her hair. She held out a hand to Edmund; he took it, gave a curt bow, made the briefest of enquiries about her health and turned away to join his father and hers, who were standing by the large east window discussing the uprising in Russia earlier in the spring and whether it would lead to a ceasefire between Russia and Germany. He sensed his mother's reproachful look and Philippa's disappointment. A few moments later he heard Philippa chatting to Mrs Winthrop, with false brightness, about her voluntary work at a Red Cross canteen.

His mother came over to the window, bringing him a glass of sherry. 'You'll take Philippa in to dinner, of course,' she instructed him in an undertone.

All this ridiculous formality! Each woman had to be escorted the few yards to the dinner table by a previously allocated male, as if she might lose her way unaided. He drank his sherry in one gulp and thumped down his glass. Whisky was what he needed, a good double tot of it, not this sweet stuff. His mother fixed him with a warning look.

He performed his duty of settling Philippa in her chair and sat gloomily in his adjacent place. Food appeared in front of him, and wine in a cut crystal glass. God, how tedious! He toyed with his dinner, barely speaking. He was aware of Philippa to his right, pale-faced, clearly upset but doing her best not to show it, and of his mother's frequent glances from the end of the table. On Edmund's left sat Mrs

Winthrop, who was twittering on about some nephew of her sister-in-law's who was an officer in the Epping Foresters and just might have come across Edmund at the training camp in Étaples. As she was one of those speakers who rarely gave pause for an answer, Edmund let her ramble without paying much attention. Finding his wine glass empty, he nodded to the manservant, who came over and refilled it. A snatch of Mr Fitch's conversation with his father at the head of the table reached his ears: '. . . might be over by *this* Christmas, God willing, now the Americans are joining us.'

Edmund leaned across Mrs Winthrop. '*So fair a fancy few would weave in these years . . .*'

'What was that, my boy?'

'I said, *So fair a fancy few would weave in these years.*' It was a tongue-twister.

'I'm afraid I don't catch your meaning.' Mr Fitch's big, good-natured face was creased up in puzzlement. How red his nose was, Edmund noticed; studded with large pores like a strawberry with its pips.

'I mean that God is not willing. God takes no interest. I think you must believe in fairy-tales, sir – the American army swooping to our rescue like the genie of Aladdin's lamp. Has it not occurred to you that the Americans will take many months to train, let alone to arrive in France, by which time hundreds of thousands more will have been thrown into the slaughter?' Edmund paused, aware of the startled silence that hung over the table; everyone was looking at him. He swallowed. 'God has nothing to do with it, since there isn't a God. We'll just fight it out till there's no-one left alive to fight, and then the politicians can pick over the remains.'

'Isn't that rather defeatist?' Mr Fitch said.

Oh, *observant*! Edmund broke a few grapes from the bunch on a silver platter. He saw his father's outraged expression, but his mother was first to speak.

'I'm afraid Edmund's been under a lot of strain,' she announced, with a brittle smile. 'I do wish we could keep him here at home for another week. It's such a short leave.' She turned brightly to Mrs Winthrop. 'Have you heard from Lady Cumnor at all?'

Philippa plucked at Edmund's sleeve. He turned, saw her pale anxious face, her eyes shining. 'I'm so sorry, Edmund,' she whispered.

He swallowed. 'For what?'

'That you're so . . . upset. Bitter. I wish I could help.'

'You can't.'

'My letters.' She spoke so quietly that he almost had to lip-read. He saw Mrs Fitch looking at them, her flabby, double-chinned face softening into an indulgent smile. *That's better*, she was clearly thinking. God! All these useless, ugly, over-fed people – what gave them a right to live when Alex had died? Why did he have to exhaust himself being polite to them?

'My letters,' Philippa repeated in a whisper. 'I wondered if you'd received them.'

'Oh, I received them.' Her tedious letters, week after week. Elegantly written on high-quality paper, discreetly perfumed. Solicitous, understated, clearly waiting for the merest hint of encouragement from him to become more intimate.

'You never answered.' She had a way of looking at him from under her eyelashes, doe-eyed. Presumably she thought it was appealing.

Edmund fiddled with a grape-stalk. 'No. I never answered for the very good reason that I've nothing whatever to say to you.'

Philippa's hand flew to her lips; she gazed at him, stricken. Edmund's words had unfortunately dropped into a pause in several conversations; he had spoken more loudly and certainly more harshly than he had intended. Everyone was looking at him. He saw his mother's mouth open slightly; for once, the smoothing-over, perfect-hostess remark eluded her.

His father spoke first. 'Edmund! Have you taken leave of your senses? I insist you apologize.'

'Apologize for what? For speaking the truth?' The pressure in his head was unbearable. 'Can't any of you tell the truth? Why don't you come out with it, instead of manipulating me? Why must you keep pushing, nudging, insinuating? Can't you leave me to myself?'

Abruptly he stood up, knocking his plate and fruit-knife to the floor and his chair tipping; Philippa's glass of dessert wine poured its contents into her lap. She moved her chair back from the table with a cry of alarm, colliding with Edmund, who pushed her roughly back into her place. 'I'm sorry,' he said, recollecting himself, giving a mocking little bow to the table at large, 'but I must go outside and get some air. Please excuse me.'

He blundered out, seeing his mother rise to follow him, and his father restraining her. He heard her start to speak, her voice unsteady: 'I'm so very sorry. Edmund's really not quite himself . . .'

Not quite himself! For once she had got it precisely right. Indeed he was not quite himself, the self she thought she knew. But perhaps he was only beginning to become himself, his true self.

Outside, at the top of the steps to the garden, he filled his lungs with cool air. It was dusk. Lights from the windows fell on the stone terrace, and a fountain played. Its soft, regular trickle ought to have been soothing, but nothing could soothe him; he had to get away, down the steps, out of sight of the house. Trimmed lawn welcomed his feet, yielding silently to his tread. The cool roughness of cypress leaves brushed his face as he pushed through a row of conifers; the air smelled of grass and damp earth. He closed his eyes as memory surged through him like the delayed after-shock of pain. He felt detached from his body: from his walking feet, his breathing lungs, his mind registering smells and sounds.

In the lower garden he paused for a moment to listen, facing in the direction of London, thinking of Kent beyond, and the coast, and Alex in his grave (*his cold body laid in the ground, his eyes closed for ever, a spade shovelling earth and stones, covering him, burying him, smothering him – unbearable, unbearable*) at the edge of the hopfields. People said that you could sometimes hear the guns, even at this distance. Nothing. He was disappointed; listening for Alex in the muted voice of the heavy artillery, he heard only the whirr of moth wings, saw the quick flickering shape of a bat; an owl hooted down in the woods. Nothing else disturbed the silence.

Silence and nothing. Nothing. It threatened to swallow him, smother him, swirl him away into black depths.

He lowered his head and walked on across the orchard, down a flight of steps towards the glimmer of water, along the path to the grotto by the silent lake. No-one would follow him down here.

A sound – the soft plop of a stone into water – alerted him. Another, spinning out of the grotto, dropped in, sending ripples. Edmund dragged himself out of his lethargy to wonder who was in there. A trespasser? A poacher? With a gun or a knife? The hairs on the back of his neck tingled, the instinct for self-preservation stirred from dormancy. But why should he care? He walked closer, keeping his footfalls silent; then, intending to startle, he strode to the front of the building, peering in, expecting a tramp or a local farm-worker after an illicit duck or trout. Funny way to go about it, though, flicking stones . . .

The person sitting inside made an incoherent sound, a clumsy scrambling movement. In the gloomy light, Edmund made out the broad face and squint eyes of the gardener's son, the idiot boy.

'It's all right. You needn't be afraid,' Edmund said, relieved.

The boy made a gargling sound that might have

been an attempt at speech. He was large for his age, fourteen or fifteen. Edmund had seen him engaged in simple tasks around the grounds, under the supervision of Baillie senior, moving with slow, ponderous concentration. He was too stupid to attend school, presumably. But should the boy be sitting here in semi-darkness? Was he capable of looking after himself?

'Come on,' Edmund said, deciding. 'I'm taking you back up to the cottage.'

He stepped closer and took the boy's arm, urging him to his feet. The boy shrank back; Edmund saw the gleam of fear in his eyes. Then he submitted, lurching heavily to his feet. Edmund had no idea whether or not the boy recognized him, or whether he was capable of recognition.

It was a struggle. The boy was poorly co-ordinated by day, even more so in this half-light. Edmund managed to coax him up the steps, talking to him, encouraging him as he might an elderly or slow-witted dog. When the boy reached the top of the steps, he gave a little chuckle of triumph and leaned for a moment against Edmund. Both touched and repelled by the human warmth, Edmund said briskly, 'Come on. Let's get you indoors before it's dark.'

They lurched across the orchard together, the boy breathing hard, tripping on the rough grass. When they finally reached the gardener's cottage behind the stables, he gave Edmund a pleased look as they stood side by side on the doorstep, a look of complete acceptance and trust.

Baillie came to the door in shirtsleeves, startled to see his employer's son at this late hour. Looking past him, Edmund saw lamplight, a fire in the grate, and a wooden table set with a teapot and a slab cake. Mrs Baillie got hastily to her feet and bobbed a curtsey.

'I . . . was down by the lake,' Edmund said, 'and found the boy in the grotto. I was afraid he might fall in, so I've brought him here.'

'Thank you, Mr Edmund, sir. That was very kind, I'm sure.' Baillie grabbed the boy by the sleeve of his tweed jacket and pulled him indoors, ruffling his already untidy hair. 'Come on in, Joe, you great gossoon! How many times have I told you not to go wandering down there? Thought he'd gone to the stables, to sit with the pony, sir,' he explained to Edmund. 'He loves that pony.' Then, to the boy again, 'Time you was tucked up in bed! Not roaming about, bothering Mr Edmund. You've to be up early for work tomorrow.'

'Does he enjoy his work here?' Edmund said.

'Yes, sir.' Baillie looked at him curiously. 'He's never going to find work nowhere else, not being like he is, so he helps me out here with what he can manage. He's our only one at home now, with Jim in the army. Thank you so much for your letter, sir, after Georgie got killed. It meant a lot to both of us, that did.' He gestured towards a photograph on the mantelpiece, a broad-smiling Georgie Baillie in uniform.

Edmund nodded, swallowed. 'I'm very sorry.'

'Joe here's the only one of the three what's a bit

234

simple, like,' Baillie said in a confiding undertone.

'He doesn't speak?'

'Never has. He makes noises, and some of them we know what he means.'

Joe had sat in a chair near the fire and was rocking, his arms cuddled round himself, apparently quite happy. He gave little grinning noises at Edmund and his parents, chuckling. Edmund saw, in the warm light of indoors, the face that looked somehow out of focus, the eyes asquint, so that he could never quite tell whether the boy was looking straight at him or over his shoulder.

'I'm very sorry you was troubled, Mr Edmund,' said Mrs Baillie. 'I'll make sure it don't happen again. Good night, sir.'

'Good night, sir. Much obliged. And – good luck,' her husband added.

Edmund nodded; the door was closed. He walked away slowly. For the last fifteen minutes or so he had had contact with another human being, had been taken out of his own preoccupations. The little tableau inside the Baillies' cottage, the simple supper and the fireside chair, reminded him of the idyll he and Alex had planned for themselves in France. If Mr and Mrs Baillie had invited him to go in and sit down, he would have done so. He felt oddly moved by the glimpse of a family life that was lived in such close proximity to his own. But of course it would never have occurred to them to ask him. He was the young master of Graveney Hall, removed from them by wealth and social position.

Where to go now? Was there any comfort to be found anywhere?

'You spent the night in the *stables*? For pity's sake, boy, what's got into you?'

'I like it there. I'm very sorry if I spoiled your dinner party.'

'You most assuredly did!'

They were in the book-lined study, Mr Pearson seated behind his desk, Edmund standing, feeling like a schoolboy again, summoned to account for himself. But his father was not so much stern as dismayed.

'Should I send for a doctor? Should you postpone your return?'

'There's nothing wrong with me, Father.'

'The way you've been behaving is hardly normal!'

'I couldn't stand it last night. The guests. Being polite.'

Henry Pearson put down his glasses on the leather-topped desk, and rubbed his eyes. 'Edmund, I know you're under strain. But snubbing Philippa like that was quite inexcusable.'

'I'm not trying to excuse myself.'

'I insist you apologize before you go back to France. Philippa was extremely upset. Worried for you. Your mother was hoping . . .' Henry Pearson sighed, tapped a pen on the blotter. 'But never mind. What in God's name induced you to sleep in the stables?'

'It wasn't in God's name!'

Edmund saw impatience and concern struggling for dominance in his father's expression.

'Must we have this constant quibbling? All right, then – what the devil made you go and sleep in the stables?'

Edmund laughed. 'That's more like it!'

He could not explain in any way that would make sense to his father. He had stood outside the Baillies' cottage for some while, undecided, wondering whether to go back to the lake for the solitude he had longed for; but now he wanted not solitude but company. The warmth of another body. Nothing that could be found in the frigid spaciousness of the Hall.

He had wandered to the stables, without knowing why; he had looked at the scrubbed empty stalls and had mourned for the sleek beautiful horses whose care had required a team of grooms before the outbreak of war. Horse-riding was the one thing Edmund could do far better than Alex. On the fortnight of riding-school drill included in their officer training, Alex – to whom horses were merely a means of transport – had refused to be impressed by Edmund's ability: 'Of course, the young master of Graveney Hall would have been born in the saddle and ridden to hounds from the age of five,' he teased. 'I suppose you were a daring young thruster in the field? Had your face daubed with fox blood when you were in at the kill?' The hunting days seemed long ago and the horses were gone: the lovely, spirited creatures had been taken on a bewildering journey across the Channel that even now could provoke Edmund's pity.

Hearing a nickering whinny from the far end, he went to investigate. Baillie's pony, a tubby black creature with eyes that peered through a bushy forelock, lay on its bed of straw, alone in the stables meant for pampered hunters. Its head raised, it was about to brace itself on its forelegs to get to its feet; Edmund let himself in, soothed and stroked it, buried his face in its neck. The pony nuzzled his back. Comforted by its warm animal smell, he settled in the straw next to it, thought for a while, then found, blissfully, that he was no longer thinking, and slept.

'Maybe you'd better go to your room and get some rest,' his father said now, at a loss as to what to do with him, 'since it appears we can't have a sensible conversation.'

Next afternoon the Reverend Tilley arrived for tea, summoned to find out what was wrong with Edmund.

Send/Receive

Greg's mental snapshot: Tanya in a leather jacket, which she wears unzipped over a cropped vest top. She stands, hands in jeans pockets, leaning back from the hips. Her long hair is pushed back behind her ears, with a strand falling over one eye. She is looking directly at the viewer. Her lips are pressed together in a sardonic half-smile.

Greg arrived home, panting.

'Is that you, Katy?' his mum called from the front room.

'No, me. I'm going out again. Came back for the bike.'

He rang Gizzard's number. Gizzard was out, of course, it being Saturday night. 'He's gone to High Beach with some friends,' Mrs Guisborough told Greg. 'There was a group of them going to the pub up there.'

'See you later,' Greg called to his parents, tripping over his father's golf bag in the hall and ignoring his mother's call of 'Where are you—'

He had to keep moving, he didn't much care where to. He pushed away on the bike, cursed it for not being his own, reached the main road and cycled hard, raising a sweat. He wanted mindless pub atmosphere, a few beers, head-banging music, to drive the last couple of hours out of his mind.

High Beach was a clearing in the forest, set on high ground, with an open hillside plunging into a tree-lined valley: a favourite spot for visitors, picnickers and bikers, with a pub and a summer café. Greg locked the bike and shoved his way into the Forest Tavern. It was packed, as always on a Saturday. A leather-clad biker holding two pint mugs above his head dripped froth down Greg's sleeve, and smiled at him, amiable, unconcerned: 'Sorry, mate.' Hopeless, trying to find Gizzard in this lot. Anyway, they might have gone on somewhere else. Greg gave up trying, bought himself a pint and drank it at the bar. 'You on your own, then?' the bloke next to him asked, another biker, twentyish, with a ponytail. He looked Greg up and down, as far as he could manage in the crush.

'Looking for a mate,' Greg said.

'Well, here I am,' said Ponytail, with a lascivious grin. 'Look no farther.'

'Stuff that!' Greg downed his beer; he'd never finished a pint so quickly. He moved away, out to the door. Bloody queers! God, what *was* it about him tonight? Was he wearing a pink badge or something?

What now?

He went outside. It had been so hot in the pub that the air struck cold at first, but really it was quite a mild night for early October. He didn't want to go home, but neither did he feel like going on a crawl of all the forest pubs in search of Gizzard; anyway, it wasn't long till closing. He stood for a few moments by his bike, looking at the cloud-lightened sky and a half-moon above the impenetrable darkness of forest, thinking of Graveney Hall standing beyond on its rise of ground, isolated in moonlight, forbidding. Maybe he should have gone there. Then he heard a yell from across the road: 'Oi, Frogspawn!'

It was Gizzard, sitting with two girls on the curved shoulder of trodden grass that looked down the hillside towards the lights of Waltham Abbey below. 'Thought you must have left the country,' Gizzard called as Greg walked over. 'What you up to?'

'Looking for you.'

'Hi, Greg,' said Sherry/Cherie, giving a rolled-eye look at the other girl.

Tanya. It would have to be, wouldn't it? She wore a zipped leather jacket and was cradling a pint mug; she eyed him, aloof and unsmiling. 'Do Mummy and Daddy let you stay out this late all by yourself?'

'It's not my bedtime yet,' Greg said. 'But any time's yours, isn't it?'

'Ooh! Sharp,' Tanya said. 'For a schoolboy.'

'Sit down.' Sherry shuffled up to leave a space between herself and Tanya, and patted the grass. 'It's all right, she's just sharpening her claws.'

'Don't let me interrupt your cosy threesome,' Greg said, looking at Gizzard.

'In my dreams,' said Gizzard. 'I'm not that lucky.'

241

Sherry raised clenched knuckles to his chin. 'Sex on the brain!'

'And not only on the brain—' Gizzard pulled her towards him, hands roving octopus-like.

'Gizzard's always been known for his subtlety and romantic charm,' Greg remarked.

Tanya laughed. 'Better watch, Greg. You might pick up some useful technique. Don't know why I bothered to come out with these two – gooseberry fool, that's me. They need me like they need a cold shower.'

'I expect you could pick someone up in the pub if you put your mind to it,' Greg suggested.

'You think so?'

'But now here's Greg, like the genie of the lamp,' Sherry said, shoving Gizzard aside. 'Chance for you to win your bet, Tan?'

'Oh?' said Greg.

Tanya looked at him archly. 'You'll find out if you're lucky.'

'When you've finished sniping,' Gizzard said, 'I was about to ask if anyone wants a refill while I'm getting a beer in for my mate Greg.' They all had glasses from the pub, but only Gizzard's was empty.

'Cheers,' Greg said.

'Why do you let him call you names all the time?' Tanya asked, when Gizzard had crossed the road.

'Greg *is* my name.'

'Clever! I meant Frogspawn, Dungheap, Cowpat – all those things.'

'Gives him a chance to show off his verbal

ingenuity,' Greg said. 'Anyway, you ever tried stopping him?'

'Sit down if you're staying,' Sherry said. 'I'm getting neck-ache craning up at you.'

Greg sat, and Tanya moved in. 'So, why are you out on your own on a Saturday night?' she asked, shuffling up to him. 'What's happened to St Ursula – at home polishing her halo?'

Greg almost asked, 'Who?' before remembering his lie to Gizzard. 'Oh, that. Bit of an on-off thing.'

'Which at the moment?' Tanya asked.

'Off.'

'You mean you dumped her at a party?'

Sherry giggled. 'I'm not sure Tan's going to forgive you for that.'

'I might,' Tanya said, 'depending how things turn out.'

Greg's mother woke him with a mug of tea.

'You were late last night,' she remarked, opening her curtains. 'This morning, rather. Where did you get to?'

It was a second or two before Greg tuned in; then, remembering, he felt hot and cold prickles all over. Would she be able to tell by looking at him? He pulled his duvet up to his chin.

'Oh, nowhere much. Met up with Gizzard and some friends.'

'And?' She picked up his jeans from the floor and folded them over a chair.

'Had a couple of drinks. Hung around a bit after.'

'Was Jordan with you?'

Oh, God. *Jordan.*

'No, only for the swimming meet. Why d'you ask?' He peered at her suspiciously.

'His father rang, very late. Said Jordan came home for his bike – just like you did – then went off again without saying where. He was a bit worried, his dad, I mean.'

'What time was this, when he phoned?'

'Gone midnight – I'd already gone to bed. I assumed Jordan was with you, so I told him that. I'd have checked when you came in, only I'd dozed off by then.'

Greg sat up blearily and swallowed some tea. 'How'm I supposed to know where he went? I'm not his keeper, am I? Went to the pub with the swim team, most like.'

'His dad said he seemed upset.'

'Yeah, well, he lost his race, that's why.'

His mother gave him a shrewd look. 'Have you fallen out with him or something?'

'No! Why would I?'

The phone rang downstairs; she went down to answer it, spoke briefly, then came back up to the bedroom. 'It's all right – that was his dad again to say sorry for bothering us so late. Jordan got in just after.'

'That's OK, then.'

'I'm cooking bacon in about ten minutes. Come down if you want some. Oh, and Faith rang last night as well. Said she'll see you at the Hall today.'

She left him to get dressed. Greg lay back and stared at the ceiling.

Last night. God, what a mixture! He was dizzy with memories: jealousy, longing, relief, anger, resentment, bewilderment, frustration, lust, ecstasy, triumph – he'd been through the lot, on fast-forward. And now? He was a washed-out wreck, with a head that felt as if six radio stations were playing simultaneously.

He had done it. With Tanya.

Seen Dean Brampton in Intensive Care. Been harangued by his Scud Missile of a Mum.

Quarrelled with Jordan. Walked off and left him.

He shoved all but the first of these out of his head. He had done it. Pulled. Scored. Proved himself not a poofter.

After the pub closed, to a steady roar of motorbikes away from High Beach, Gizzard and Sherry found they had urgent business to conduct under cover of the trees behind the Conservation Centre. 'Can you two amuse yourselves for half an hour or so?' Sherry said, giggling.

'I'm sure we can think of something.' Tanya's fingers were already intertwined with Greg's; she was *paddling his palm*, as Greg had read somewhere. 'Greg's too much of a gentleman to clear off and leave me waiting on my own.'

'See you *soon*,' Sherry called suggestively.

And for the second time Greg found himself being led away purposefully by Tanya. She was seeking not the cover of trees but the open hillside, a dip of

245

ground some distance from the road. She went straight to it, making Greg think she had used the place for the same purpose before. 'It's better in the open. You going to play this time? Might as well, there's nothing else to do.'

'Wait – are you serious? I haven't got a—'

'Don't worry, I have.' She reached into her jeans pocket and pulled out a condom in its packet, which she dangled in front of him. 'You ought to be better prepared. You never know how things'll turn out.'

No, you never did.

She had to win her bet, Tanya explained afterwards. She won it spectacularly: taking charge, guiding his hands, doing the most breathtaking things with her own. No clothes, she insisted, chucking his jeans and underpants away down the slope, throwing her own after them; you feel more naked in the open, beds were for prudes, she said. True, he had never felt so stripped naked: the cool air and the darkness, the sweep of her long hair brushing his skin, her teasing fingers touching him everywhere, all stirred him to a pitch beyond his imaginings. His erection was a salute to the night sky. 'Don't forget this,' Tanya said, tearing open the condom packet with her teeth, fitting it for him with practised deftness while he almost burst with restraining himself. She pulled him over on top of her, reversing their positions, and parted her legs and guided his fumblings and there was no need for restraint, all rational thought swept out of his head by the urge to thrust, the bloodheat inside her, her body writhing beneath his, her sharp teeth nipping his ear, her hands clawing his

246

back and oh oh oh oh *ohhhhh* – a spasm of mindfuzzing cockthrobbing limbtingling delirium.

He lay still, breathing hard against her hair. *Stuff you, Jordan!* he thought, when capable of thought. *Get out of my head.*

'Mmmm,' Tanya went, a sound he took for approval; then she laughed. 'Not bad for a beginner.'

'You could tell?' he said shakily, his mouth in her hair.

'Guessed. Doesn't matter. I won't tell Gizzard, don't worry.'

They found their clothes, brushed grass and leaves off their skin, dressed. In Greg's case rather drunkenly, they made their way back to the pub car park. Tanya, now that the intimacy was over, was brisk and matter-of-fact. She zipped her leather jacket right up to the neck; they walked without touching.

'Well?' Sherry was already in the front seat of her car, Gizzard beside her, grinning at Greg man-to-man.

Tanya held up five fingers of one hand and two of the other; then, considering, flicked up a third.

'Not bad, then,' Sherry said approvingly.

'You owe me.'

In the shower, Greg looked down at himself with new respect. A major initiation had been passed, after all, and quite creditably. But even now Jordan was irritatingly inside his head. *You have to be sure what you want. It's too important to be thrown away at the first chance. It ought to mean something.*

Fuck off, Jordan.

Jordan *would* say that, wouldn't he? Greg was all too aware of what Jordan wanted: an exclusive blood-brotherhood, a soul-baring two-in-one, a let's-discuss-everything openness, a binding tie. Jordan had offered to share the sea and the stars, darkness and dawn; Tanya had offered only sex, but for the moment sex was enough. Jordan wanted love; he had as good as said so. More than Greg could give, or take.

Greg *had* been sure what he wanted, and last night he had wanted Tanya. What about Jordan's *will to live*? The will to live had never been more rampant, and Greg had followed where it led. Jordan couldn't have it all ways.

He got dressed, went down and ate his bacon, and wondered why he felt suddenly morose.

'You going to the Hall, then?' his mother asked, assembling flour, eggs and sugar, going into Julie's Party Cakes mode. 'You don't seem in much of a hurry.'

'No. Don't feel like it today.'

'Faith's expecting you.'

'Thought I'd just go out on the bike for a bit.'

'Why don't you go with Dad to the golf club for a change? It might cheer you up, and you know how chuffed he'd be.'

Greg shook his head; his mother darted an anxious glance at him. He knew she knew there was something wrong, but she did not pursue it. Fifteen minutes later, cycling away down the road, he saw another cyclist coming towards him through early mist. He looked, did a double-take. Jordan. He was

248

angered by the thump of pleasure in his chest, swiftly converting it to irritation.

Blast! Not knowing how to avoid him, Greg pulled over to the kerb. Jordan swerved across the road and stopped with the bikes head to tail. He looked at Greg, looked down at his foot on the pedal, and back again, quizzically.

'Look, I'm sorry about yesterday.'

Greg shrugged in a way calculated to annoy. 'Doesn't matter.'

'It does.'

'Where d'you get to last night?' Greg asked.

'Where did you?'

'Went to the pub with Gizzard. Met up with that girl I told you about. Tanya.'

'Oh,' Jordan said flatly. 'And?'

Afterwards, Greg didn't know what made him answer as he did; in that instant he wanted to hurt Jordan, and see him hurt. The words came readily. 'You really want to know? Scored. Screwed. Shagged.'

Jordan's eyes met Greg's, searching his face as if to ascertain whether he was joking; then he looked down, studied his hands gripped on the handlebars, scuffed a foot on the road. 'Oh,' he said again. 'I hope it was – a good experience.'

'That's the understatement of the millennium. You ought to try it. Get yourself sorted out.'

Later, when Greg replayed this conversation again and again in his mind and heard the hard, taunting note in his voice, what he most remembered was the way Jordan had betrayed neither anger nor shock, though he must surely have felt both, but had gazed steadily towards the end of the road as he said, his voice calm: 'OK, Greg. I get the point – no need to hit me over the head with a sledgehammer. I suppose you haven't read my email?'

'No?'

'I sent you one last night – this morning. But I'd prefer you not to read it after all. The problem with e-mails, you can't unsend them, can you?'

And you can't unsay. Greg had plenty of time, later, to wish his words unspoken. He watched Jordan turn his bike round and head back fast the way he had come. Greg, who had not expected the conversation to end as abruptly as this, considered following; but while he was considering, he sat on his bike by the roadside, and Jordan receded into distance, turning the corner out of sight. Greg shivered. It was much colder today, clammed with dampness, the mist hugging the ground, the air breathing the first hint of approaching winter. It seemed unbelievable that a few hours ago he'd been naked on a hillside, and still hot.

And now there was nothing to do but go back home and download that message. Indoors, he hurtled up the stairs and into the study, and logged on. He could do what Jordan preferred and delete the message unread. Or he could read it.

He clicked the mouse.

From: JMcA@zoom.com
Date: 6 October 2002 02.45
To: greghobbs@mercury.com
Subject:

Greg,
I can't sleep and can't phone you in the middle
of the night, so I'm doing this instead.

After you left the hospital I went home for
my bike and went up to Graveney Hall. I
thought you might have gone there, but you
hadn't, so I stayed there for a while by
myself, by the Panless statue, where we
talked. That was only on Friday but it feels
like about two years ago. I wanted to go down
to the lake and find that grotto you told me
about, but it was too dark and I couldn't
find the way through the bushes and trees. So
I went back to Pan's place.

I can remember everything we said on Friday.
Most of it came from me. I was talking and
talking about everything except what I most
wanted to say. It took Dean Brampton and his
horrendous mother to bring that out. More
about that in a minute. I was thinking of
what you said about the power of wishing.
(Doesn't seem to work for me. More often it
has the opposite effect.)

251

According to the fictional God we should love our neighbours. That would mean we have to love Dean Brampton, mouth and all. I'm not saintly enough to do that. You did better than me. You tried to break his fall, even though you could easily have got injured yourself. And you knew how to look after him. You did those things instinctively. That's a kind of loving your neighbour, a practical kind. And I'm glad you did, because I wouldn't have been so sure what to do or not do.

Since you asked, I've been wondering if I'm really, genuinely sorry about what happened to him. It was a shock, it would be if it happened to anyone. But I'm only as sorry as I would be if it were something I read in the paper – basically a what-if-it-were-me response. It doesn't mean anything. Going to the hospital was only to make myself feel better. Which it certainly didn't, as things turned out.

Perhaps the fictional God thinks that giving Dean Brampton a fright and sticking him in a hospital bed might turn him into a better person. But that's too neat, isn't it? All the evidence suggests that luck and bad luck are dished out at random. I might possibly have been a Christian if I lived a couple of hundred years ago, but for me the First World

War and the Holocaust and Hiroshima and the World Trade Center have finished off all that. My dad told me this – in the concentration camps, the rabbis held a trial. God was the one in the dock, for cruelty and neglect. They found him guilty. Human wickedness wasn't enough to account for what was happening.

What's worse? For there to be a God, but one who didn't care, one who could watch that happen and turn his back? Or for there not to be a God at all?

I'd rather there was no God.

So – I don't blame any made-up God for Dean's accident but I don't blame myself either. We can't be responsible for other people's actions. Our own are enough trouble. I prefer Gaia and the will to live, which leaves guilt out of it. If Dean is a survivor, the will to live will keep him going.

I wish you hadn't walked out. I wish we could have talked for longer. I wish I'd explained things better. Perhaps I'll get the chance. I don't think what I said could have been a total surprise to you, but I'm very sorry if it was. Thanks for reading this, if you have.

Jordan

Greg read the message, too fast, and a second time more slowly. His first thought: Jordan on his own at Graveney Hall last night. If Greg had thought of going there, then what? Reconciliation by moonlight? No. It couldn't happen. Whatever Greg wanted from Jordan, it was less than Jordan wanted from him. It must have been eerie, the solid slabs of the house frontage broken by its black eye-sockets. No-one there but Jordan and whatever ghosts might haunt the place. Had he been afraid?

His second thought: Jordan going down to the lake, alone in the darkness. It made him uneasy. In case he fell in? But Jordan of all people was unlikely to get into trouble in the water . . .

His third thought: Jordan did not want him to read the message, not now.

He returned a single word: *Sorry*. But it was too late for sorry. He thought of the two bikes aligned in the road, himself wanting to hurt, succeeding; saw the horrible smug smile that had twitched at the corners of his mouth while he flung crude words at Jordan. It made him want to throttle himself, to choke off any more brutal things he might find himself saying.

I made it happen, he thought. I wanted to know, and now I do know. I wanted Jordan to tell me, and he did tell me. Why did I want it? So that I could chuck it back in his face.

The phone rang downstairs. He listened, held his breath. His mother called up, 'Greg? Is that you up there? It's Faith.'

Disappointed, relieved, Greg clumped down.

'Aren't you coming?' Faith's voice said. 'I've been looking for you.'

'Look, I can't make it today—'

'Please come. Now. There's something I've got to tell you.'

Faith

Photograph from the local paper, black and white: a group of elderly people standing around a birthday cake on a table. All are smiling. The cake bristles with lit candles. At the centre, seated in an upholstered chair, is a very old man. He is smiling fiercely: an almost toothless smile.

Greg found Faith near the grotto, hacking with a curved blade at brambles and suckers that trailed over the path. When he called, she put down the sickle and walked slowly towards him. She had on a fleece jacket, bright red, which suited her so well that Greg stopped for a moment to look at the picture she made: dark hair flowing over scarlet, against a backdrop of berried shrubs. *Focus, click.* He was surprised she wanted to see him, after Thursday.

'Hello,' she said – rather aloofly, he thought. 'Dad asked if we'd clear the path round the lake. They want to bring visitors down next Sunday, on the guided tour.'

'Visitors? Down here?'

'I know. I don't like it either. It's mine – ours – this place. I don't want other people, with their noise and chat. But it's only for one day.' She fetched secateurs and a pair of long-handled loppers from the bench in the grotto. 'Will you help? I've got a flask of coffee, so we can stay down here all morning.'

'OK. All the way round, though? It needs one of your dad's chain gangs.'

'I've made a start,' Faith said. Greg saw that she had already cleared a few metres of path, throwing the cut grasses and brambles onto a heap on the bank. 'I'll slash, you chop up the tougher stuff, then we can swap when my arms ache.'

'What are we going to do with all that?' Greg nodded towards the heap of vegetation.

'Burn it, later.' Faith began swinging the blade again. 'I haven't even seen you since the accident to that boy. What an awful thing to happen! Horrible to think about. Dad says you were heroic,' she added.

'What, for doing what anyone else would have done?'

'You took charge. You knew what to do.'

'Could hardly clear off and leave him, could I?'

'Dad went to the hospital again this morning with some books and sweets for Dean. Poor thing – fourteen and never likely to walk again. How terrible! I know it was his own fault, and he shouldn't have been here, and there are plenty of Danger notices and all that, but all the same it's tragic, isn't it? We've been praying for him at home . . .' She stopped; Greg saw an expression of pain flicker over her face.

'What's wrong?'

'Nothing.'

He looked at her; she swished her blade fiercely. He picked up the loppers and severed a few elder saplings that were too near the path, then dragged them to the pile. When he returned, Faith said, 'I wanted to say sorry for the other day. You know. I made a fool of myself, didn't I?'

'No,' Greg said, embarrassed. 'It wasn't your fault.'

'It was wrong of me to throw myself at you like that. I got what I deserved,' Faith said. 'You were just . . . being kind, that's all. You're too nice to say *Leave off, I don't fancy you.* But don't worry. I'm not going to humiliate myself like that again. And what makes it worse is that I was using you.'

'Using me how?'

'I wanted to – to be like other girls. I wanted a boyfriend. And I didn't really tell you the truth before. I didn't lie either, but I let you think I've been out with boys.'

'You haven't,' he stated.

'No.' She looked at him. 'With parents as strict as mine, and going to a girls' school, I just don't *meet* boys. People's brothers sometimes, but hardly ever a boy I really like. Even if I did, Mum and Dad would never let me stay out late or go to parties, the way most girls at school do. I know it's because they care about me, and I know it's not right, the things some of the others do, but honestly, Greg, it's hard being a girl! All the time, everywhere you go, there are magazines and adverts telling you how you should

258

look, what you should wear, how you're nothing if you don't have boys flocking round you. And the stupid thing is I don't even believe it! I know it's wrong, and manipulative, and turns people into anorexics. But when it comes down to it, I want – *wanted* – to be a Christian *and* a normal teenage girl. And when I met you, and I thought you liked me a bit, and I liked you – I just wanted to see if I *could* be. It was wrong and stupid, and I'm sorry.'

'Don't put yourself down! Of course I like you. A lot. And don't start thinking you're not fit enough, 'cos you are. The thing is . . .' Greg reached for a handy excuse. 'There's someone else. *Was* someone else.'

'Oh?' Faith asked dully. 'Who is she?'

'No-one you know.'

'Why didn't you tell me? We know each other well enough, don't we?'

Greg pulled a dead branch out of the tangle of vegetation and hauled it over to the pile. Faith, resting for a moment, watched.

'Is it a secret or something?' she asked, her face sharp and curious.

He wished he hadn't opened his mouth – thought of fobbing her off with Tanya, and decided not. Tanya was an obliging body, that was all; she didn't figure.

'Dad told me you were with Jordan McAuliffe on Friday night,' Faith said. 'Jordan as in river, McAuliffe as in Michelle. That's something else you didn't tell me! Why didn't you let on that her brother's your friend when we talked about Michelle? I asked Dad about him. Quiet, serious, he said. Rather handsome.

You're weird, you are, talking about the meaning of life but not even telling me who your friends are or who you're going out with . . . *Oh!*' She stared at him open-mouthed. 'That's not what you're telling me – is it? *He's* the someone else? You don't mean—'

'No! Definitely not. Do me a favour!' Greg pulled out a mesh of dried goose-grass that had tangled itself round his legs. 'It's just – things have got a bit complicated, one way and another.'

'How do you mean?'

'Oh, nothing. The accident and everything. The other girl – *girl*, OK, got it? – is just someone I met. It's finished now.'

She glanced at him; they worked in silence for a few moments. Then Faith said, 'That woman – the boy's mother – was trying to blame you, Dad said, accusing you of all sorts of things. As if you could have made him break in here!'

'I know. She's got it all completely twisted, saying I terrified her poor innocent boy. I bet she'll be at school first thing tomorrow complaining to the Head.'

'He won't believe her, surely?'

'Well,' Greg said, treading down nettles, 'I did have a go at him once – that time I found them chucking stones at the caryatid. Didn't exactly hit him – I grabbed him, he ducked away and I ended up ripping his anorak. But I could easily have ended up throttling him, arrogant little git.'

'I don't blame you for grabbing him. I'd have done the same if I saw him damaging my caryatid.'

'If she wants to make something of that I suppose

she will.' Greg remembered the fury that had gripped him, the urge to hurt and to take pleasure in hurting – with hands and fists then, with words this morning. 'You can pray for him in spite of that? I suppose it makes things easier, being a Christian.'

'No!' Faith said sharply. 'It doesn't and it didn't! When I said we've been praying at home, I meant Mum and Dad have. Not me, because I don't know how to.'

'But you're always praying!'

'Not any more. There's no-one there!' Faith looked at him, fierce, accusing. 'I talk to God and He's not there to listen.'

'Are you serious?'

'Would I joke about something like that?' Faith carried on hacking the grass, swinging from her shoulders. Greg stepped back, well out of range.

'But I thought – I thought it was part of you, your belief in God.'

'Yes, so did I!'

'What's happened?' he asked, dismayed. 'Is it my fault?'

'Of course it's not your fault! You don't think you said anything I couldn't have thought of for myself, do you?'

That put him in his place. He worked in silence for a few moments, cutting bramble suckers, waiting for her to say more.

'Tell me how it happened, then,' he said, since she offered no explanation. 'Was it . . . a sudden revelation, or what?'

'The road back from Damascus? I suppose it was. A conversion in reverse. I don't know if I can explain.'

'Try.'

'Well.' She straightened, sighed. 'In our house we're always having conversations with God, and with Jesus, as if they're extra members of the family. Always there. I've never known anything different. I've never even doubted it before, but last week I did.'

'Why last week?'

'It was something we were doing at school about the Arab-Israeli war. It'll sound stupid—'

'No, go on.'

'We were watching a documentary. It was one still photograph that did it. There was a Palestinian woman whose little boy had been shot dead by Israeli soldiers. The boy was only about ten and his mother was quite young – beautiful, you could see that, even though she was crying, sitting on the ground, with two other women trying to comfort her. It looked sort of biblical: the weeping woman with her shawl draped over her head. And in her face there was – oh, it sounds stupid, but it struck me that in her face there was all the suffering the world has ever known, all focused on this one woman. One of the others was holding up her hands to Allah. But what could Allah do? What could God do?'

'I don't get it, though. You must have seen photos like that before, you must know – why should that one—?'

'I don't know, I don't know. Knowing something isn't the same as feeling it. Suddenly I felt as if I'd always been sort of buffered by this – this air-bag of faith. There was all that despair, the pointless killing of one little boy, and the gesture – hands up to Allah, asking for revenge, when it's only humans who go out for revenge. It goes on and on and on. And this is happening in the holiest places in the world – Jerusalem, and Bethlehem, and Jordan, and Nazareth. It sort of underlines how useless it all is – how little difference Jesus made, when it comes down to it! I've always wanted to go to the Holy Land. I wanted to stand where Jesus stood and walk where He walked. But I can't – because it's a war zone, a modern war zone. And I know now that if I did, those places would be spoiled for me for ever. Not only because of the war – that's just an excuse. War or no war, the real reason I don't want to go is because I know those places will just be ordinary. I won't find Jesus there. I won't find Him anywhere. Like you said, I don't even know what He looked like. The picture I've always had in my mind is completely untrue.'

She stared at him. He saw the look of glazed panic in her eyes.

'But Faith—'

She gave a humourless laugh. 'Yes, what am I going to call myself now? Faithless? I suppose my parents christened me Faith as a sort of insurance policy to keep me on the straight and narrow. It's worked, so far. Now—'

'Have you told them?'

'Course not. How can I?'

263

'You'll have to, though, won't you? Unless you go on pretending.'

'I can't do that.'

'But – perhaps it's only a sort of temporary blip? Even saints had those, didn't they – dark nights of the soul? Can't you pray to get your faith back?'

'I've tried that. But who am I praying to? To emptiness. To a black hole. It's just words. I might as well try a Ouija board or reading tea-leaves. How can I pray to a God I don't believe in any more?'

'You've got to tell yourself there still is a God, even if the lines are out of order and you can't get through at the moment.'

'How can you say that? *You* don't believe,' Faith said angrily. 'If you tell me to pretend there's a God, you're just . . . going along with it, like I'm a child with an imaginary friend, who needs to be humoured. The point is – the whole point is that if I can lose it so easily, it must mean I never really had it, mustn't it? I've been kidding myself all my life.'

'But you *did* have it – you did believe when we talked before, truly! You weren't pretending then.'

Faith pulled off her scarlet fleece and chucked it on the bank, and carried on cutting grass with a wearied, mechanical motion. 'No, I wasn't pretending. That's because I was like a trained parrot. I knew my lines. I knew what I was supposed to believe. And all that made me think I *did* believe, because there was no alternative, was there? But it's only like a house built on sand – no, it's hollow, a shell house, like the one up there! *In my father's house are many mansions,* Jesus said. You could walk around in it, there'd be plenty of room for everyone. But it's not like that! You might think so from the outside, but when you get close you can see it's only a shell, no real rooms at all. Nothing inside except crumbling staircases, no warmth or life, no light at the windows. And I thought it was everything.'

'You can get it back! I bet you can.'

'There you go again. You can't tell me that unless you've got it yourself, and you haven't. How would *you* know? Without, it's just like telling me to believe in Father Christmas, or looking for fairies at the bottom of the garden – you think if I want it badly enough, I'll be able to hypnotize myself. The thing is, it's all been so easy – too easy. Doing what I'm told to do, going to Sunday school, going to church, saying my prayers. And Jesus – He's been everything, too much. I'll be your friend, I'll listen to you, I'll do your thinking for you, I'll die for you. I *wanted* that. I wanted Him to be everything, the centre of the universe – my universe, anyway, not yours; you prefer black holes. But now I don't, because I need to think things out for myself, not lean on someone who saves me from having to and isn't even there. He was just someone who died two thousand years ago, like you said. This – this thing I always wear, this cross—'
She threw down her blade and tugged at the crucifix round her neck. 'It's – it's *too much* – it's like Jesus is asking too much of me, the way I was asking too much of Him!'

'But how can he if you've stopped – hey, don't!'

She had pulled the clasp round to the front and was unfastening it. Guessing what she was about to do, Greg sprang forward to stop her. Too late: as he grabbed her wrist, she transferred the cross and chain to her left hand and threw it clumsily overarm into the lake. He saw her eyes shiny with tears and then the slow trajectory of cross and chain, whirling through air, hitting the water with a slap, sinking. Immediately he plunged in. Cold wetness wrapped the legs of his jeans and surged inside his boots as he snatched up the cross from the sandy bed. The water came only to his knees, but as he turned to show Faith the chain in his hand, the sand shifted and gave way beneath his feet. He overbalanced, staggered, too late to save himself: toppled backwards in a wild flailing of arms, a comic windmilling, a fall of slow-motion inevitability. He heard Faith's shriek, and in an instant the shock of water embraced him, closed over his head, dragged at his clothes, filled his eyes and ears with coldness. Spitting, spluttering, gasping, he got his head above water and thrashed for a foothold. Faith splashed in to help him, extending a hand. His feet sank in deep as she pulled. He lurched to the bank, dripping, streaming, shaking tendrils of waterweed from his boots.

'Greg! Oh, Greg!' They stumbled against each other, Faith laughing and crying. They stood on the path, hugging, while a puddle formed at their feet. 'You were so *funny* – like a gun-dog, straight in!'

'Did you get that on camera? Shall I do it again?'

'Oh, you're *soaked* !'

'Now you mention it, yes. I hung on to your chain, though. Here it is.' He dangled it in front of her. 'Hey, you're going cross-eyed.'

'Ha ha.' She looked away with an effort. 'I don't want it. You can have it.'

'What, after I've swallowed a couple of gallons of lake fetching it?'

'No.' Faith shook her head.

'OK,' Greg said, stuffing it into his pocket. 'I'll look after it till you need it.'

'But what shall we do about you?' She grabbed one of his hands and started rubbing it between both of hers as if he were at risk from hypothermia. 'You'll get cold – here, put this on.' She fetched her fleece jacket from the bank and draped it round his shoulders, tugging it round; she picked a piece of weed from his hair.

'You're nearly as wet yourself.'

'Shall we go up to the Coach House? There might be some blankets or something up there.'

He quite liked her fussing round like this, but shook his head. 'I'm OK if you are. We'll warm up if we carry on working – after I've emptied out my boots.'

'Me too.' Faith looked down at her soggy trainers.

They sat side by side in the grotto, wringing out their socks and their jeans. Faith was downcast again; Greg's sousing in the lake had raised her spirits but, he saw, only temporarily. She hadn't tried to blame him, but this *must* be his fault; he was the one who'd started questioning her faith, picking holes in it. Why had he done it? Whatever he had wanted, it wasn't this. Noticing that she was starting to shiver, he gave back her jacket, guided her hands into the sleeves and zipped it up to her chin; then he sat with an arm round her. She leaned against him reluctantly. With hesitant fingers he pushed her hair back from her face and kissed her cheek; when she did not resist he held her closer and bent his mouth to hers.

She pushed him away. 'Don't! Stop it.'

'Why?'

'I don't want to. And you're only doing it as a consolation. Don't think you can make up for—'

'I don't. And don't think I went floundering in the lake just to make you laugh, either.'

'I didn't.'

'Tell you what,' Greg said, with complete serious-ness, 'I'll make a bargain with God.'

She looked at him, startled, pulling away. 'A what?'

'A bargain. Like this.' He raised his eyes to the curved ceiling of the grotto. 'OK, God, are you listening up there? If you give Faith her faith back, I'll believe in you too.'

The sun had broken through the mist while they were talking; it reflected ripple patterns on the curve of the wall. She sat shrugged into her jacket, her hands tucked up inside the sleeves; her eyes were dark and intense. She was a girl in a shell, cupped and held like a pearl in an oyster. He saw her as part of an accidentally beautiful composition: dark hair and eyes, scarlet fleece, tiles arranged behind her in swirls.

'You can't do it,' she told him. 'You can't make a bargain with God. He doesn't make bargains.'

'How do you know that? Besides, you're contradicting yourself again. You're telling me what God does and doesn't do when you've just been saying you don't believe in him.'

'Habit.'

'Well, we'll see if God wants to play.'

'You shouldn't talk like that!' Faith reproved.

'Why not, if he doesn't exist? Who's to mind? And if he does exist, he won't mind a bit of straight talking, will he? Or does he only listen to *thee*ing and *thou*ing?'

'You're cold.' Faith rubbed his arm. 'Let's get back to work.'

Greg stood up slowly, his attention caught by the EP initials in shells. 'What if—?'

'What if what?'

'What if he's *here*? Edmund?'

'In the grotto? What are you talking about?'

'Has it ever occurred to you that he could have drowned in the lake?'

Faith stared. 'Drowned himself, you mean?'

Greg nodded. 'That would explain the vague wording, wouldn't it, if no-one knew for sure? *At the time of the fire.* Not *in* the fire. Not on the Western Front, either.'

'What made you think of that?'

'Being in the water just now. What's in there? What's under there?'

The idea, he realized, had been prompted by Jordan's email, though he did not say this to Faith.

Jordan had tried to find his way through the bushes, in darkness, looking for a way down to the lake. Greg had not seriously suspected Jordan of having any thought of drowning himself, but nevertheless he had been uneasy, picturing it.

'Well, he *could* have done,' Faith conceded. 'But why?'

'You don't have to look far for a reason! Shell-shock . . . unable to face going back . . . best friends killed . . . And then there's the house! Imagine it – he comes back from the Western Front, from who knows what, for home leave, and finds the place a smouldering ruin.'

'Mm. I suppose.' Faith turned to look out at the water. 'How odd if he's in there, so close, after all the wondering we've done . . .'

'It's just an idea,' Greg said. 'You know when people talk about that footsteps-on-their-grave thing – a kind of premonition? That's what it felt like, only in reverse – not the future, but something that happened here years ago. We'll never know, though, will we?'

'I don't like thinking about it,' Faith said. She reached for a damp trainer and pushed a sockless foot inside it.

By lunch-time, when they went up to the Coach House, both had dried out enough to look only mildly dishevelled, though Greg wasn't sure his Timberland boots would ever recover. Preparations were already in progress for next weekend: tables and chairs assembled inside, and a long row of display stands showing photographs past and present.

'There's one I want to show you,' Faith said. 'Maura's put these up – she's in charge of the old photos as well as the new ones. But they're precious, the archive ones, so they only come out for special occasions.'

Maura, who had pure white hair cut in a youthful style and was dressed as if for yachting, smiled vaguely at them and carried on sorting through a box. On one of her stands she had mounted photographs in matched pairs: old black-and-white or sepia, showing Graveney Hall's former splendour, and colour prints of present dilapidation. Greg's eyes went straight to a shot of the caryatid, full-on in blank sunlight and not as good as his own, in his estimation; but Faith was pointing to the black-and-white photo on the next panel.

'Greg, look at this – it's him, Edmund! I've seen this picture before, last year, but I didn't take much notice then.'

Greg looked: a family of three, in a posed portrait. *The Pearson family by the Pan statue in about 1914,* said the caption in amateurish calligraphic script; and, with dubious accuracy, *Edmund Pearson was killed in the First World War.* Mr and Mrs Pearson, stiff and formal, sat upright in garden chairs, dressed in light summer clothes that nevertheless looked restricting. Behind them was a tall young man. Greg stared, for the first time, at the face of Edmund Pearson.

'Nineteen fourteen – so he's eighteen, just a year older than me. He's got three years to live.'

Edmund Pearson gazed out of the portrait. He

stood behind his seated parents with a hand resting on each wicker chair-back. He was lightly-built, and wore an open blazer, no tie, and cricket trousers. His hair, which looked as if it would be light brown, fell across his forehead; he had strongly-marked eyebrows and a steady gaze. His mouth could have been smiling, but not quite; he seemed about to speak to the photographer.

Wonder if I'd like him, Greg thought, if I met him?

'A real Mona Lisa smile,' Faith said. 'Find me if you can.'

'Summer nineteen fourteen. They must have known by then that war was likely.'

Faith's father Mike came up to them, all smiles. 'How are you two getting on with the scrub-bashing down there? Got you hard at work, has she, Greg? I'll come down later and see for myself. Good to see you again. No better news about Dean, I'm afraid – awful business. Thank God you were here with your friend, though I should disapprove, strictly speaking, as you were trespassing, all of you. But come and have a look at this! We're all very excited—'

On one of the tables the local newspaper was spread out: two of the women were bending over it, exclaiming to each other. Ushered towards it by Faith's father, Greg read JOE'S CENTURY, and the sub-heading LOCAL PENSIONER CELEBRATES 100TH BIRTHDAY. There was a photograph of a withered old man, beaming gappily by a huge birthday cake. Greg immediately recognized the cake as one of his mother's; he'd seen her icing the words

One Hundred Not Out, and packing it in its ribboned box ready for delivery to the old people's home on the edge of the common. Nothing exceptional about that had struck him at the time, but Mike Tarrant urged him and Faith to read the article, and one of the women said to the other, 'How astonishing!' as they moved away.

Greg read:

It was a hundred candles and a telegram from the Queen for Mr Joseph Baillie, oldest resident of Oak Grove Retirement Home, last Saturday. Sprightly Joe enjoyed a birthday bash with fellow residents of the Epping home, where the Foresters Brass Band played golden oldies while Joe blew out the candles on his cake.

'Joe's a bit of a golden oldie himself,' quipped Hazel Thorne, matron of Oak Grove. 'He's always in good spirits and he thoroughly enjoyed his party. It's amazing to think that he's lived in this area all his life. What changes he must have seen!'

Joe Baillie was born at Graveney Hall, near Epping, where his father was employed as head gardener. Joe, whose two elder brothers were killed in the First World War, also worked in the Hall gardens until the fire which destroyed the mansion in 1917. Later, Joe worked as station gardener for London Underground on the Epping–Ongar line (now closed), a job which he held throughout the 1939–45 war and until his retirement. For most of his working life he lived at Toot Hill, near Epping, until the death of his parents. He never married and has no living relatives.

'Joe's marvellous for his age,' said fellow resident Mrs Elspeth White, who is due to celebrate her own hundredth birthday in June next year. 'I hope he'll still be around to help me blow out the candles when my turn comes.'

'Amazing, isn't it?' said Faith's dad. 'I'm going to visit him – see if he's fit enough to come for Open Day. He could be our guest of honour; we might even get him to say something. If his memory's good, he can give us all sorts of information about the gardens and the household. Old people often do have the most marvellous memories, especially of things that happened years ago. I'll make a tape recording and transcribe it for our records – I bet we'll get something to put in the next guidebook. This is such a fantastic find. And to think he's been there all these years, a couple of miles down the road, and we might never have known!'

'Mike, do you know where those boards are, for the entrance signs?' someone interrupted.

'Oh, yes, I'll come and show you – you'll need the key, and be careful of the stepladder.'

Greg and Faith looked at each other.

'He was here – he must have known Edmund!' Faith exclaimed. 'Oh, why didn't we think of that – there still being someone alive who was here at the time!'

'Because you don't really expect people to live to a hundred and stay in the same area all their lives,' Greg pointed out.

'We've got to go and see him! He might know what happened!'

'Your dad's going, and if he gets his way the old codger'll be here next week.'

'No, on our own! We've got to ask him about Edmund. We can't ask him that in the middle of Open Day. We need to get him to ourselves. Tomorrow, after school? I'll ring first and make sure it's all right.'

Greg couldn't match her urgency. 'What are you hoping – that he stood by the lake and watched Edmund drown himself?'

'He must be able to tell us *something*,' Faith insisted. 'Give us some clue.'

'Well, OK.'

Greg glanced back at Edmund in the photograph, framed, frozen and caught. Edmund in 1914, who did not know the dates of the Somme or Passchendaele, who had never seen a tank or heard of mustard gas, who had no idea what *over the top* would come to mean.

Instead of cycling straight home, Greg took the longer route to Jordan's house. He had no idea what he was going to say, and was almost relieved when Jordan's dad, Stuart, told him Jordan wasn't at home. But Jordan had been out all day, no-one knew where, and his father was anxious, Greg saw.

'Come in for a few minutes, anyway.'

Not really wanting to, Greg followed him indoors. Michelle was sprawled in an armchair, reading. She looked up, surprised and pleased, but her father led the way through to a book-lined study that adjoined the main room, evidently wanting to talk to Greg in private. He sat on a swivel chair and gestured Greg towards a small sofa.

'Any more news of that boy, from the hospital?'

Greg shook his head. 'No change, as far as I know. Michael Tarrant went in this morning.'

'You don't know where Jordan might be, I take it?'

'No,' Greg said. A wrench of regret grabbed him somewhere in the middle. 'I saw him on his bike, earlyish, about ten, but only for a minute. That was near my house.'

'Not since then?' Stuart McAuliffe was watching him closely. 'He went out about then – hasn't come back or phoned since, and his mobile's switched off. Where was he heading?'

'Didn't say. Back here, I thought.'

Jordan's father compressed his lips and gazed out of the window. 'He seems very upset about something. I'm worried, Greg, to tell you the truth. It's not like him to go off without telling us.'

Greg swallowed. 'Last night, you know, when you rang, he'd gone up to Graveney Hall. But he's not there now, 'cos I've just come from there. And there are lots of people about. He'd want to be on his own, I expect—'

'You've had a disagreement, I take it?'

'Sort of.'

'Tell me it's none of my business, if you like. But maybe I can guess.'

Greg looked down at his hands. There wasn't much point pretending; Jordan's dad already knew most of it. 'It's like – we're mates, and that's it as far as I'm concerned.' He picked at the edge of his thumbnail. 'I mean, I'm not – you know – gay or anything. Definitely not! And there was nothing to make him think so. Only he must have thought – he got it all wrong—'

'Ah.'

'Then this morning, I told him I was with a girl last night,' Greg said, to the nearest bookshelf. He didn't know how to explain that Jordan was simultaneously the last person he wanted to hurt, and the one he wanted to hurt most. And what he'd just said – it sounded like bragging. Perhaps it was. He wasn't even sure that his face wasn't wearing a horrible smirk of self-congratulation.

'I see,' Stuart said; 'yes, he'd take that badly. But then, if that's how things are, he needs to know.'

Greg looked up cautiously. He almost added: I told him to sort himself out. He felt prickly with the shame and unfairness of that too-easy taunt.

Jordan's dad sighed. 'I'm sure it's not the last time he'll have to face this, but it's the first time, and that makes it hard. It's not going to be easy for him – he doesn't take things lightly. Not that it's particularly easy to be straight either, but being gay, at his age, still at school – I'm just grateful he had the courage to tell me. I'd hate to see him upset and have no idea why.'

'I didn't mean to . . .' Greg stumbled, hearing how pathetic he sounded.

Jordan's father looked at him. 'No, I'm sure you didn't. Difficult all round, I can see that.'

'I can't seem to help it. I open my mouth and upset people. My other friend, Faith – you know, Michael Tarrant's daughter – she's not the one I was with last night but she's my friend, and she used to believe in God till I started arguing with her and asking questions to prove she'd got it all wrong, so that's my fault too . . .'

He blathered on, wondering what had impelled him to start on this. Didn't Jordan's dad have enough to worry about, without being Greg's agony uncle? But he listened attentively until Greg had finished, then appeared to give careful thought before saying: 'It sounds to me as if you're blaming yourself too much. This girl – Faith, did you say? – is bound to come up against problems and doubts sooner or later, and if you hadn't made her question what she believes, someone or something else would have done. I'm a Jewish agnostic myself, and Ann – my wife – is a lapsed Catholic. We're a family of lapsers, so I'm not the best person to talk to about matters of belief. But it may not be as drastic as you think. Faith may get her faith back, if that's what she wants. Maybe you've raised doubts she already had. She'll have to sort them out for herself.'

The study door opened and Michelle came in. 'Mum says does Greg want to stay and eat with us, and wait for Jordan?'

Greg looked at Stuart; a glance confirmed that it would be better if he was not here when Jordan came home. 'No. Thanks, but I've got to go.'

He cycled around aimlessly for a while. It was dark

and getting cold; eventually, driven by hunger, he went home. His mother met him at the front door. 'Jordan's dad just phoned again. He says to tell you Jordan's come home.' She looked at him suspiciously. 'Mind if I ask what's going on?'

'Oh, nothing,' Greg said. 'Bit of a misunder-standing, that's all.'

Oak Grove

Greg's photograph (colour), close-up, enlarged: Faith's cross on its chain. The crucifix is of plain design; its cross-piece catches the light. The links of the chain necklace loop out of the frame. The piece of jewellery is photographed against a fabric background of matt green (Greg's pencil case).

```
From: JMcA@zoom.com
Date: 7 October 2002 06.25
To:   greghobbs@mercury.com
Subject: Re: sorry

Never express yourself more clearly than you
think. Nils Bohr.
```

That was all. Greg stared at the screen, scrolled down to see if there were any more, stared at it again.

Typical bloody Jordan – clever, indirect, baffling. But it didn't sound friendly, whichever way he looked at it. He turned off the computer without replying.

The weather had turned wet and gusty. Arriving early in the sixth-form common room, Greg found Jordan in his usual place in the corner, reading a *Guardian* which Greg could see was last Friday's copy.

'Hi,' Greg said, trying to pretend nothing had changed.

'Hi.' Jordan looked up briefly and went back to his reading.

'Got your e-mail,' Greg said. 'Nils Bohr?'

Jordan lowered the paper for a second. 'Physicist.'

'I know that, but what was he on about?'

'Theoretical physics.' This time Jordan didn't even look out from behind the *Guardian*.

'Where d'you get to yesterday?' Greg tried.

'Out.'

Still Greg hung around, counting out coins for the coffee machine. 'Want a drink?' he asked.

Jordan inclined his head towards the steaming cup on the table which made the question redundant. Greg got his own coffee and sat down two chairs away, remembering that he was supposed to have gone to the pool this morning for training; had Jordan expected that? He sat in silence, undecided; Jordan read on, taking no further notice of him.

People began to trickle in, Monday-morning subdued, moaning about the wet weather and undone homework and looming deadlines. Ben

Cousins dumped his bag and came over. 'Hey, you two – where were you Friday?'

'Friday?' Greg echoed. The day of Dean's accident, the evening he and Jordan had talked by the Pan statue – he wasn't sure he wasn't going pink in the face.

'Cricket! I had you two down to play. We were two short—'

'Sorry,' Jordan said. 'Forgot all about it.'

Ben's glance swivelled to Greg. 'You as well?'

'Yeah, sorry, mate. Went right out of my head.'

'We lost, in case you're interested. I'll find someone else next time, as it's too much trouble to show up.' Ben gave them a withering glare. Greg looked at Jordan, hoping to find that Ben's scorn had reunited them as friends, but Jordan had turned away and was fastening his rucksack.

First lesson was English with Mr O'Donnell. Jordan, arriving first, went to sit in the spare seat by Maddy, which left Greg with Bonnie. 'In favour, am I? Wossup?' she hissed, interested. 'You two had a row or something?'

Greg shook his head, aware that Bonnie's stage-whisper was loud enough to carry to everyone in the room. She was the second person today to use the phrase *you two*; now that it was no longer applicable, he wondered if people said it all the time, and how it was meant. God, did everyone know? But what was there to know? Did everyone *assume*, then? Maddy didn't, obviously; her cheeks were glowing with pleasure because of Jordan's choice of seat. She was heading for disappointment, Greg thought with malicious amusement.

'You know this thing teachers have about mixing up boys and girls?' he answered Bonnie. 'To stop boys from under-achieving? Thought I'd give myself the benefit of your scintillating insights into world literature.'

Bonnie goggled at him. 'Scintillating? It'd take a couple of pints on a Saturday night for me to do that. First thing Monday, you can forget it.'

Mr O'Donnell came in, observed the new seating arrangements without comment, and started the lesson.

'A diversion to start with,' he told them, handing out sheets. The class was used to what had become known as his free-range slot, roaming from Pliny to Sylvia Plath to Primo Levi. Refusing to be hemmed in by the syllabus, he often read them something just because he liked it, or to make an interesting point, or to encourage them to read widely. 'We looked at the extract from *The Return of the Native* a couple of weeks ago, and some of you know Thomas Hardy as a novelist – yes, Maddy, *Jude the Obscure*'s been filmed, as well as some of the others. But Hardy was also a very prolific poet. This one – *The Oxen* – is one of my favourites.' He cleared his throat and read:

'Christmas Eve, and twelve of the clock.
"Now they are all on their knees,"
An elder said as we sat in a flock
By the embers at hearthside ease.

283

We pictured the meek mild creatures where
They dwelt in their strawy pen,
Nor did it occur to one of us there
To doubt they were kneeling then.

So fair a fancy few would weave
In these years! Yet, I feel,
If someone said, on Christmas Eve,
"Come; see the oxen kneel

In the lonely barton in yonder coomb
Our childhood used to know,"
I should go with him into the gloom,
Hoping it might be so.'

Mr O'Donnell paused at the end, looking at the students over the top of his glasses. 'You know, I've read that poem countless times, but reading it again just now the ending sends a tingle down my spine.'

Next to Greg, Bonnie gave a little snort of derision, which she swiftly converted to a hiccup when Mr O'Donnell looked at her. 'Bonnie? What do you think? Any tingles for you?'

'I don't get it.'

'OK, who does?' Mr O'Donnell scanned the class for offers. 'Jordan?'

'Well, it says at the bottom *Nineteen Fifteen*. That gives a context to the line *In these years* . . . the First World War. Hardy seems from this to be an agnostic who'd like to believe in God if he could—'

'An atheist, you mean,' Bonnie interrupted.

'I mean an agnostic,' Jordan said, not looking at her. 'An atheist is someone who definitely doesn't believe in God. An agnostic thinks God's existence can't be proved but can't be disproved either. Thomas Hardy – or at least the person in the poem, not necessarily Hardy himself – can't believe. I don't think it was just because of the war, but because of Darwinism and advances in science – that could be implied. He thinks the idea of the oxen kneeling on Christmas Eve is like an old-fashioned fairy-tale, but all the same if he could see them do it for himself . . . he's *hoping*, not just going along to see . . .'

Greg listened in some astonishment, as did Mr O'Donnell, while Jordan, who rarely volunteered to speak in class, explained the poem so well and fully that even Bonnie got the gist.

'Thank you, Jordan. That's very good,' Mr O'Donnell said when he had finished. 'It's a subject that preoccupied Hardy – what kind of God could God be, if he exists at all, since he seems indifferent to human suffering? On Wednesday I'll bring you *The Convergence of the Twain*, Hardy's take on the sinking of the *Titanic* . . . And now we'd better get back to our war poets, though the poem we've just read is certainly relevant, as Jordan says.'

Afterwards, Greg understood that this unusual volubility was Jordan's way of showing that Greg wasn't going to get him down. Greg could be crude, hurtful, disloyal if he liked: Jordan had self-respect and a sense of his own worth, that was the subtext. Greg thought about this later, during afternoon registration, when they were both summoned to the Head of Sixth. They knew what it was about, but neither spoke while they waited outside Mrs Leeson's office, Greg sitting on a hard chair, Jordan standing, looking out of the window.

When she arrived, Mrs Leeson led them inside and asked Greg for an account of what had happened at Graveney Hall on Friday; then she explained that Mrs Brampton had phoned the Head to accuse Greg of bullying her son. It wasn't really a school matter, she added, but she needed to get Greg's and Jordan's versions before replying.

'It's complete rubbish about the bullying,' Jordan said. 'If anything, the Year Nine boys were bullying us – following us, throwing bricks and yelling insults. Besides, Greg's a trained first-aider – he was the one who looked after Dean till the ambulance arrived. I suppose she missed that out?'

Mrs Leeson asked a few more questions, said she was glad to have got things straight, and the interview was over.

'Thanks for that,' Greg said in the corridor outside. They had different lessons now: Greg Art, Jordan Geography.

Jordan shrugged, aloof again. 'What else was there to say?'

Greg scuffed his feet. 'You could have made things difficult for me if you'd wanted to.'

'Not half as difficult as you could make things for me, if *you* wanted to,' Jordan said, unsmiling, and walked away towards the Humanities block.

God! Greg screwed up his face, staring out of the rain-spattered window, unable to face his Art lesson just yet. That was true, of course – he could spread rumours and gossip about Jordan if it had occurred to him to do so. But did Jordan really think so little of him as to fear that he might? He wished he'd been quick enough to come back with *I'd never do that. You know I'd never do that.*

But even if he'd said it, why should Jordan believe him? What Jordan had offered, he'd chucked back in contempt. He banged his head against the glass and stood for a moment leaning against the streaming window, then Mrs Leeson's door opened abruptly behind him and he stomped off to Art.

It was still pouring with rain when he met Faith by the church. She had taken cover in the bus shelter, but produced an umbrella as he approached and held it over both of them as they walked. Greg pushed his bike – his own bike, which he had just collected from the repair shop, grudgingly handing over a wad of notes.

'I phoned the matron, Mrs Thorne,' Faith told him, 'but she said we won't get anything out of Joe because he hardly talks. It's for a project, I told her. Which it is in a way, though I expect she thinks I meant for school.'

'I wondered about him talking. In the article there were quotes from two other people but not from him.'

'It said *sprightly*, though, and *enjoyed his party*. So he can't be completely ga-ga.'

Oak Grove was a large Victorian house set back from the common. Inside the lit front room, Greg saw a number of elderly people in armchairs angled at a TV set with the colour turned up to glaring brightness. Mrs Thorne, who looked almost old enough to be a resident herself, answered the doorbell. 'Our Mr Baillie's very popular at the moment!' she gushed. 'Never had so many visitors in twenty-five years as he's had this week. Now I did warn you, didn't I,' she added to Faith, 'that he's not going to understand much.'

Greg mouthed, *'Twenty-five years!'* at Faith as they followed the matron through the hallway. Longer than they'd been alive! Strident TV noise blasted out of the lounge door as Mrs Thorne opened it. Faces looked round, some of them alert, several completely vacant.

'Now, Joe,' Mrs Thorne said very loudly, approaching a large wing-backed armchair that seemed to have no occupant. 'Here's your visitors I was telling you about. Faith and . . . er—'

'Greg,' said Greg.

'Greg. Isn't that nice?'

One of the old ladies made a cooing noise; another started to clap her hands with great concentration. The first Greg saw of Joe Baillie was a gnarled hand, corrugated with blue veins, blodged with liver-coloured spots, that clutched the armrest. Moving closer, he saw a skeletal frame and a slack face with drooping eyelids. The head moved slowly round to face the visitors. The eyes did not flicker, though Greg noticed the squint: one eye seemed to look at him, the other over his shoulder, making him want to turn round to see if there was someone behind him.

'You can't talk in here – I'm going to pop you in the visitors' room,' Mrs Thorne said. She had the kind of tirelessly cheery voice that people must get from dealing with infants or the elderly, Greg thought. The old man nodded slowly, took the arm she extended and heaved himself out of his chair. His clothes – thick trousers and a knitted pullover – hung on his bony frame. Mrs Thorne supported him, matching his slow steps towards the door, talking all the while. 'That's the way! Just along the corridor – walking quite well today, aren't we?'

Sprightly? Greg thought. This was going to be hopeless, a complete waste of time. He grimaced at Faith, glad to get away from the blaring TV and the overheated room, and the stares of those residents capable of being curious. The visitors' room was much smaller, with four chairs. Mrs Thorne settled Joe Baillie in one of these, then fetched a rug and tucked it round his legs. 'I'll leave you to have a nice chat,' she told them. 'Call me if you need anything.'

Faith pulled out a large white envelope and a box of chocolates from her school bag. 'Happy Birthday, Mr Baillie,' she said, loudly and clearly. 'I'm sorry this is late. My name's Faith and this is Greg. We've brought you some chocolates, soft centres. Shall I help you open the card?' she added as Joe Baillie stared, not seeming to understand what it was. When she took out the birthday card and held it up to him, his face creased into a smile that showed more gaps than teeth, the smile of the photograph; he nodded slowly and reached out his hand, making a sound that Greg couldn't recognize as a word. Joe opened the card; inside Faith had written, in large letters, *With congratulations and very best wishes from Faith and Greg*. Greg thought it odd, this business of congratulating people for managing to stay alive. He'd never have thought of getting a card or a present.

Faith was good with the old man, talking to him slowly and clearly about his party and the article in the paper. Joe's mouth hung slightly open, and one of his watery eyes rested on her face in puzzlement while the other looked off at a tangent. Brown in colour, his eyes seemed overlaid with chalky blue, giving them an odd opaque look. His head seemed to wobble on his neck, as if it were an effort to hold it up. Occasionally he replied with an incoherent sound that was almost a groan.

'This is pointless,' Greg said to Faith in an undertone. 'What can he possibly tell us?'

Faith ignored him. 'We've come to ask you about Graveney Hall,' she enunciated. 'About when you were a gardener there.' Joe Baillie stared at her blankly.

'Write it down,' Greg suggested.

Faith rummaged in her school bag and pulled out a red exercise book and a zipped pencil case. She knelt on the carpet in front of Joe's chair and wrote on the back page: *We want to ask you about GRAVENEY HALL.*

Joe took the book from her and stared closely at the letters. Greg shook his head at Faith; this wasn't going to work either. But then Joe made a grunt of recognition and reached for Faith's pen. Gripping it, breathing hard, he wrote laboriously underneath in shaky capitals: *MINE ALL BURND*.

Mine all burned? 'What's he on about?' Greg muttered. 'The gardener's cottage? But that didn't burn down, did it?'

'Wait,' Faith muttered back, then said gently to Joe, 'Yes, that's right. Were you there?' She wrote it, passed the book back to him.

YES.

Was Edmund Pearson there at the time? Faith wrote.

This time, after scanning the letters for some moments, Joe looked blank.

'Wait.' Faith went back to her school bag and took a photograph from between pages of a Geography textbook: the picture of Edmund Pearson with his parents.

'You stole that?' Greg asked, impressed.

'Borrowed. OK, without asking. Important visual aid, I thought.'

Faith held out the photograph to Joe, and wrote *EDMUND PEARSON* in the book in large capitals. Now Joe became agitated: stabbing a forefinger at Edmund in the picture, looking at Faith, making incoherent noises.

'He knows something! Get him to write it down!' Greg urged.

What happened to Edmund? Do you know? Faith wrote.

They both sat with eyes fixed on Joe while he slowly composed his next message. He handed back the book.

DIS APERED, they read.

'Try again,' Greg said.

Do you know where he went?

Joe looked at Faith, shook his head. Then, in renewed agitation, he took the book from Faith and wrote again.

GAV IT TO ME.

Gave what to you?

GRAVNY HALL MINE.

'Mine all burned!' Greg pointed to Joe's first written message. 'He was saying the same thing there!'

What do you mean?

Joe pointed again at Edmund in the photograph, then wrote: *HE GAV IT TO ME.*

'Edmund gave him Graveney Hall? But that's senseless! Ask him more.'

Did you ever see Edmund again after the fire? Faith wrote.

Joe looked at her and slowly shook his head.

How did the fire start?

PARFIN.

'Parfin – paraffin!'

Did you start it?

'Faith!'

'Uh . . . uh . . .' Joe pushed the exercise book away and began to writhe in his chair, grabbing at the arms, turning his head towards the curtains.

Greg and Faith looked at each other. '*A servant's carelessness*,' Greg said. 'That's what the guidebook says. Carelessness, or . . .?'

'But why, if he thought the house belonged to him?'

Joe snatched the book back and wrote one word: TOLET.

'Told, told someone?' Faith guessed.

'No – toilet! Quick! I'll get Mrs Whatsit, before—'

Mrs Thorne showed them to the door. 'I don't suppose you got much for your project? It was nice of you to come and see him, anyway – I think he really enjoyed it. But it doesn't take much to tire him out. I hope you don't mind me shooing you away like this.'

'How long is it since he stopped talking?' Faith asked.

'Oh, he's never talked. He makes noises, and sometimes we can understand what he means. We manage.'

'He told us – wrote down – that Graveney Hall belongs to him,' Faith said.

Mrs Thorne laughed. 'Did he really? Well, he rambles a bit – he's very confused, you know. But the things he comes out with! Lovely to see you.' The door was already half-closed. 'Bye now.'

Rain was still plashing steadily on the leathery shrubs by the gate. The pavement was wet and shiny, scattered with the first leaves to fall; cars on the main road already had their headlights on. Greg unlocked his bike.

'Well, where does that leave us? Anywhere, or just where we were before? Can we believe any of that?'

'The fire started with paraffin. We didn't know *that*.' Faith put up her umbrella.

'Off-putting, those squinty eyes. You don't know which one to look at.'

'Let's go home,' Faith said. 'My house, I mean. You don't have to rush off, do you?'

Greg balked. 'Is your mum there?'

'So what if she is?' Faith gave him a scathing look. 'It's OK, you don't need a chaperone.'

That was not what Greg had meant. Faith's crucifix was in his pocket; did her parents know she wasn't wearing it, and why not? They'd hardly welcome him into their home if they knew – the heathen boy who had demolished their daughter's faith.

'Oh, come on,' Faith said impatiently. 'I'm getting damp and frozen.'

Faith's house, as Greg had guessed, was much larger than his: detached, in one of the quiet roads on the opposite side of the main road, near the tennis club. Her mother – Greg now knew her as Margaret – sat at the dining-table, marking exercise books. 'It's all right, we'll talk in the kitchen,' Faith said when she started to move the books aside.

The kitchen was huge, with another big table, shining utensils dangling from a ceiling rack, and everything tidy. Faith made tea and brought cake in a tin. 'How on earth can Graveney Hall be his? What could he have meant?'

'Henry Pearson left it to him after Edmund died?

But why would he? Anyway, we know it went to a cousin. It wouldn't have been Edmund's to leave, would it? Not while his father was still alive.'

'And the paraffin. Did Joe start the fire? And if so, by mistake or on purpose? He got upset, didn't he, when I asked him?'

'*A servant's carelessness*. His? Spilling paraffin? They could have used it for lamps, or heaters, or for drying washing. But he was a gardener, so why would he be lighting paraffin stoves in the house? And I think the getting upset was because he needed the toilet.'

'So,' Faith said, frowning as she cut a large slice of cake, 'the fire started with paraffin, whether by accident or on purpose, and it was the last straw for Edmund – his inheritance going up in flames – so he drowned himself? Just like you said? *Disappeared*, according to Joe. Disappeared into the lake?'

'You don't think – *believed killed at the time of the fire* – Edmund died *in* the fire, after all? Joe killed him, then claimed the house as his own?'

Faith stared. 'You're suggesting Joe's a *murderer*?'

'It's obvious he's always been a bit peculiar, isn't it? Never talking, and hardly literate—'

'Lots of people are a bit peculiar. It doesn't make them murderers. Besides, I can't believe he'd have been clever – or devious – enough. How would he have managed it, let alone covered it up for all these years?'

'Body burned in the fire – a handy way of covering up!'

'But then Edmund would have been found,

surely?' Faith objected. 'A body, however badly burned – it would've been found and buried.'

'Mm, the lake idea's better. Less chance of anyone knowing.'

'Suicide,' Faith stated. 'Not murder.'

She darted a warning glance at Greg as the kitchen door opened. It was Margaret, taking a break from her marking: 'I hoped you were making tea. Cut me a piece as well, please, darling.'

She reached across the table for the plate; a crucifix on a silver chain, swinging forward from her open-necked shirt, caught the light. Greg reached into his pocket to check that Faith's cross was still there. He hadn't yet liked to ask whether she wanted it back. Till she did, he felt an obligation to keep it with him. When Margaret had gone back to her marking, Greg ventured: 'What did you do about church on Sunday?'

He wished he hadn't spoken. Faith stared back at him, then sat down at the table and covered her face with both hands.

'I went,' she said. 'I said the prayers. I sang the hymns. I thought that would help, but it didn't. I felt like a total hypocrite. And I can't keep going – I'll have to tell Mum and Dad.'

Greg reached across to touch her arm. 'Sorry,' he said, inadequately.

She shrugged him off. 'Not your fault.'

Remembering this morning's poem, a ridiculous picture slipped into his mind: himself and Faith, on Christmas Eve, tramping across muddy fields, searching the countryside for oxen in a shed, hoping to find them kneeling. 'There,' he would say, when they found them. 'There's your proof.' And he would fasten the cross round her neck, and one of his wrongs would be righted.

It rained hard all evening and into the night. Greg woke up in darkness, lay listening to the rain, tried to sleep, couldn't. Not in the mood for reading or listening to music, he turned on his bedside lamp and looked at his watch. One-forty.

He pulled on pants and jeans and went downstairs. The kitchen tiles were cold under his bare feet; the cats yawned at him from their basket. He got himself a glass of water, then stood by the patio doors. Rain battered the glass, steady rain, as if it was never going to stop; as if it would always be night-time and raining.

There was nothing to do but go out in it. Quietly, he slid the door open. The ground was wet and gritty; something crunched underfoot as he felt his way to the grass, avoiding the low wall. He stood on the lawn and turned up his face while the rain beat down hard, soaking his hair, running over his shoulders and down his back, clamming his jeans against his legs. It seemed the obvious place to be: outside, not cocooned in bed. The sky was too overcast for stars, but some clear night he'd come and stand here and look. How often had he done that? Not often enough. The universe put on its amazing space-show and he hardly ever bothered to spare it a glance. And the rain was something else, a kind of blessing: the strange, relentless force, the ground receiving it, drinking it thirstily, and the sense of giving himself up to it, letting it drench him. He stretched up his arms, opened his mouth and tasted it.

'Greg? Greg, is that you?'

He swung round. The downstairs hall light was on, silhouetting the shape of his father in the patio doorway, in his dressing-gown.

'What the hell are you doing? I heard the door open – thought we had burglars—'

'No, only me.'

'What – what are you—'

'Nothing,' Greg called back, shivering.

'Hey, what—' His father came out to him, put an arm round him. 'Come on in, you're soaked! You weren't sleepwalking, were you? You haven't done that since you were little!'

Greg allowed himself to be ushered indoors; his father took off his dressing-gown and put it round Greg's shoulders. Greg noticed that it was his mother's pink satin one, streaked with rain.

'Dad! What's—'

His father grinned. 'Picked up the wrong one in the dark.'

'You were going to tackle burglars, wearing pink satin?'

Shared laughter was a release: muffled, trying not to wake the sleepers above.

'Greg, what's worrying you?' his father asked, abruptly serious. 'Something must be. You're not in trouble of some sort? You would tell me, wouldn't you? You know I'm always here to listen.'

'I'm fine, Dad, thanks. Honest. I just felt like standing out in the rain.'

'Why?'

'Don't know, really,' Greg said, sheepish. 'It seemed like a good idea. Didn't realize how cold it was.'

'Get those wet jeans off. You'd better have a shower before you go back to bed, warm yourself up,' his dad said, pushing him gently towards the stairs. 'I'll bring you some hot chocolate.'

Greg heard footsteps from Katy's room; her bleared, incredulous face appeared over the banisters. 'Has someone chucked a bucket of water over your head, or what?' she demanded. 'And why are you wearing Mum's dressing-gown?'

'Greg felt like a midnight excursion,' their dad said, jollily.

'Oh, fine. My brother's a screwball,' Katy said. 'Did I hear you say hot chocolate, Dad?'

1917, Good Friday

To A.C., 1895-1917

I've crossed to France to find your grave,
Too many years gone by,
And find you on a sward of green
Beneath an April sky.

In the strip of fertile soil
Before your marker stone
There blooms a fragile Lenten rose,
A gift from one unknown.

Such dignified remembrances –
Inscriptions, flowers, peace –
Are meant to offer solace
To those who bring their grief.

I only know – my dearest love
Lies here beneath the ground.
My hopes, my youth lie with you,
By faithful promise bound.

And now – the skies are dark again
While Europe holds its breath.
One and twenty years of peace
You paid for with your death.

Edmund Pearson, April 1939

'Good afternoon, Edmund,' said the Reverend Tilley in a bracing tone.

'Is it?' Once the veneer of politeness was thrown off, how easy it was to be rude! As soon as Edmund had seen the vicar's pony-trap arriving, he had come out to the summerhouse, but the Reverend Tilley had followed him there. Edmund wished he had made a more effective escape, down to the lake. 'Father's in his study,' he said curtly.

'I shall speak to him in due course, but it's you I've come to see. Your father's very concerned about you. Your . . . state of mind. Your behaviour. Your attitude. He thinks you ought to be persuaded to see a doctor.'

'Pointless. There's nothing wrong with me that a doctor could cure.' Edmund would not look at the vicar. He stood with feet astride, looking up at the left-hand caryatid with her garland offering. Her beautiful impassive face gazed over his head. Edmund would readily have let himself be turned to stone in exchange for such untroubled serenity.

'Edmund, I share your father's concern. You seem deeply perturbed. What is it?'

Edmund looked at him. 'The war isn't enough?'

'Of course, of course, we know you're under strain. But your position is a privileged one, you know – you're young, physically capable, able to take an active part in this conflict. When it's over you will feel justly proud to have served your country, especially if you can keep your spirits up till the end. Some of us can only watch from the sidelines and offer up our prayers.'

'So I'm to consider myself lucky? I shall remember that next time I'm taking cover in a stinking shell-hole.'

The vicar frowned: stinking shell-holes were not part of his view of warfare. 'Edmund, you must not allow these hardships to make you bitter. You're perfectly fitted by background, education and training to lead your men into battle. They look to you for an example of strength and courage. Don't let them see bitterness and weakness.'

'I can't help it,' Edmund muttered, hearing his voice like that of a petulant child.

'Has something in particular happened to upset you?' The vicar spoke more kindly. 'You can confide in me, you know that. I've known you all your life, Edmund, and I'd like to think that I can share your burden. Shall we walk?'

He steered Edmund towards the long central path. Edmund hesitated; then, suddenly reckless: 'Yes, there is something.'

'I thought so! Go on.' The vicar bent his head to listen.

'My closest friend was killed. Not killed outright. He was caught by a bursting shell and he died slowly, in agony. He took three days, dying. I watched him.'

'My dear boy, I'm so sorry.'

'Yes, no doubt you are, but in a moment you'll tell me that he had the great privilege of dying for his country, dying a hero's death. It wasn't. He died the death of a tortured animal. God – your God – showed no mercy—' Alarmingly, Edmund's voice wavered and broke into a sob. He covered his face with both hands. The vicar put a hand on his shoulder; Edmund moved away.

'How terribly distressing for you.'

'For *him*!'

'Yes, for him of course. You must console yourself with the thought that he's at peace now, with God—'

'No! There is no God! How can there be?'

'You must not speak like this,' the vicar said calmly. 'I will pray for your friend, and for you—'

'Keep your prayers for yourself! I won't have you interfering!' Edmund burst out. 'I loved Alex, I still love him, and you can't bring him back with your prayers, or make it a fraction more bearable—'

'You must avoid dwelling on it. Pray for him, if you can. If you cannot, think of your blessings. Think of all you have here at Graveney, to return to,' the vicar said, waving an expansive hand. 'This beautiful house, marriage, a loving wife, if you would only—'

'*Wife!* I shall have no wife. Neither Philippa Fitch nor anyone else. Don't you understand? I've just told you I love Alex.'

'Love, yes,' said the vicar, 'but not of the same kind as for a wife – the love of a good friend is a blessing, but of a different kind.'

'It isn't different.' Edmund spoke in a whisper. 'I won't let you take away what we had together, with your words. We loved each other body and soul. That was our blessing. We planned a future together – away from Graveney, if that was what it took.'

'Edmund, recollect yourself! What are you saying?' The vicar had recoiled as if from a noxious drain. 'Are you implying that you – you and this man – knew each other carnally, shared physical intimacy?'

'Yes!'

Edmund heard the vicar's hissing intake of breath. 'And you call that a blessing! It's depravity – bestiality!'

'It was not!' Edmund met his gaze, chin high. 'It was love – freely given, freely received. I refuse to view it in the way you do! Killing other men with grenades, killing with bullets, killing with bayonets, killing with poison gas – is that not depravity? Is that not sinful? No – according to your twisted logic, to kill is right and to love is wrong!'

'*Thou shalt not lie with mankind as with womankind; it is an abomination!*' the Reverend Tilley quoted fiercely. 'So it is written in the Book of Leviticus. And what is wrong in God's eyes cannot be made to seem right or justifiable, whatever the situation. I will not listen while you make excuses for your sin – if it is repulsive to me, imagine how much more repulsive to the Lord! You must realize, man, that not only is it morally repugnant, it is also a crime in the eyes of the law! Have you no shame?'

'No,' Edmund said, although he felt the uncomfortable stirring of a reminder that he *had* felt ashamed. 'You said I could confide in you,' he reproached.

'Yes, but I did not for one moment imagine what you were about to tell me – tell me with such relish, such exultation!' The vicar turned away to look over the ha-ha. 'I don't propose to carry on discussing your filthy indulgence. It is highly distasteful to me, as it would be to any decent human being, let alone a minister of God's Church. It would be quite wrong of me to encourage you to carry on talking in this way. If your father knew of this, he would disinherit you—'

'I'd willingly have disinherited myself,' Edmund said, his voice breaking, 'if Alex had lived.'

'But God has seen fit to take him to Himself – this – this Alex. And let us hope that he repented at the last. As you must, now. As for this talk of disinheritance, of betraying your family's love and trust, their hopes for you – Edmund, Edmund, you must cure yourself of this!'

'There's no cure,' Edmund muttered.

'Nonsense, boy! Do you know what tomorrow is?'

'It's Good Friday.' Easter marked the end of Edmund's leave. On Monday he would set off for Folkestone and the crossing to Boulogne.

'Indeed it is.' The Reverend Tilley looked at him accusingly. 'The day when our Saviour willingly died on the Cross for our sins – for *your* sins. What better day to make clean of your life, to ask for forgiveness, to throw yourself at the feet of your Saviour and ask Him to deliver you from impure thoughts? I suggest that you spend some time in prayer and contemplation before coming to the service. I will also pray for you.'

'I don't want prayers,' Edmund said sullenly. 'I've told you.'

'My boy, to sin is one thing, to persist wilfully in clinging to your sin is another. This stubbornness – this spiritual blindness – will do you no good; you must open your heart to God's healing love. I won't tell your father about the details of our conversation,' the Reverend Tilley summed up. 'You needn't worry yourself that I will break your confidence. Not only would it be one of the most repellent tasks I have ever had to undertake, it would break your parents' hearts if they knew how you have repaid their devotion. I will merely tell them that we have had a good talk, and that I hope – as indeed I do – that the Easter services will send you back to France in a more dutiful frame of mind, at peace with yourself. Good afternoon – until tomorrow, then.'

The vicar gave Edmund a last cold look before walking quickly back to the house. Edmund followed as far as the summerhouse, and stood as before looking up at the caryatid. How many conversations, arguments, pleadings, disputes had been overlooked by her imperturbable gaze? She was a godless, pagan figure, her sole purpose to offer her beauty and her self and her garland of vine leaves. Edmund preferred her to the vicar's God, the forbidding God who could be shocked and appalled by the instincts of the humans he had created. But as God did not exist, Edmund need not worry about him. He was more concerned that he had betrayed Alex, letting the vicar's filthy mind label him as depraved, bestial, perverted. He had allowed the vicar to speak his name, allowed his memory to be tainted. He leaned against cool stone and closed his eyes to the spring morning. 'Why did I speak?' he murmured to Alex. 'Forgive me. Please forgive me.'

On the day of the Armistice, nineteen months later, Edmund sat with other soldiers drinking in an estaminet near St Omer. A church bell – not English peals, but the French intoning of a single, sonorous note again and again – announced that the war was over. It seemed impossible: the war had sucked him into its vortex, draining him of youth, of vitality, of love, and now it was going to regurgitate him and spit him out. Without caring whether he lived or died, Edmund had somehow come through, and the men with him had come through, and the Armistice had ended the purpose of their lives together and they must all find something else.

What now?

He had no home to go to, no family awaiting his return, no real name. He must build some kind of life for his new self, the self he had invented over the last year and a half.

He drank his beer, thinking of England in November: mists, and the opening meet, and the trees scattering their gold over the grass; the denuded garden showing its outlines, its bare hedges and skeletal trees. But Graveney Hall too was skeletal, a burned-out hollow. There would be no more opening meets, no more teas on the terrace, no more elegant guests spilling out to the lawns. It was a shell house, not a home any more.

When Edmund thought of Good Friday it was like watching the actions of a madman. He pushed his memories away from him and ordered another beer. They were part of his old life, not of this one.

He refused to go to church the morning after his conversation with the vicar. No amount of pleading or reproaches from his parents could make him change his mind. The Reverend Tilley would be looking out for him, he knew – would be looking for signs of shame and contrition. He would see none because he would not see Edmund.

'Very well! Since you are so obstinate, we will see you at luncheon,' his father said coolly, getting into the motor car. Edmund's mother merely gazed at him sadly. Baillie, who became chauffeur on church days, touched his cap to Edmund and drove them away. Edmund stood watching as the Crossley made its steady, rocking progress along the track to the lodge gates.

He stood by the holm oaks on the eastern front and

turned back to look at the house. It was waiting for him, waiting to claim him, body and soul. He belonged to it: it was nonsense to think of it the other way round. He had been conceived and born for Graveney; it dictated the course of his life. It was a great, sprawling excrescence on the face of the earth, a magnificent shell with coldness within. He hated it.

If there were no Graveney Hall, there would be no need for an heir. He would be free. The idea struck Edmund – simple, appealing – and took hold.

With most of the servants at church, there were few people about: only two or three maids and the cook, preparing luncheon. He went to the stableyard and into the harness room. There was a paraffin stove here, used in winter to take the chill off the air and prevent the leather from going damp and mouldy. There must be stores of paraffin, in cans. He went into the adjoining store room and rummaged around amongst tins of saddle-soap, neatsfoot oil and liniment.

Squat containers. Cans and cans of it. He screwed open a lid and sniffed.

On the shelf opposite he found matches.

So easy! Everything laid out for his convenience, as if it were meant.

There was no-one to see him return to the house and mount the back steps, with a can of paraffin in each hand and matches in his pocket. He did not hesitate. In the drawing room, he sprinkled a trail of paraffin across the carpet and dropped a lighted match. The flames licked up brightly, blue then yellow.

He did not stay to observe the effects, but crossed to the dining room and tipped a liquid trail across the linen cloth that was spread in readiness for luncheon, striking a match and lobbing it at the centrepiece of spring flowers. The leaping flames were a fanfare of light, a triumph. Then it occurred to him that he should have started upstairs, or risk trapping himself if the blaze took hold. He ran up the broad staircase to the upper floor.

As he went from room to room, pouring, lighting, he developed a kind of reckless artistry: igniting a bowl of pot-pourri in his mother's room, making a neat pyre of books in the centre of his father's. With a lighted spill of paper, he torched the damask curtains that draped his mother's four-poster bed, and made a bonfire of the crested and embossed stationery on her writing desk. It was an act of creation. *Let there be fire: and there was fire. Let the fire be gathered unto one place: and it was so. And it was good.*

Down again to survey the results of his work. Yes, taking hold nicely. He ran down the stairs and into the library. A slosh at the dry ranked books, his father's collection, all leather-bound with hand-tooled titles: the encyclopedias, the essays, the bound *London Illustrated* and the books on botany and ornithology and horses and hunting. The pungent, oily smell of paraffin filled his nostrils. He struck a match and threw it, heard the satisfying *whoosh*, saw the steady blue flames turning gold, consuming. Good. The temperature was rising: sweat trickled on his forehead and down his neck.

He ran out through the hot tunnel of the main reception room and down the steps to the garden, carrying his cans. The servants would still be working in the kitchens, safe along their corridor, oblivious. By the fountain he turned and looked back at the dining room, seeing flames beating at the window, and a pall of black smoke.

He turned away, composing himself for the second part of his plan. He had sacrificed the house; now himself. Death by fire, death by water – he had chosen fire for the house, water for himself. It was really rather pleasing that it was Good Friday. Walking quickly through the gardens, he realized that he would never see them again: the fountains, the statues, the summerhouses, the ha-ha. But still he did not stop for a last look. He had to make sure he was gone when the fire was discovered.

Across the lower lawn went his feet, down the steps to the lake. He threw the paraffin cans in, one after the other, hurling them as far as he could. Then he went into the grotto and sat on the bench. As an afterthought, he unwrapped his pocket-book and pencil from their protective oilskin, tore out a page and wrote a bland farewell message to his parents. He placed the note and pencil on the bench, weighted by a stone; then he sat leafing through his own poems and Alex's letters, his most precious possessions.

No-one must find them after his death. He should have given them to the flames.

He kissed Alex's signature and traced the flamboyant capital A with his fingertip. Then he folded the loose sheets inside the notebook and wrapped the oilskin tightly around. Standing, he tossed the package into the water: the words and eventually the paper would dissolve them, and all the feeling in them. Now he undressed, removing his jacket, his tie, his shirt, his boots and socks, breeches, undergarments. He smoothed his finger-tips over the initials EP, marked in tiles. He had a memorial here, ready-made.

Now.

He stood naked by the water's edge. It felt like a gesture of bravado, exposing himself to the air: he could not rid himself of the notion that there might be snipers behind the trees and machine-gun posts on the slopes facing him. Across the lake the trees were beginning to come into leaf; he looked at the delicate colours, the pinky-browns, the first shadings of green, a frosting of wild cherry-blossom. The woods were full of birdsong: birds going about their business of nesting and living, while he went about his business of dying.

He closed his eyes and thought of Alex diving into the river near their Picardy farmhouse, where green weed flowed like hair. Alex was a strong swimmer; Edmund was not. It was time to follow.

The water was colder than he would have believed possible. He dipped one toe, stepped in with both feet, waded on yielding, sandy mud. There were creeping shocks of coldness as the water reached his testicles, stomach, chest – how *wet* it was! Now the final chilly clutch over his shoulders, ears, hair, and he was in, swimming. He would have to combat his instinct to keep afloat, deliberately fill his lungs with water. He raised his head, took a deep breath (why?) and ducked, sweeping with his arms to take him deep, out to the middle of the lake where weeds would entangle him and keep him down.

He was so busy concentrating on drowning that it took him a while to register a commotion in the shallows behind him. Annoyed, he surfaced, and the same instant a hand grabbed him painfully by the hair. He turned his head as best he could and came face to face with a pair of bulging eyes, goggling, asquint, level with his in the water.

Joe Baillie, the gardener's boy.

'On't! On't!' Joe shouted, and then he sank, his arms, in heavy corduroy, flailing wildly. Edmund realized that the boy could not swim. Having plunged in to save him, Joe was now in danger of drowning.

Damnation! Edmund had no choice but to postpone his suicide. He pushed and shoved the boy's unwieldy body back towards the edge. As Joe still thought he was the one doing the saving, the result was a locked-together thrashing and stumbling, to shallower water and then the muddy path. They stood there, gasping, the boy's eyes flicking down at Edmund's naked body. They were both cold, starting to shiver.

A new idea struck Edmund: pleasing, mischievous. He guided Joe towards the shell grotto.

'Take off your clothes, Joe. Put on mine,' he told him.

Joe stared at him, his head moving from side to side, one eye on Edmund's face and the other over his shoulder. Edmund helped him off with his sogged corduroy and wool, and on with the officer's uniform. Joe, getting the idea, began to chuckle, thinking this a good dressing-up game. It took an age to do up all the buttons and fasten the tie.

'Your own boots,' Edmund said. Joe pulled them on and spent some moments puzzling over the laces. Then he stood up, fully dressed, looking like a parody of a soldier: smartly-clad but bedraggled, wearing badges of responsibility and a half-witted, lopsided grin.

'Good. Now my turn.'

Joe Baillie was large for his age and his clothes were baggy and worn. Edmund wrung water out of the trousers and pulled them on, then the checked shirt and finally the ill-fitting jacket. Joe looked at him and sniggered.

'One more thing. Let me . . .' Edmund reached for the pencil-stub he had left on the bench in the grotto. To the note he had written for his parents, he added: *I name Joe Baillie as my heir. I bequeath him Graveney Hall and its estate.*

'You're welcome to it, Joe – what's left of it. I've done with it. I hope it makes you happier than it's made me.' He took the boy by the shoulders. 'Now, Joe, I want you to go back to the cottage and wait there for your father. Do you understand?'

He had to repeat his instruction twice before the boy nodded.

'And give him this.' Edmund handed Joe the note. 'Give it to your father. You understand?'

A slow, uncertain nod.

'Go, then. Now!'

Edmund stood watching while the boy climbed laboriously up the steps, pausing at the top to wave. Waving back, Edmund turned and walked along to the farthest end of the lake; then he took a narrow path that led up a gradual slope and out to the barley field beyond.

He had made a decision.

His life as Edmund Pearson had ended when he plunged into the lake, though not in the way he had planned. Since Joe's arrival had dragged him back to life, he would have a new identity. Edmund Culworth, he decided: a kind of marriage, his name with Alex's. Edmund – no, better change it to Edward – Edward Culworth, farm labourer, would concoct some story and serve out the war as a private soldier.

His new resolve had almost driven the fire out of his head. Four fields away he paused, looked back and stood shocked and horrified at what he had accomplished: Graveney Hall was ablaze, flames leaping from the roof, the gardens obscured in a drift of smoke. The fire that had started with a few matches was as big as the house, ravaging, consuming. As he gazed he pushed away his moment of panic, and a smile spread slowly over his face. There was no room for regret. He was escaping, triumphant. Graveney Hall would never claim him now. For so long pushed and manipulated, he was leaving with this spectacular gesture of self-assertion.

'*He saw what he had done,*' he muttered, '*and behold, it was very good.*'

A dry ditch and hedge at the edge of the field marked the limit of the Graveney estate. Edmund stumbled and half-fell in the long grass and nettles, picked himself up, pushed through the twiggy mass of the hedge and was free, in his neighbour's cow-pasture. Wiping dried cow-pat from his boot, he hurried on across the grass. He did not look back.

Henry Pearson felt sick and faint. He stood by the fountain, gazing at the smouldering ruins of his house. What paintings and bits of furniture the servants had been able to save were dotted crazily about the terrace and around the fountains. He had the ridiculous feeling that if he asked Baillie to drive him back to church, if he repeated his journey home, he would see Graveney Hall standing proud and unblemished, as he had left it. This – this was *impossible*! His home charred and smoking, disembowelled by fire . . . And Graveney was more than his home; it was his past, his future, his life's purpose. Where was Edmund? He needed Edmund; he felt so old and suddenly frail that Edmund would have to take charge . . .

'I'm very sorry, sir, to trouble you in your distress, but I think you should see this.'

He turned slowly, dull-witted; saw George Baillie holding out a scrap of paper. 'Yes, Baillie, what is it?'

The gardener approached him reluctantly. 'It's Mr Edmund, sir. I – I believe he's drowned himself in the lake. He left this note.'

Henry Pearson stared, unable to take in this second shock. He snatched Edmund's note and tried to make sense of the words:

To my parents.

You will have realized that I have not been myself since returning from the Front. I am most sincerely sorry for the anguish this will cause you but I cannot face returning to France and am taking the coward's escape route.

Your loving son,
Edmund.

I name Joe Baillie as my heir. I bequeath him Graveney Hall and its estate.

Henry Pearson made a gargling sound and sagged at the knees; Baillie realized with alarm that he was about to faint. Supporting with strong arms, he helped his employer to a low wall and sat him down, then called to one of the servants who was dithering by the steps to fetch brandy and a rug. Shortly after, Mrs Pearson appeared and took her husband away to the groom's apartment which was being made ready as temporary accommodation. George Baillie wondered whether he should break the news to her too, then decided not to. He had tucked the suicide note into Mr Pearson's pocket. Sadly he thought of young Mr Edmund, two nights ago, at the cottage door. He had been kind to young Joe, sure enough, and standing there he had looked for a moment so wistful that George Baillie had thought of inviting him inside. He wished now that he had. Who knew what was going through the young gentleman's mind, for him to do away with himself? Nothing that a chat and a cup of tea could have put right, but all the same . . . Baillie sighed, shook his head and went back to his work, helping to carry furniture up to the apartment above the stables.

Next day Henry Pearson summoned Baillie to his makeshift rooms to discuss the matter further. Baillie, having got from Joe that he had seen Edmund plunge into the lake and that the young master was now gone, had to confess the rather embarrassing detail that Joe had appeared wearing Edmund's uniform. Where Joe's own clothes were, he had been unable to establish. George suspected that Joe had thrown them into the lake.

'This note,' Mr Pearson said curtly. 'I think we can assume that my son was of unsound mind when he wrote it.'

'Yes, sir.'

'I'd be most grateful if you'd refrain from mentioning it to any of the other servants – and Joe won't, of course. I shall have to report my son's death to his regimental headquarters but apart from that I would prefer to let it be believed that he has returned to the Front. We shall have to try to find the – the body . . .' He held out a hand over his eyes and breathed deeply in and out.

'I'll do my best, sir.'

'Suicide – it's a bad business. My wife's devastated, of course – we both are. We wouldn't want it known.'

'Of course, sir. I understand.'

Baillie, who suspected that Joe had had something to do with the starting of the fire, was relieved that his employer did not go on to raise similar doubts. Dismissed, he said, 'There's one other thing, sir.'

'Mm?' Henry Pearson, haggard, exhausted, managed a flicker of interest.

George Baillie handed over Edmund's pocket-book.

'I went down to the lake, sir – took Joe with me to see what sense I could get out of him. He seemed to say it must have been near the grotto, so I had a good look round, even waded in, to see if I could find Mr Edmund's ... er ... body. I couldn't, but I did find this near the edge of the water. It's his notebook, sir, and this bundle of letters – wrapped in an oilskin, and fortunately not too damaged. You'll want to have them. I hope they may give you some comfort.'

'Thank you, Baillie.'

The gardener left. Henry Pearson opened the pocket-book and took out the damp bundle of letters tucked inside its back cover. The edges of the paper were stained with water, and some of the ink had spread, but most of the writing was quite legible.

Carefully unfolding the first, he started to read. *My dearest Edmund*, it said in Alex's swooping black handwriting.

Refraction

Greg's photograph: a huge eighteenth-century mansion standing alone. It is built in classical style: weighty, monumental, symmetrical. The frontage is of Portland stone; twin flights of steps rise to the pillared main entrance. The central section is surmounted by a decorative triangular panel sculpted with reclining figures and a Latin inscription. At a glance, you'd think you were looking at a stately home – a National Trust property, perhaps. Only when you look properly do you see that the door and windows are blank, that there is no roof, and that the house is an empty shell.

Jordan walked into Greg's room and took off his clothes and got into bed with him.

They lay side by side, facing each other, looking, looking. Jordan's eyes were sea-green, night-warm. Greg was afloat with happiness, pillowed and billowed by it, his brain awash.

'I love you,' he whispered; and then, because the

words sounded so awkward in his mouth, 'Is it all right?'

'Yes, it's all right,' Jordan said. 'I know.'

Greg reached out a hand to touch Jordan's face: curve of browbone, eyelid, straightness of nose, shapely upper lip: a facescape familiar and strange, his to explore. Parting teeth nipped his fingers and held them: gentle, teasing. The eyes opened wide, fixing gleefully on his, and he saw what a stupid mistake he had made. The face was not Jordan's but Tanya's – bright smiling teeth, glittery eyes, sparkly hair. The body was hers too: smooth, inviting.

'I don't love you, stupid. Come here.' She pulled him on top of her. 'What's love got to do with it? It's just sex. You need practice.'

He could not answer. He could only bury his head in her neck, and thrust and thrust, give himself over to his body's urges . . . she was moving with him, and laughing, and her nails and teeth were so sharp . . . *oh, let me let me . . . ohhhh . . .*

And then he was looking at the dawn-grey curtains, finding himself alone in his bed, dizzied with the shock of waking. Warmth tingled through his limbs, nice . . . he felt the hot stickiness on his thighs and on the sheet, rapidly cooling. *Damnation!*

He thrust back the duvet and stripped the under-sheet, bundling it into a heap. A glance at his watch showed that it was only six-thirty, much too early for anyone to be up, thank God. He stuffed the sheet into the laundry basket in the bathroom and took a clean one from the airing-cupboard, then got into the shower.

He squeezed a dollop of minty Energizing Body Gel, turned the shower dial so that the flow was hot and needling, and remembered what day it was. Sunday, Open Day at Graveney Hall. While he washed and minted and energized himself, the dream lingered in his mind, vivid and disturbing.

Truth? Nonsense? Which?

He stood under the shower until the bathroom was filled with steam and the mirror clouded over.

Now what?

He had promised to meet Faith at the Coach House, to help set things out. But it was earlier than early. On Sundays the pool opened at seven, and Jordan would be there. The team didn't train at weekends, but he had told Greg that he felt restless and lethargic unless he began each day with a hard swim. *Mental*, Greg had said; didn't he like a lie-in once a week? No, Jordan replied; he was conditioned to wake up at six-thirty and go straight to the pool without even thinking about it.

Greg remade his bed, then dressed in his swimming shorts, with jeans and a sweatshirt, and rolled clean underpants into a towel with his goggles. Quietly, he let himself out of the house.

Sunday morning was for the keenies: no children, length-swimmers only, the pool marked off into lanes. Greg nodded to Paul, who was on the lifeguard's chair, and saw Jordan in the far lane, recognizable by his dark head and streamlined front crawl. He knew Jordan would not notice him, head in the water, intent. Finding a space two lanes away, Greg dived in.

The water was not at all cold, but the shock of wetness jolted him into action. He adjusted his goggles and settled into his stroke, enjoying the rhythm, the push into blue water, the silky flow over his skin. He had not so far taken up Sandy's suggestion of coming to a training session, but now he thought he might. Jordan had said no more about it, but that wasn't surprising. Jordan had hardly spoken to him all week.

Now?

When he judged that Jordan was reaching the end of his session, and the pool was beginning to be taken over by casual swimmers, Greg moved over to the far side, ducking under the red discs of the lane marker. Jordan swam up fast, grabbed the rail and stopped. He looked at Greg in some surprise through the blue-tinted plastic of his goggles. 'Oh,' was all he said, lapped by backwash.

Greg thought of his dream; courage failed him. 'Thought you'd be here,' he said feebly.

'So?'

'Give you a race?' Greg suggested. 'Two lengths, front crawl?'

'If you want.' Jordan half-smiled – a fleeting ghost of one, but still the nearest thing to a smile Greg had seen for over a week. They lined up, feet against the side, arms back, hands grasping the rail. Jordan let Greg give the nod to start. He swam level with Greg for the first length, almost lazily, not even bothering to do a tumble-turn at the end, just pushing off the side. Then, on the return, he moved into a different gear; he was not going to let Greg win.

Struggling to catch up, Greg glimpsed him from both above and below the surface: upraised arm arrowed at the water, head pillowed by it, legs kicking below, and the long slim body, fluent and beautiful in motion. Jordan was in his element: swimming, alone, absorbed. He was ahead, out of reach, while Greg floundered behind.

The church, Faith's church, was ahead of Greg as he pedalled up London Road. It served as a useful landmark, its square tower dominating the skyline; the bus stop next to it was a convenient meeting place. He hadn't been inside since junior school, when a yearly carol service had been held there. Last time he had been inside a church was for his cousin's wedding in the spring, and then he'd felt silly and dressed-up, expected to sing hymns he didn't know and join in the prayers.

But this was Faith's church. He wanted to see what she saw every Sunday.

Self-consciously he locked his bike by the stone wall. The town was almost deserted this early, but what if anyone saw him? Gizzard, say? He'd have to pretend to be interested in the Roll of Honour or something. There was probably a service going on, anyway. The heavy wooden door opened to his push, creaking loudly; he saw warm light inside.

He hesitated in the porch. No voices, no organ music. Cautiously he went in, closing the door behind him. He smelled polished wood and hundreds-of-years-old coldness, and faint dusty warmth from an inadequate heater. Looking up, he saw daylight cut into shapes by stained-glass windows. On the wall opposite was a Memorial Tablet listing the dead of both wars – some three dozen for the Great War, fewer for the Second. Greg went across to look, glancing at the place where Edmund Pearson's name would have been, but there was no Pearson. There were two Baillies: G.E. and J.P. Both Joe's brothers! Joe had started life as one of three, ended up an only child. That could have been enough to send him half-demented . . .

By the lectern someone had made an arrangement of autumn foliage: scarlet berries, and green and golden leaves, and the silvery tufts of old-man's-beard. An altar-cloth showed loaves and fishes in embroidered silk. Above was a large crucifix of carved wood, with a Christ-figure attached, skinny and suffering. Greg looked, wondering what he was seeing: a torture victim, an executed prisoner, a Middle-Eastern Jewish man who had lived and died two thousand years ago, made to look European for easier appeal to English eyes; the man who said he was the son of God. Faith's Jesus. He was not Greg's Jesus, but nevertheless he – or the myth he had become – would not be diminished by unbelief. Greg looked at the sideways-tilted face, with cheeks hollowed out by the woodcarver's chisel, and a crown of thorns gouging the forehead.

'Who are you?' Greg asked aloud.

If it were true that Jesus was God's son and that he

showed the way to heaven – if it ever had been true –
then it was true for ever. And if it was not true now, it
never had been. It was a mass delusion. Greg sat
down in the front pew, and looked, and waited to see
if a revelation would prove him wrong.

His thoughts wandered. Edmund Pearson must
have sat here, he thought, spreading a hand over the
cool grain of the wood. It was all hierarchical, wasn't
it? People didn't sit anywhere they chose – they had
their own places, and a wealthy family like the
Pearsons would have been at the front. What had
Edmund thought, the last time he sat here?

He called himself back to attention. Now that he
was seated in the pew, facing the altar, he had to make
an attempt at saving Faith's faith, however stupid and
self-contradictory it sounded.

He cleared his throat. 'Look, if there's anyone
listening,' he began, speaking so quietly that he could
barely hear his own words, 'could you do something
for Faith? You know her, don't you? Could you show
her you're there? I mean, you wouldn't want her to
lose it, would you? You don't turn people away,
specially not people who want to believe. And it's my
fault, whatever she says, so if you could put it right I'd
be really glad. I hope you don't mind me asking; it's a
bit of a cheek, really. Anyway, that's it. Thanks.'

What a prat, eh? Asking favours of a wooden
effigy.

Behind him, the door opened with a creaking
sound.

The back of his neck tingled; the air felt alive with

electricity. It's him, he thought. He's come to find me. He knows. But it seemed impossible to turn round, as if his head were held in a neck-brace.

Heeled shoes clopped on the stones of the aisle. Half-standing, Greg saw an oldish woman, carrying a water-jug and a bunch of leaves and berries. He blundered out of the pew, clumsy with disappointment. The woman, smart in a grey coat with a scarf at the neck, stared at him, curious and wary. She doesn't know if I'm here to pray or to nick the brass candlesticks, he realized, glad that she hadn't come in a few moments earlier to hear him mumbling to himself.

'Good morning?' she said. She wasn't used to teenagers, he could tell.

He tugged at his sweatshirt. 'Just looking round.'

He was still early at Graveney Hall, though he could see from the number of cars parked along the frontage that the helpers were here in force. 'Marvellous news!' Margaret, Faith's mother, greeted him by a striped pagoda set up as the official entrance. 'Have you heard?'

'No?'

'That young boy, Dean. He's started to get the feeling back in his feet and legs. They think he might make a full recovery after all! What a relief for everyone.'

But I didn't pray for Dean, Greg thought for a confused second.

'There's a card inside,' Margaret went on. 'We're all signing it, and we've got him a present. Make sure you put your name. It looks like rain, but if we're lucky it'll hold off till this afternoon. I don't know where Faith is. She's around somewhere.'

Greg found her in the Coach House, getting Maura to sign Dean's card. She waved him over: 'You as well, Greg!' People had already written things like *So glad to hear you're making progress* and *Hurry up and get yourself out of there*, as if they were Dean's favourite uncles and aunties, and Dean a nice little boy. Greg wrote *Get well soon. Greg.*

'Not paralysed after all,' he said to Faith. 'He's going to take up his bed and walk! Did your prayers do that, or what?'

Faith shrugged. 'Who knows? Would have happened with or without them. I'm glad, though.'

'A bit of a miracle, you could say?'

'Who do you want me to say that for – for me or for you? What's a miracle anyway?'

'Something that goes against the laws of Physics. Something that can't be explained.'

'Well, this can be explained,' Faith said. 'His spine wasn't as badly damaged as they thought it was at first. Easy.'

Her mother brought up another whole box full of jam and lemon curd and chutney, all in jars with frilly caps, and each needing a *Friends of Graveney Hall* sticker with the price written on; then the postcards and guidebooks had to be set out. Then Mike came over to say that the numbers were already more than expected, and could Greg go out to help supervise parking along the front drive. Greg stayed there, guiding the cars into neat lines and stopping people from backing into each other, until Phil came out to relieve him.

Back on the garden side of the house, he stopped to take in the scene. A wind quintet, arranged with their music stands in a semi-circle on mown grass near the steps, played something elegant and classical. There were people everywhere: gazing into the ruins, sitting on white plastic chairs with their refreshments, wandering around the garden, gathering for the next guided tour and looking up at the uncertain sky, which promised rain. Children ran across the grass, parents pushed buggies, one couple had a pair of identical King Charles spaniels on leads. A second pagoda displayed raffle goods, and a queue had formed at the entrance to the Coach House, where sandwiches, cakes and quiches were set out in a spread far in excess of the usual Sunday offerings. What would the Pearsons have thought of all this?

I hope the Friends never restore the place too much, Greg thought. I like it as it is.

Faith came across the grass with a plate of sandwiches and cakes. 'I know,' she said.

'What?'

'Feels like the place has been invaded, doesn't it? It's nicer when we have it to ourselves. But think of all that money rolling in! This many people – loads of money at the gate, and that's before they spend anything else. Here, I've brought our lunch – Maura's taken over the jam and stuff so we can have a break.'

They sat on the low wall to eat, but were sent scurrying into the Coach House by a sudden fierce shower of rain. 'Good!' Faith said, trying to run with two wedges of chocolate gateau still on the plate.

'Why good?'

'It brings everybody inside. And when they're inside they'll spend money.'

For the next hour and a half, while it rained steadily, the Coach House was packed. 'Like the Harrods sale!' Margaret beamed, pushing her way through to collect the notes from the bottom of the cash-box. 'Our extra publicity this year has certainly paid off.' Quite why wet weather should provoke a rush for green tomato chutney Greg had no idea, but he and Faith were fully occupied with taking money, sorting change and replenishing their tables from the boxes underneath until there was little more to be sold. When the rain eased and the visitors began to drift outside or back to their cars, Margaret came to take over the stall. 'Go and have a wander round. You've done well here.'

Outside, under the dripping trees, there was just a straggle of people, some smugly clad in Goretex and boots, others less suitably in shorts and open sandals. Automatically, Greg and Faith made their way across the orchard and down the steps to the lake. The last guided tour was making its way ahead of them, led by Faith's father. He gathered his group around the grotto, where Greg and Faith caught up; they heard the exclamations of people seeing it for the first time.

'This is the grotto,' Mike Tarrant informed them. 'One of the last features to be added to the grounds, in the late nineteenth century. Henry Pearson – the owner of Graveney at the time – had it made in memory of his baby son, Edmund, who died in infancy. We think he did the tile decorations himself. It's not obvious at first, but when you look you can see EP, for Edmund Pearson, again and again in the pattern – here, and here. His surviving son, of course, was the next Henry, the last owner, who lived here until the fire in 1917. Sadly, he had no heir – his only son died in the First World War . . .'

The old lie, Greg thought. People said that so often that they believed it.

The people stared and touched and exclaimed, some of them taking photographs, some gazing blankly, chewing gum. Mike Tarrant looked up at the darkening sky. 'I think we'd better hurry if we don't want to get drenched again. We'll just do a quick walk round the lake, then up to the sunken garden . . .'

As soon as the crocodile moved on, Faith darted inside the grotto and sat on the marble bench, reclaiming it for her own.

'I keep forgetting about that other Edmund Pearson – the first one.' Gently she touched the tile pattern. 'How weird if our Edmund really did drown himself here. I bet he came in here first, don't you? And saw his own ready-made memorial. Perhaps that's what gave him the idea.'

'No grave, but a grotto. It's better than most people get, isn't it?' Greg stood looking out at the ruffled water.

331

'We'd have to drag the lake – that's the only way we could ever prove anything.'

Greg shook his head. 'No. Let him stay.'

'I wasn't *serious*!'

The line of visitors had reached the farthest end; one of them, a boy, skimmed a flat stone that pinged across the surface. Then a fresh spatter of rain sent them all scurrying up the log path into the shelter of trees. The water was steely-grey, pitted with raindrops. Greg retreated into the grotto and stood looking as the last straggler disappeared, and the lake and its trees became theirs again. There was something very peculiar about the light, dull but intense, as if gathering itself; about to remark on this, Greg saw that the rain had stopped as suddenly as it had begun, and the lake was lit almost theatrically by vivid sunlight. Half a rainbow appeared in the retreating rain; from where they stood it looked as if it touched the ground precisely where the shell of the Hall was hidden from sight by the rise of ground. Greg stood looking at the eerie, beautiful light, wishing he had his camera. The trees opposite looked spotlit, every leaf and stalk and branch clear. And the rainbow – according to the Bible, hadn't God used that as a promise, after the Flood, setting his seal in the sky? It was the nearest thing to kneeling oxen Faith was likely to get.

'Can you see the rainbow's end?' he said.

'Nearly. But is the rainbow really there? Or do we only think we're seeing it?'

'It's an illusion, and we're both seeing it, but we're not seeing exactly the same because of the distance between us. I'd have to see through your eyes to see exactly the same rainbow you're seeing.'

'Are you saying more than you're saying?'

'I'm not sure. I'm a Physics student and I know that what we're seeing is sunlight refracted by moisture in the air. But can you believe that's *all* it is?'

'What, then?' Faith said. 'You'll be telling me next you think there's a pot of gold buried at the end.'

'Did you know that it wasn't till Isaac Newton that we understood about rainbows – about how light gets dispersed into different colours? And then he was criticized for spoiling the mystery of it.'

Faith nodded. 'Understanding isn't the same as wondering. It's fading – look. Going, going . . . gone.'

'There's still a bit left, if you want it,' Greg said, looking towards the trees. 'Anyway, 1 don't believe that. When you understand something you get something else to wonder at. We know now what makes a rainbow, but that doesn't mean it's not worth looking at. Looking properly. And we ought to think *Wow!* and say thank you, because the world is arranged the way it is.'

I sound like Jordan, he realized; that's a Jordan thought. For the first time he understood the meaning of the word *gutted*. He felt a physical pain deep inside, as if his intestines were being slowly pulled out, leaving him hollow.

'But the world has evil things in it as well, not just sunshine and rainbows. You gave that as a reason not to believe. And anyway,' Faith said, 'who should I thank?'

'Who do you think you should thank?'

'You want me to say that God's put this show on just for me? And therefore I have to believe in Him again? *Except you see signs and wonders, you will not believe.* That's what Jesus said to the man at Capernaum whose son He had healed.'

'OK, so that means you might not get signs and wonders – it doesn't tell you to take no notice when you *do* get them. Jesus performed miracles, didn't he?'

'Yes, for healing! Not conjuring tricks.'

'OK then. Dean's going to take up his bed and walk, and we've just seen a rainbow. What more do you want – loaves and fishes?'

'You're making it too simple,' Faith objected.

'And you're making it too complicated.'

'But if I believe, then you have to believe as well,' Faith said, 'because of your bargain. I have to drag you with me. And you don't want that.'

'But I do want *you* to believe,' Greg said, with certainty.

'Why?'

'I want to know it's possible.'

'You want me to save you the effort of believing for yourself? Sorry, I can't decide to believe because you want me to. And you can't decide to believe because of a bet.'

'No, but I can be a – a wondering agnostic.'

'There's nothing stopping you from being that. It doesn't depend on whether I believe or not.'

'OK, then.' Greg moved nearer to the shore and felt in his jeans pocket for Faith's crucifix. He leaned out over the water, dangling it. 'A rainbow's just particles arranging themselves in a certain way. Dean's getting better because he was going to get better anyway. So neither of us believes. Either there is a God behind everything or there isn't – there's no half-way, a God who's only partly there, or a God who can't make up his mind whether he exists or not. And we've both decided he doesn't. In which case you won't be needing this tacky piece of jewellery. There's no point hanging on to it, is there?'

'Wait—'

'Let's donate it to Edmund.'

God doesn't make bargains, he thought, but I can make one with myself. If Faith gets her faith back, I tell the truth – to myself, to everyone who matters. And if she doesn't, I don't have to. Simple.

He glanced at Faith. Intensity sharpened his actions as he whirled the chain around like a lasso, preparing. Faith watched him uneasily. Taking an exaggerated breath, he swung his arm back, watching her from the corner of his eye. Like an Olympic discus-thrower, he balanced himself for the throw.

'No!'

Faith grabbed his arm at the moment of lunging. The crucifix whirled over the water, catching the light.